ELIZABETH WEBSTER
AND THE
COURT OF UNCOMMON PLEAS

WILLIAM LASHNER

ELIZABETH

WEBSTER

AND THE
COURT OF UNCOMMON PLEAS

WILLIAM LASHNER

DISNEY • HYPERION

LOS ANGELES   NEW YORK

First Edition, October 2019
10 9 8 7 6 5 4 3 2 1
FAC-020093-19242
Printed in the United States of America

"Sealed with a Kiss"
Music by GARY GELD
Words by PETER UDELL
Copyright © 1960 (Renewed) CHAPPELL & CO., INC.
All Rights Reserved
Used By Permission of ALFRED MUSIC

This book is set in 12 pt. Sabon LT Pro/Monotype
Designed by Phil Buchanan

Library of Congress Cataloging-in-Publication Data
Names: Lashner, William, author.
Title: Elizabeth Webster and the Court of Uncommon Pleas / by William Lashner.
Description: First edition. • Los Angeles ; New York : Disney Hyperion,
2019. • Summary: When popular Henry Harrison asks twelve-year-old
Elizabeth to help dispel a ghost that speaks her name, she calls on her
estranged father and learns he is an attorney for the damned.
Identifiers: LCCN 2019002973 • ISBN 9781368041287 (hardcover)
Subjects: • CYAC: Ghosts—Fiction. • Fathers and daughters—Fiction. •
Friendship—Fiction. • Hell—Fiction. • Mystery and detective stories.
Classification: LCC PZ7.1.L3725 Eli 2019 • DDC [Fic]—dc23
LC record available at https://lccn.loc.gov/2019002973

Reinforced binding
Visit www.DisneyBooks.com

For my father,
the senior partner of Lashner & Lashner

The Jungle

Sometimes it feels like a cold breath against the back of your neck. Sometimes it shakes you awake in the middle of the night. One day you're all la-de-da, thinking you've got life figured out, and the next day you're racing down a grassy hill in the dark, being chased by your own screams, because you know what is out there. And what is out there is terrifying and it is calling your name.

Welcome to my world.

My name is Elizabeth Webster and my story, like every mystifying and horror-filled story in the whole of human history, begins in a middle school cafeteria.

See me there gripping my tray, black hair falling over my eyes. Among the tables of gazelles and rhinos, I am the lost meerkat, trying to find a sheltered place to sit so I won't get gored. Lunch at my school is like a program on Animal Planet: *Wild Beasts of Suburban Phildelphia.*

"Lizzie."

In the middle of the jungle I spied Natalie Delgado waving me forward like a gym teacher encouraging me to run faster, jump higher.

"Lizzie, over here!"

The louder she called my name, the more kids swiveled their heads, and the more I wanted to disappear.

Natalie had been my best friend since the first day of kindergarten—we had bonded over coloring books and the taste of glue. A seat beside her was normally a safe enough spot, but Natalie was sitting with the Frayden twins, two sixth graders who were as annoying as a cloud of gnats. Charlie was short and blond with large front teeth, wearing a red plaid shirt. Doug was short and blond with large front teeth, wearing a blue plaid shirt. They looked like a pair of chipmunks dressed for a rodeo. I glanced around quickly to see if there was anywhere else—

"Come on, Lizzie. I saved a place for you."

I took one last look for a rock or something to hide behind and eat my gruel in peace before heading over to Natalie. Just as I was slipping between two rows of tables to the open spot, I tripped over a chair leg, rattling my silverware and spilling my apple juice.

"Squeak, squeak," someone shouted out, followed by a chorus of laughter.

Ha-ha. We were such a happy bunch of comedians at Willing Middle School West. So here's the sad story about that. For the winter concert last year, I was given a clarinet solo that ended with an epic squeak that froze the entire orchestra in shock. In the suddenly silent auditorium, you could hear the mice chewing on our shoelaces. Such fun.

Now, with the laughter still ringing in my ears, I hurried over and dropped into the chair next to Natalie.

"Nice landing," said one of the Fraydens in that grating Frayden voice, like a cross between an air horn and a bumblebee.

"Be quiet, Doug," said Natalie. "Hey, Lizzie. The twins were just trying to get me to join debate club."

I picked at the macaroni and cheese on my plate, which looked suspiciously like chunks of rubber hose in a yellow industrial sludge.

"Both you guys should join," said Charlie.

"Pass," said Natalie.

"But we have so much fun," said Doug. "We laugh and laugh."

"Have you ever noticed that when you guys laugh you sound like hyenas?" said Natalie.

"How do hyenas sound?"

"Say something amusing, Lizzie."

"Something amusing," I said.

The boys snorted.

"Like that," Natalie said.

The Fraydens were smart and cheerful and beyond my comprehension. First off, they seemed to like everyone, which made no sense to me, since I pretty much knew everyone they knew and I barely liked anyone. They were also always so excited about the most boring things, such as debate club. If instead of a debate club there had been a silent club, I would have been right on it. When the mood struck I could out-silent a rock. But the thought of standing around arguing about something with other people who were arguing back, and doing it on purpose—for fun—just seemed wrong. Like if someone told me she had joined the falling-off-the-roof club. *I mean, if it wasn't for the broken arms . . .*

"What do you debate about?" I asked.

"It doesn't really matter," said Charlie. "You don't pick your topic or your side. It's all in how you argue."

"That sounds like dinner at my house," said Natalie.

"What about you, Elizabeth?" said Charlie. "We could use some brains on the team."

"Obviously," said Natalie.

"You mean you want me to stand in front of a bunch of people I don't know," I said, "and argue for something I don't care about."

"Exactly."

"You see this fork?" I said, holding up a piece of silverware spearing a drippy piece of yellow macaroni. "I'd rather stick it in my eye."

"Better yet, stick it in Charlie's eye," said Natalie.

"We need that aggressiveness, Elizabeth," said Doug. "You're a natural."

"I have got to find something to do after school," said Natalie. "Even debate would be better than going home on the early bus. I was thinking of trying out for cheerleading in the spring. You want to do it with me, Lizzie?"

"Give me an 'N,' " I said. "Give me an 'O.' "

"But they give us pom-poms," said Natalie. "Who doesn't

like—" She stopped talking and lifted her head, before saying in a soft whisper, "Yikes alive."

And there, right there, in Natalie's breathless little *eep*, was the beginning of everything.

A Sketchy Proposition

I searched the lunchroom for some horrible creature running loose, a wild boar, maybe, with two-foot tusks. It would take something truly awful to stop Natalie in the middle of a sentence.

"Could he get any better looking?" said Natalie when she finally caught her breath.

"Who?"

"Him," said Natalie. "Henry Harrison."

Ah yes, now I saw. Henry Harrison was walking toward our side of the lunchroom. Hooray, hooray. Everyone knew Henry Harrison, the swimming star who went through girlfriends like Natalie went through shoes, who played bongos in the talent show, and who each morning before school was already training with the high school swim team. He was almost as big as a high school kid even at thirteen, dark skin, broad shoulders, and a sharp high fade for a haircut.

"Is he looking here?" Natalie asked. "Oh my God. He's looking here. He's looking right at me."

"Doesn't he have a girlfriend?" I said.

"Debbie Benner, a tennis player. But nothing lasts with Henry Harrison. And tell me he's not coming right here."

As impossible as it sounded, Natalie was right—Henry Harrison was walking toward us. And what was more, he was looking right at Natalie. And it wasn't just Natalie who noticed. The whole lunchroom hushed as Henry Harrison slowly made his way to our table.

"What did you do?" said Charlie Frayden in a nervous voice.

"Nothing," said Doug. "I swear."

"Did you hear what he did to Grimes?"

"They had to spread him with butter to get him out of the trash can."

"And Grimes is a vegan! What did you do?"

"Got to go," said Doug before he grabbed his tray and fled the table, his brother right behind him.

I lowered my head and let my hair drop over my eyes like a shield as Henry Harrison walked the final few feet to our table, sat down across from Natalie, and stared at her for a moment.

I had seen him in the halls and on the talent show stage, but being this close to him was disconcerting. As I plowed my fork through my macaroni, I could feel the force field of his athleticism and popularity.

"Hey," said Henry Harrison.

"Hey, yourself," peeped Natalie as she put on her most charming smile. She was trying so hard I was embarrassed for her, but I understood. In Natalie's world, to be swooped upon by a popular eighth-grade sports star was as delicious as a chocolate Pocky—and is anything more delicious than a chocolate Pocky?

"People have been talking about you," said Henry.

"About me?" said Natalie. "Nothing bad, I hope."

"Nothing bad at all."

"Then maybe you've been talking to the wrong people." She laughed nervously.

"I heard you're some kind of math genius."

"Hardly. Math's like way down on my list, somewhere between square dancing and hang gliding."

"Do you hang glide?"

She shook her head. "I don't square-dance, either."

"So, no math?"

"No math. *Pero, soy bastante buena en español.* And I play guitar, if that counts."

"I'm a little confused," said Henry. "Aren't you Elizabeth Webster?"

"Oh, you are confused," said Natalie, her smile disappearing bit by bit, like the sun slowly setting below the horizon. "You don't want me. You want her."

Henry Harrison turned his gaze from Natalie to me. "You're Elizabeth?"

"Since I was born," I said in a low, embarrassed mumble.

"What do your friends call you?"

"Elizabeth."

"How about Beth?"

"How about not."

"Okay. I'll call you Webster. So you're the genius I've been hearing all about. You're studying ninth-grade Geometry with Mr. Pepperton, right?"

"You don't have to be a genius to learn ninth-grade Geometry. I mean, Mr. Pepperton is teaching it."

"I don't know, I'm having a hard enough time with linear equations."

"Stick with it," I said. "I'm sure you'll get them straightened out."

This Henry Harrison laughed a little too loudly at my joke before drumming a bit on the table. "Here's the story," he said. "I'm having trouble with math, and my swim coach is hassling me about my grades. I was hoping you could help me with—"

Thunk!

Henry jerked back at the sound as I turned to face Natalie, who had just smacked her head on the table.

"Are you okay?" said Henry.

"Why wouldn't I be?" said Natalie, still facedown.

"Don't worry about Natalie," I said, having seen this act before. "You know that thing where you fall asleep in the middle of a conversation? Narco something?"

"Narcolepsy?"

"That's it."

"You have narcolepsy?"

"I wish," said Natalie.

Henry looked at me, at Natalie, back at me. "So, Webster,"

he said, barreling on despite his confusion, "what do you think? Could you tutor me, just until I catch on to the basics? Please? I'll pay you."

Natalie's head lifted from the table as if raised by the scent of money. "How much?" she asked. I turned and gave her a low growl.

"How about twenty bucks for the first session?"

"Twenty-five," said Natalie.

"Done," said Henry. "Do we have a deal, Webster?"

"I don't know," I said.

"All right," he said, flashing his famous smile. "Is tonight good?"

"Tonight?" I said.

"No time to waste. Eight at my house. We're at the top of Orchard Lane. Two one three."

"The pile of—"

"That's the one," he said quickly. "See you then." And just as quickly as he had appeared he was gone, heading back across the lunchroom as if being chased by my regret.

What had just happened? One moment I was sitting peacefully, trying not to get sick at lunch, and the next moment I had been signed up to spend hours trying to explain linear equations to some jock who lived in a heap of stone high on a hill. We had all heard things about that house. And Henry Harrison seemed too anxious. The whole thing sounded way sketchy.

"I have got to get better at math," said Natalie as she watched Henry walk away.

"Nice face-plant," I said.

"Thanks. I've been working on it. You are so lucky."

"What do you want, a commission?"

"I'm not talking about the money, silly."

"It's just tutoring," I said.

"It's never just tutoring, not with someone like Henry Harrison. He is totally hot."

"And a zero at math."

"Sometimes, Lizzie, you are just so dense."

Maybe I was, because Natalie was right that this wasn't about math. But it wasn't about Henry Harrison and me, either. What it was about was a glimpse into another, terrifying world where my name was being tossed around like a basketball.

TRIP TO THE MOON

Shortly after my mother got remarried, she arranged for me to have a talk with a nice psychologist. At the time I didn't understand why I needed to talk to anyone. Do you think maybe it was because of the way I acted at the wedding?

I told my mother I didn't want to go and see the nice lady. I buried my face in a pillow and screamed when she insisted. And then, in the doctor's office, I sat on the couch with my arms crossed for the entire "talk."

"I feel some anger here," said the doctor.

You think? Like I said, she was nice, and she tried really hard, but there was all this stuff swirling in my head that made dealing with her impossible. I mean, how do you put a tornado into words?

"Tell me about yourself, Elizabeth," said the doctor.

And right there, at her very first question, I was stumped. What could I say then? What could I say now? When I thought about myself, I only thought about who I wasn't and what I couldn't do. I wasn't an actor or a singer—my grandmother once described my voice as frog-like. Yes, my grandmother! My math was okay, sure, and I liked to read manga paperbacks, stories about wide-eyed girls with supernatural powers—everyone needs heroes—but I couldn't dance or write poetry, my clarinet was a certified instrument of torture, and I certainly wasn't a sparkling conversationalist, as my mother pointed out to me every night at dinner.

"So how was school today, Elizabeth?" she asked after dishing out the meatloaf, potatoes, and peas.

"Fine."

"Did anything exciting happen?"

"No."

"Nothing."

"It's school."

"You must go to the most deadly dull school in America," said my stepfather, Stephen Scali, in his slow voice. Stephen, bald and thin, suffered from an incurable disease called boringitis. "Gosh, I remember all my adventures in junior high. I might have to call the principal and tell her that they need to liven up the place."

"Please don't. Tell him, Mom, please."

"Don't get into such a huff," said my mother. "More mashed potatoes, Peter?"

"What's a huff?" said my little brother, Peter.

"You know the big bad wolf?" said my mother. "Well, he huffs before he puffs."

"He smokes?" said Peter.

"No wonder he couldn't blow down that house," I said.

Peter laughed. Unlike me, Peter, who was in the second grade at my old elementary school, laughed a lot.

"We don't want to embarrass you, Elizabeth," said Stephen. "We're just trying to be part of your life."

"Why?" I said. "Even I don't want to be part of my life."

My mother looked at Stephen with that look. You know the look. I was one step away from another talk with the nice psychologist, when my brother flew to my rescue.

"We went into space today," said Peter.

"Was it exciting?" said my mother.

"Not really, until we almost ran out of fuel and started falling back to Earth. The lights flicked on and off and some kids started shouting until Mrs. Swinton just happened to remember to fire up the booster rockets."

"Thank goodness for Mrs. Swinton," said Stephen.

"She sure saved the day," said Peter, giving me a glance to let me know who was really being saved. "If she can flick the lights fast enough, next week we're landing on the moon."

"That sounds like fun," I said. "I could use a few weeks on the moon myself. Can I go with?"

"You have to bring your own lunch," said Peter. "Moon pies."

"Yum," I said.

"And Mrs. Swinton told us we need to bring moon boots."

"What's a moon boot?" I asked.

"I think it's just a sneaker with duct tape all around it."

"Stylish," I said.

"I'll ask for you, Lizzie," said Peter, "but there might not be enough seats. And with you on board, we would need more fuel. Mrs. Swinton is a little crazy about the fuel."

I glanced up to see my mother smiling at me, as if I had just had a breakthrough. Peter sat back with a smirk like he had arranged it all, which he had. He was a sharp little weasel, my brother.

Mom remarried two years after the divorce. Two years of it just being her and me. When Stephen appeared, I didn't get why we needed this new guy around. I even insisted—with a series of endless arguments that my mom and Stephen still shake their heads about—that I retain my original last name. I don't remember why I was fighting so hard, but eventually I got my way.

Since then, to be honest, I hadn't been so nice to Stephen. At first it was to punish him for coming between me and my mom, and then later it was just out of habit. I even called him Stephen so I wouldn't have to call him Dad. But there was no question that the greatest thing Stephen ever had done, or could do, for me was to give me Peter.

For the rest of dinner, as mom talked about this and that, and Peter laughed, and Stephen droned on about something boring that happened at work, we were almost like a happy family, the three Scalis sitting around the table, tolerating the Webster in their midst.

"More cake?" said my mother.

"Can't," I said. "Have to go."

"Where to?"

"I'm tutoring some kid in math."

"Good for you, Elizabeth," said my mother. "Who are you tutoring?"

"No one." I stood, grabbed my plate, and took it to the sink. "Bye."

"Sweetie?"

"It's just some guy who asked for help with linear equations."

"Yes. But which guy?"

"You don't know him. Henry Harrison."

"The swimmer?" said Stephen, suddenly alert.

"That's the one."

"There was a front-page article on him in the sports section. He won his age group in the state. They say he's a potential Olympian."

"So what?" I said. "If there's anything I care less about than sports I haven't found it yet."

"What about patents?" asked Stephen, a patent lawyer to his bones.

"A close second." A patent is like this little piece of paper that lets you build things but that keeps other people from building the same— Sorry, I have to stop. If I keep explaining this right now I'll fall into the most boring coma of all time. "See you," I said.

"You want a ride?" Stephen asked hopefully, as if he was anxious to meet the swimming hero. How embarrassing would that be?

"No," I said, "absolutely not."

"Elizabeth?" said my mother.

"I've been walking alone to my friends' houses since I was nine," I said. "This is no different." Before either of them could say anything more I was out of the kitchen and reaching for my coat.

If I had known then what was in store for me, I wouldn't have been in such a rush. I might have bagged on Henry Harrison completely and stayed at home. I would have planned our trip to the moon with Petey or done homework in the kitchen while my mother graded papers. It would have been a night like every other night—calm, and quiet, and eye-crossingly dull.

Instead, a few minutes later I was hurrying along the sidewalk to Henry Harrison's house.

AN ANNOYING
THING TO LEARN

Henry Harrison's house always gave me the creeps—even before Henry Harrison lived in it.

It was a stone mansion built on top of a hill a hundred or so years ago. By the time I was old enough to first notice it, the house was deserted and falling apart. A pillar was slanted, the roof was collapsing, vines were crawling everywhere.

And there were stories about it—of a teen gone missing on Halloween night, of shifting lights and eerie howls coming from the ruin. But the house didn't need stories to make it frightening. There was just something sour about it.

And then, for some cracked reason, the Harrisons came along and bought the place.

They tried to spiff it up. The pillar was straightened, the roof was fixed, vines were chopped down. But the gloomy never went away. The pillars still looked like huge, gaping front teeth, and the shuttered windows still looked like evil eyes. At night, dimly lit, the house was the head of a giant monster with the body buried deep beneath the ground.

The sight of the monster's head up on that hill convinced me again that I should have said no when Henry Harrison asked for math help. I actually thought I had said no. I hugged myself in the chilly fall night and headed up the long driveway. I told myself I was just there to make a quick twenty-five bucks and then run right on home.

I banged on the front door. A dog barked. There were no lights on inside. I hoped for a second that no one was inside. But then the door opened with a creak, and there he was, Henry Harrison, in jeans and stockinged feet. A little dog yapped noisily.

"You came," he said. "I wasn't sure you'd show."

"You didn't give me much choice."

He pushed away the dog with his foot. "Don't mind Perky. He's still just a pup."

"Perky?"

"It seemed to fit."

"I hate perk." The dog kept jumping and yelping. "Maybe you could give it a pill."

"Let's work in the kitchen. My folks are out."

"Oh," I said. The house was dark, the parents were out, the dog was yelping. This didn't seem right. Not at all. "My stepfather's picking me up when we're finished. He's waiting for my call."

"Good," he said. "I thought we could work on some word problems."

We set out his textbook and some writing pads on a wooden table in the kitchen, and got right to it. The word problems from the first few chapters were easy as pi. I taught him how to create equations from the stories, and then how to the flip the equations to make them easier to graph. I moved baby step by baby step so his chlorine-filled brain could keep up.

Perky lay on the floor beneath the table, whimpering. Henry asked a few questions here and there, but they were less about the problems and more about me, which was sort of annoying. And then every once in a while, in the middle of one of my explanations, he would abruptly get up from the kitchen table and run upstairs to check on something.

He was so distracted that I got distracted and I started making mistakes. I actually had to scratch out wrong figures on the paper, which bugged me. I was working in pen, of course—I mean, it was only math.

"I thought you were supposed to be a genius," he said.

"Pay attention. Shirley has a plant a half a foot tall that grows an inch each month and she wants to know how big it will be after a year and a half. Now let's build the equation."

"What kind of plant is it?"

"It doesn't matter."

"It matters to Shirley."

"But it doesn't matter to us," I said. "It's just a stupid plant."

"Is it pretty? Does it have flowers?"

"I don't care."

"That's just sad, Webster. Everyone likes flowers. What do you do for fun?"

"Math."

"Do you ever just hang out, play video games, throw balls against the wall?"

"No. Can we get back to work?"

"I'm just trying to get to know you a bit. You know, to help the learning process."

"What helps the learning process is doing the learning."

"You're good at this," he said, "because you figured out my problem right there."

"Can we just do this equation?"

"No need. I think I get it now."

I looked up at him. "I think you got it from the start."

"It's only linear equations, Webster. It's not rocket science."

"It is if you want the rocket to go up," I said before slowly closing the book. I wasn't even angry at him, I was angry at myself for getting roped into this. How could I have expected anything else? "So this was all one big joke, right?" I said as coolly as I could. "You're planning to haze me like you hazed Grimes."

"Who?"

"The kid you stuck in the garbage can."

"Oh, him, yeah," said Henry. "I didn't do that, but I didn't stop it, which is just as bad."

"So . . . what? Is something going on upstairs? Are you setting up a prank for the math geek so all your friends will have something to snicker about tomorrow? I'm sorry

I won't be able to provide hours of entertainment. I'll take my twenty-five dollars now."

I thought he'd be mad, or embarrassed, or even break out in laughter. But what he did instead was smile sort of sadly.

"You'll get your money," he said. "I promise. And you're not geeky, or at least not as geeky as I thought you'd be. And I wasn't punking you. I asked you here because I need your help."

"But not in math."

"No, I've had that pretty much down since second grade. But there is something upstairs I need to show you."

I pulled my phone out of my pocket and started to unlock the screen. "I'm going home."

"Please don't," he said. "It's not anything like you think, I promise. I really need your help, Webster. Really. If there was any other way, I'd take it, but there isn't. Help me, please."

Part of my brain told me to get out of there as quickly as possible. But I didn't listen to that part of my brain, the sensible, responsible part that sounded so much like the voice of my mother. Instead I put away the phone.

What was it that made me stay? Had I somehow caught Natalie's ambition of being friends with the popular swimming star like you catch the flu in homeroom? I don't think so. I think it was something else, something even more troubling.

I could tell by his sad smile that Henry wasn't trying to play a trick on me. He seemed just then like nothing more than a scared kid who needed help. My help. And here's the thing. In a way that I couldn't explain, just his asking for help made me feel responsible for him. Talk about an annoying thing to learn about yourself. It would have been so much easier to turn my back and walk away, but instead I was face-to-face with a truth as undeniable as a wart: He needed my help, and because of that I felt like I had no choice but to give it.

"Okay," I said. "But no funny stuff."

"There won't be any funny stuff, I promise," he said. "At least not from me."

FLOWERS

Henry led me out of the kitchen and through a path of shadows to the dark center hall. He turned on the light and the stairwell appeared, all twists and turns, rising at a crooked angle. With Perky yapping at my heels, I followed Henry up the stairs, but when we reached the top he flicked the light off again.

"I know electricity is expensive," I said, "but really?"

"She likes the dark."

"Who, Perky?"

"Don't be silly," said Henry as he led me through the unlit hallway. "Perky's a boy. This is my room."

He switched the light on in his bedroom. The room was lined with rocket ships and trophies. There was a drum set in a corner, a blue easy chair with a lamp for reading, and a carpet with a map of the solar system.

"Sweet rug," I said.

"Go ahead and take the chair."

I waited for a moment to see the trick he was about to play, but nothing happened, so I lowered myself into the chair. Perky yapped once and jumped onto the bed. Henry turned out the light again. I could just make out his shadow as he slid onto the bed next to the dog.

"Now what?" I said.

"Now we wait."

"In the dark?"

"Don't fall asleep."

"Don't worry. What are we waiting for?"

"You'll see," said Henry. "So, Webster, of all subjects, why math?"

"I don't know. It just makes sense to me. And I like that you can't fake math."

"Unlike English, right? I can make up anything I want in English class and Mrs. Benjamin will say, 'Good point, Henry,' like I just discovered a cure for cancer."

I laughed. "With math there's always a right answer and a right way to get there. And somehow, in the middle of working through a problem or a proof, I feel like—I don't know—myself. Does that make sense?"

"I suppose so, sure," he said. "And you're good at it."

"That helps."

"But did you ever wish you weren't?"

"Weren't what?"

"Good at math."

"Why would I ever wish that?"

"The pressure, maybe? Worrying about the moment

you'll run up against someone who's better at math than you? All I know is the older I get, the more they expect from me. I was named after my mother's grandfather. He was a Tuskegee Airman who was shot down over Berlin."

"I'm sorry."

"A real-life hero. That's a lot to live up to. Maybe too much. Sometimes I think I'd just as soon stay this age forever. It's not like the adults are having so much fun. Would you want to trade places with your parents?"

"No way."

"See what I mean? Thirteen forever, that's my motto. Although it changes every year. Last year it was twelve forever. There might be a flaw in my motto system."

"I think to be trapped like this forever would be a crime."

"What's wrong with the way you are now?"

"Don't get me started."

"No really, what?"

I paused for a moment. I was blabbing to Henry in a way I hadn't blabbed to anyone else in a long time, not even Natalie. Maybe it was because he was a total stranger, or maybe it was because of the darkness, or maybe it was because he actually seemed interested. But the peculiar Henry Harrison was way different than I had imagined him to be. I had misjudged him, which was funny because I hadn't thought I had judged him at all.

"It's just like I'm in the wrong place all the time," I said. "That I'm saying the wrong thing all the time. That I'm thinking the wrong thing all the time."

"Join the club, Webster. Everyone feels like that."

"You too?"

He thought for a moment and then laughed. "Nah. I've always fit in. That's my trouble, I guess."

"It doesn't seem so bad."

"Yeah, and everybody smiling in the hallway is really so wonderfully happy all the—" He stopped talking for a moment and then said, "Uh-oh."

"Henry?"

"Shhh."

I shut right up and stared into the darkness, seeing nothing. A moment went by, then three. I closed my eyes for what seemed like only a second and snapped them open when I heard a growl, low and angry, coming from the dog.

The growl exploded into barks as I felt a breeze sweeping through the room.

"You smell that?" said Henry.

"I think so," I said, and I did. It was sweet and bright, fruity and innocent. Flowers?

I couldn't figure out where the breeze was coming from. The window was closed and the door was shut, but still it darted from this corner to that as if it were alive. It swirled about the ceiling before diving down again, rushing over the cymbals of the drum set with a quivery sound, then sweeping around the chair so that it prickled the hairs on the back of my neck.

"Hold on to your belt," said Henry, "because here she comes."

And just then something began to shimmer in the middle of the room. It was at first just the tiniest bit of grayish light, but it grew bright and brighter. As I looked on with wonder, two glowing balls of pale smoky blue emerged out of that shimmer.

The balls of light became two eyes staring at Henry. Slowly a face to hold those eyes came into view—a girl's face, with a beauty mark beneath her eye like a movie star, and long, curly hair. A sweater appeared below the face, a tightly fitting sweater, and then a skirt with a poodle design sewed on. It was so amazing I couldn't take my eyes off the sight.

Smack in the middle of the room was a glowing teen ghost reaching her hand out to Henry Harrison. And out of her ghostly mouth came a syrupy, ghostly moan.

I laughed and clapped, like at a magic show when a card was plucked out of the air.

"This is so cool," I said. "What a great trick."

"It's not a trick," said Henry.

Just then, as if a switch was flicked, the sweet floral scent soured. The ghost's glowing skin peeled away. The reaching hand became all bone. The sweater drooped until it hung as if off a skeleton, and curly hair fell off the newly exposed skull in a rush of ringlets. The pretty blue eyes darkened to become pools of shadow, from one of which scurried a shimmering cockroach.

I jumped to my feet as the low moan grew louder and louder until it filled the room. And then the ghost in her poodle skirt turned toward me and with that skeleton hand lifted her head right off the stem of her neck, swung it behind her, stepped forward, and threw it at me underhand, like she was rolling a bowling bowl right at my face. Just before it hit me, the head exploded into a mass of sparks shaped like a smile.

What I heard next was the most terrifying scream—which became even more terrifying when I realized it was coming from me.

Ghost Story

You can bet I didn't wait for an explanation. I didn't need an explanation. The fear that had plunged into my gut like a knife told me everything I needed to know.

I tore out of that room, barreled through the darkness, stumbled down the stairs. All the way down I could hear the moans of the ghost, the yap-yaps of the dog, and my own high-pitched screams.

When I burst out the front door into the cool night air, I didn't worry about following the stone path to the long drive. Instead I charged straight down the hill, as fast as I could manage.

Until I lost my balance and started tumbling, bouncing like a loose basketball, rolling like a runaway wheel.

I landed on my back on a flat stretch of ground. Battered

and dazed from the fall, I stared up at the spinning stars and fought to catch my breath.

What had I just seen? I remembered closing my eyes for just a second. I must have fallen asleep and dreamed a terrible dream. And then maybe I had woken abruptly and charged like a spooked zebra out of the room, and out of the house, and down the hill.

Henry Harrison must think I'm a total loon.

But when I sat up and turned to look back at the house, I realized I wasn't alone anymore. Henry was standing next to me, holding my coat, and the dog, Perky, was panting by my side. Henry stooped down, put the coat around my shoulders.

"So what did you think of our ghost?" he said.

"I didn't dream it?"

"Nope."

"And it wasn't a trick?"

"Trust me, Webster, I'm not that imaginative."

"Then it's . . . that's . . ."

"What? Impossible?"

"Yes."

"But there she is, haunting me for whatever reason. I didn't think you'd believe me if I simply told you about it."

"You're right. It's unbelievable."

"And yet she keeps showing up in my room. She floats there all cute and flirty before her skin falls away. And to be honest, no matter how creepy it sounds, I think she likes me."

"She didn't like me much. She rolled her head at me."

"Yeah, weird, right? That never happened to me. She's lifted it off her neck, sure, but she's never bowled with it before."

"So you think a ghost has a crush on you?"

"Well, you know," he said with a smile, "I have some charm."

"How long has this been going on?" I said.

"I've been charming most of my life."

"I mean the ghost."

"Oh, yeah. For about two weeks now. There's other stuff happening, too—the rattling of cabinet doors, the clattering of pots. A stain appeared on the living room wall in the shape of a snake. And the faucet in my parents' bathroom let out a screech before a gush of gunk poured out. That's the stuff that has my parents freaked, but the ghost only comes for me. I tried to show my parents one night, but they couldn't see her. Instead of looking on in horror they looked at me like I was crazy. So the fact you could see her is a relief. It means I'm not cracked."

"I wouldn't go that far."

"But here's the thing, Webster. When she comes, it's like I can feel a sadness inside her. Is she sad because she's dead? Is she sad because every night her skin peels off and her hair falls out and her head comes off? Or is she sad because she's stuck here, as a ghost? I had no answer until a few nights ago when, before she fell apart, her lips began to move. And in this soft, hissing voice, she said the most surprising thing."

"What did she say?" I asked.

"One thing over and over," said Henry.

"What?"

"A name."

"Whose?"

Henry Harrison turned his head to look up to the house. Even though the rooms inside the monster's head were dark, a pale flickering slipped through the windows, a cold and gray light dancing inside those walls.

"Yours," he said.

"That's enough." I jumped up, slapped my hands over my body to wipe off the dirt and grass from my tumble, and put my arms into the coat sleeves. Henry rose with me so we were standing together, facing the big old house. "The creepiness factor has gone up to eleven. I'm getting out of here."

"She needs help," said Henry. "And my family needs help, too. I can barely sleep anymore, and with all the rattling my mother's on the verge of a nervous breakdown. We have to do something, and the only clue the ghost has given is your name. So tell me, Webster, what should we do?"

"Move," I said. "Run, like I did, only maybe with a little more dignity."

"This is our house, our home. We don't want to be chased out, and I don't want to hurt the ghost. I want to help her, actually. But we need to get her to go."

"Good luck on that. She probably doesn't take suggestions well because, you know . . ." And then I shouted, "BECAUSE SHE'S A GHOST!"

"That's why we need your help."

"What do you think I am, a ghost whisperer?"

"I don't know what you are, but you must be able to do something or she wouldn't have repeated your name."

"You heard wrong."

"No, I didn't," he said, no longer the swimming hero, just a desperate kid in a world of trouble. "She asked for you. Can you help her? Can you help us? Can you make her go away, Webster? Please?"

DEAR OLD DAD

It should have been shocking that a ghost with long, curly hair had whispered my name, don't you think? It should have been an electrified bolt out of the blue.

But somehow it didn't seem so shocking at all. And if the ghost had really said my name—and where else would someone like Henry Harrison ever have gotten hold of it in the first place?—then I was certain that this summons had something to do with my father.

I haven't told you yet about my dad. My biological dad. The truth is, what I knew about him then was muddy at best. While my stepfather, the completely boring Stephen, was there at every dinner and every squeaky winter concert, Eli Webster was an iffy presence in my life.

When I was younger he would show up here and there,

but never where you would expect to find a normal dad. He didn't attend my concerts or our holiday dinners or my birthday parties. Instead, two or three times a year, he'd magically appear, picking me up at elementary school or cheering for me in his booming voice as I indifferently kicked a soccer ball. Our meetings were always kind of awkward: my father trying too hard while I hid silently behind my hair.

"You're a talkative one, aren't you, Lizzie Face?" he'd say to me. Lizzie Face was his pet name for me, or Lizard Face when I grew angry, which often happened around him.

But even those visits had petered out a few years ago. Now I never saw him—well, maybe never.

There were times when I thought I spotted my father's wide red face and thick black glasses as he beamed at me from a sideline or in an auditorium. Yet when I went looking for him afterward, he was never there. I couldn't decide if my father was secretly keeping track of my life or if I was imagining him doing it out of some sad-sack need to have a father who cared. And I couldn't decide which possibility was worse. It was all so odd.

Then there were the stray remarks from my mother that might not have made much sense at the time but seemed to now. *Oh, Elizabeth, don't go chasing phantoms like your father.* Or, *Try to suppress the Webster in you and don't let your fantasies run wild.* Or, *I'm so glad you like math—it's nice to deal with stuff that's real, not figments of some wild imagination,* which only showed how little about math my mom really knew.

"What does Dad do?" I asked my mother after I made my way back from Henry's house.

My nerves were still jumping, as if the ghost had chased me all the way home, and my clothes were marked with dirt smudges and grass stains. Luckily my mother, grading papers at the kitchen table, hadn't seemed to notice my condition.

"You know, patents and stuff," she said.

"No, not Stephen. My real father."

My mother swiftly looked up from her work. "What happened to you?"

"I fell."

"Down a well?"

"Something like that. I'm just wondering."

"Your father's a lawyer, Elizabeth, just like Stephen."

"What is it with you and lawyers anyway?"

My mother smiled slyly, like that *Mona Lisa* painting.

"But what kind of lawyer is he?" I said, trying not to appear too curious.

"The usual kind, I suppose."

"Does he represent criminals? Businesspeople?"

"Your father always says the law is a helping profession and that's what he does—he helps those in need."

"What kind of need?"

"Oh, this and that, nothing for you to worry about."

"Anything specific?"

"How was your tutoring, dear? Was he nice?"

"Nice enough, I suppose."

"And a swimming star, think of that. Did he end up getting it?"

"Oh yes, he got it, all right."

"It always feels so good to see understanding light in a young person's eyes."

"Yes it does," I said, as understanding lit in my own.

I headed to the fridge and pulled out the jug of milk, pretending that all the questions had flown from my skull like a startled flock of bats. But after my mother and Stephen had gone off to sleep, I waited for a safe interval before slipping out of my room, down the stairs, and into my stepfather's office. Have one measly encounter with a ghost, and the next thing you know you're creeping around your own house like a burglar. But I knew what I was after.

I closed the office door behind me before turning on the light and heading straight to the storage closet. I pushed away a heap of useless computer equipment, a box of old video cameras, a crate of Stephen's vinyl records. And then there it was, like a long-lost artifact buried in an ancient tomb: a white carton with "Personal Papers" written across the cardboard in my mother's careful printing.

I dragged the carton out of the closet and sat before it like it had some sort of magical power over me. Then I pulled the box flaps apart.

Inside was a tightly packed row of files, all that remained of the Webster family records from the time before my mom became a Scali. I didn't care about bank accounts and tax records. I didn't care about the checkbooks or financial statements or letters about the mortgage. I was looking for a single file—the one with my parents' divorce papers. It took me a moment to find it, thick with paper and jammed in the middle of the box. I took hold, tugged it out, and opened it slowly.

Attached to the file with a metal clip were page after page of letters from one lawyer to another, along with documents from a court case, *Webster v. Webster*, signed by my mother and father. It was all as boring as could be and yet still it swept my breath away. These letters held my family's hidden history, revealing how it had finally been determined which of my parents would get what, including me. But those depressing details weren't what I was after this night.

Page by page I went through the file, searching and not finding what I was looking for, and page by page my disappointment grew. You would have thought there would be something directly from my father in the file. You would have thought he cared enough to write at least one stupid letter about me in the course of the divorce that had wrecked all our lives. I was letting my anger flare, the way it often did as I thought about my father, when one of the pages I was skimming through felt peculiar in my fingers, thicker than the rest.

I stopped and looked at the page. It wasn't anything important, just a notice from a lawyer about an upcoming court date, but there seemed to be some kind of printing showing through the thick paper. Then I realized there were two letters here, one attached to the back of the other as if stuck there with tears. Slowly, carefully, I separated the two pieces of paper and revealed a single typewritten letter.

Dearest Melinda,

    I'm so sorry for everything. I'll never forgive myself for all the ways I've failed you. Your lawyer is a bloodsucking vampire—and who would be able to recognize one better than a Webster—but I can't bear any more fights with you. I've agreed to everything. Be happy, please. And take care of Lizzie, she is my life.

    Love Always,

    Eli

Before I read that letter from my father to my mother, I never knew I was so allergic to dust.

I wiped my eyes and nose with the sleeve of my pajama shirt, but I wasn't searching for sentimental messages, even ones sent by my father from the distant past. I was looking for something else, something hard and specific that would help Henry Harrison in the here and now, something that I had often tried and failed to find online.

There it was on the top of the letter I had just discovered, printed in fancy type—no phone number, no website, just an address and a name. It was the address I was after, the address of my father's law office in the city. But it was the name of the firm that shook me so hard it rattled my bones:

WEBSTER & SON
ATTORNEYS FOR THE DAMNED

A Face
in the Window

Natalie was waiting at my locker as soon as the buses arrived. Her arms were crossed. The toe of her white-and-gold sneaker tapped impatiently on the floor.

"Could you, like, answer your texts for once?" she said.

"My battery is dead," I told her as I pulled a pile of books from my pack, even though my phone wasn't so much dead as off.

"It helps if you recharge it now and then. So?"

"So what?"

"Come on now, Lizzie, spill. I'm your oldest, dearest, and possibly only friend, don't hold out on me."

"It's not what you think."

"Don't tell me it was only math."

I looked left and right, noted only the usual assortment

of scruffy kids ambling by. One of them looked at me and said, "Squeak." It was a half-hearted effort, and when I growled at him, he scooted away.

I lowered my voice and said, "No, it wasn't only math."

Natalie's eyes opened in wonder, like the Easter Bunny had just fallen down her chimney with a dreidel in its teeth. "Yikes alive. Now you have to tell me. Tell me everything."

"Stop."

"Our Elizabeth Webster and Henry Harrison. No one will believe it."

"There's nothing to believe," I said. "Well, maybe there is, but not what you think. Can you keep a secret?"

"You know me."

"That's what worries me. Look, I need to go into the city this afternoon and I'm a little nervous about it. Can you come with?"

"But there's debate club this afternoon."

I grabbed Natalie's arm and pulled her close. "Natalie? Please?"

Natalie looked down at my hand, knuckles turned white from squeezing so hard, then back up at my face. "Okay, yes. I'm sorry. Of course."

"Thanks," I said, a little embarrassed by the show of desperation. *Keep it together, Lizard Face,* I told myself. Wherever I was now, I was only heading toward Crazytown from here. "I'll tell you all about it on the way in."

And that was what I did.

As the train rushed toward the city, past the neat suburban stations with their shrubbery and into the jagged mash-up of urban jumble, I told the whole shaggy ghost story to my best friend. She took it in with the appropriate nods and widened eyes.

At the end of my wild tale, Natalie thought about it all for a moment and said, finally, "So when is he asking you out?"

"Did you not hear anything that I said?"

"I heard, I heard. A ghost rolled her head at you like a bowling ball. Cool story. Tell it at the next campout. But I was hoping for fireworks."

"Her head exploded into sparks. It was fireworks enough."

"So why are we going into the city?"

"To see my father."

"Your stepdad?"

"No, my real father. I think my dad might be able to do something to help Henry."

"It's 'Henry' now, huh? Mighty chummy, aren't we?"

"I just want to help him, Natalie. But I haven't seen my real father in a couple of years and I've never been to his office before."

"Why do you think he can help?"

"I just do. He's a lawyer, right?"

"So's your stepfather."

"Yeah, but Stephen represents, like, normal people and companies. My father works at a firm called Webster and Son, Attorneys for the Damned. What does that even mean?"

"It means you don't want to be one of his clients. Maybe he'll save Henry by boiling a newt in a big metal pot. What is a newt, anyway?"

I tilted my head at Natalie and gave her a long look. "You

don't seem so weirded out about the whole ghost thing."

"In my family, if a ghost actually showed its face that would be a relief."

And somehow, Natalie's matter-of-factness put a ray of sunshine into my heart. To Natalie, stuff like shoes and cat videos were the important things in life, while the stuff that always worried me most, like grades and the future, never caused her much concern. That was one of the reasons I loved being her friend. What I was facing now felt so heavy I needed Natalie around to keep me from collapsing from the weight.

And I wasn't thinking only of the ghost.

As we climbed the stairs up from the train station, a cold breeze seemed to dart right into my face. I closed my eyes against the force of it and when I opened them again I was staring straight at the sprawling heap of stone that was City Hall.

The building's old gray walls were studded with pillars and granite statues. Its gray tower rose high and cockeyed into the air. Beneath a huge statue of William Penn atop the tower was a figure staring down at me, a stern, cast-iron Pilgrim with a great black hat.

Even as we hurried past the place, I could feel the Pilgrim's stare, as if it was a shadow in my heart. I had passed City Hall many times and never felt so creeped out by it before. Was I a little jumpy? Sure I was. But wouldn't you be?

The address on the letter from my father was a few blocks from City Hall, just off a street filled with fancy stores and bright window displays.

"Look at those shoes," said Natalie. "They're like stilts."

"You'd break your neck."

"But I'd look good doing it."

"Come on," I said, giving Natalie a good yank.

When we finally reached the building, we stopped and stared from across the street. I looked left and right, took the letter out of my backpack, and checked it again. No, this was the right address. I spun around in frustration.

"Looks empty to me," said Natalie.

"Tell me about it," I said.

Before us was a fancy stone building, seven floors high. It had surely been something in its day, but its day was long ago. The stone was filthy, the front door had wooden planks nailed across it, and the lower windows were boarded up. Handbills advertising a rock band were pasted on the plywood. A chain-link fence surrounded the building like a cage.

The date of the letter was the year of my parents' divorce. In the time since, my father had moved his office, but to where?

"Sorry," I said. "I guess my information was way old."

"Can we go shopping now?"

"Yes, I suppose."

"They have the trashiest shops on South Street," said Natalie, "with bins of bangled earrings. We have to get ourselves some . . . Wait. Look up there."

"Where?"

"That window. On the fourth floor."

"What about it?" The upper windows at the front of the building were dark, all except those on the fourth floor, which glowed dimly.

"I saw someone up there. Long pale face, beady eyes. He was looking down at us."

"It had to be a reflection or something."

"He was there, I'm sure of it."

"Maybe he's the maintenance guy."

"Exactly. If this is the last address you have for your father, he might be able to tell us where he is now."

"I don't think—"

"Don't think so much, Lizzie."

"The front door is boarded up."

"Then we'll go in the back. Come on, let's see who's up there."

As Natalie hustled across the street, I looked up at the building, seeing no life at all in the grimy fourth-floor windows despite the glow. But even if Natalie had just imagined the figure, I couldn't let her explore an abandoned building on her own. I waited for a car to pass by before I followed.

We made our way along the fence and around to the back of the building. That was where we saw the large rip in the weave of the metal. Beyond the gap was a doorway. Wooden slats were nailed over the upper part of the frame, but they left a rusted doorknob showing.

"I guess we found the way in," said Natalie.

"This is not a good idea."

"Oh, come on, Lizzie," said Natalie. The chain links rattled like chains as she slipped into the gap. "What are you afraid of?"

"My father?" I said. I hadn't meant to say that, didn't even know I was thinking it, but out it slipped.

On the other side of the fence, Natalie stood up and looked at me through the links. "Really?"

"I don't know. Maybe."

"Well, don't worry," said Natalie, pulling at the fence so the gap widened. "This building is so abandoned, even the ghosts have left. Come on."

I nodded a bit, as if that was a relief, and then ducked into the gap.

Something grabbed at me, like hands pulling me back. I let out a little shriek as I turned, expecting to see a fiend with sharp claws behind me. No fiend, just a jagged piece of wire that had speared my coat. I took a deep breath to calm myself before I freed the fabric and slipped all the way through the fence. Side by side we walked to the door.

Natalie gave me a little smile before she reached for the rusted knob. The thing turned in her hand. The door cracked open. Darkness leaked out of the opening.

Natalie stooped down so that she was below the lowest board. "Hello?" she called out.

No answer.

"Anyone?"

No one.

"Let's get out of here," I said.

"After we look around."

"Nothing's in there but rats."

"Then what's to be afraid of?" said Natalie.

"The rats!"

"Come on." Natalie ducked into the doorway and was swallowed by the darkness. After a nervous glance at the gap in the fence, I followed. The door shut with a bang behind us.

It was utterly black inside. The air was damp and smelled of wet fur. The only sounds were our own breaths and a tap-tapping, tap-tap-tapping falling down from high above us, like a coded warning from a distant world.

WAITING ROOM
OF THE DAMNED

Natalie held up her phone with one hand and held my hand with the other. From the light of the cell phone I could make out the cinder block walls and shuttered windows of the stairwell. A pigeon fluttered and cooed above us. Together we started to climb.

"What's that glow up there?" I said.

"It's from that fourth floor, I'll bet," said Natalie.

"We should turn around."

"Shush," said Natalie with such authority that I immediately shushed.

When we reached the fourth-floor landing, we saw the stairwell door had been propped open with a wedge of wood. We peered through the gap.

The long hallway beyond the door was surprisingly well lit, with green walls and splintered wooden flooring.

Natalie pushed the door open and stepped boldly into the hallway. I hesitantly followed. The tapping grew louder and more distinct.

"Is it typing?" I said. "On a typewriter?"

"Can't be," said Natalie. "Nobody does that anymore."

"Maybe it's a ghost typing."

"Cool."

The doors on either side of the long hallway were shut. But the door at the far end, its top half made of frosted glass, glowed with light. The tap-tapping was coming from behind that door.

Slowly we tiptoed forward. We were halfway to the far door when it smashed wide open.

Natalie and I froze. A giant in a hat and suit strode out, ducking beneath the doorframe before the door hissed to a close behind him. His suit and hat were brown as mud. His thick tie reached only halfway down his chest. He talked to himself as he walked toward us.

"Nothin' to be done," said the man in a deep voice. His ears were like huge slabs of roast beef. His teeth were as big as giraffe teeth.

We slid out of his way, pressing up against one of the walls as he kept coming and kept muttering.

"Twice bitten and so all is lost, she says. Velma was right, I waited too long. Velma's always right. Nothin' to be done."

"Excuse me, sir," said Natalie as he passed us by, but the man was so lost in his own conversation that he didn't seem to notice us.

"It's de law she says, and de law is de law. Twice bitten and so all is lost. Nothin' to be done."

We watched as he yabbered and jabbered to himself, until he stooped down once more and vanished into the stairwell.

We looked at each other, then turned together toward the door at the end of the hallway. We were now close enough to read what was printed in gold on the frosted glass:

WEBSTER & SON
ATTORNEYS FOR THE DAMNED

"That must have been my father's office," I said. "But who's using it now?"

"Let's find out," said Natalie.

Natalie knocked lightly with no response. Before I could stop her, she grabbed the knob, gave it a turn, and yanked the door open. Quick as that, we were inside.

"What can I do for you, dearies?" said a pucker-faced woman perched behind a desk. Even as she spoke, she kept typing away with two fingers on an old-style manual typewriter, large and black, with round keys and thin metal bars that jabbed the ink onto the paper. In front of the typewriter was a sign that read: THANK YOU FOR NOT SMOKING OR COMBUSTING IN THE OFFICE.

"We're looking for Eli Webster," I said softly. "I have this old address for him . . . and we hoped you might know where he moved to."

The woman looked at me through narrow glasses with

jewels in the corners of the frames, and then quickly down at a large calendar open on her desk, before jerking her head back up to look at me. "Do you have an appointment?"

"No."

"Then there's nothing to be done," said the woman. Her voice was fast and shrill, like the call of a crow. "Nothing to be done if you don't have an appointment."

"An appointment to see who?"

"*Whom* is the word, *whom*. And if you don't know even that, how can I help you at all? Time to go, dearies, time to go. We all have work to do."

As the woman turned back to the typewriter, I gazed about my father's old office.

Alongside the woman's desk were two rows of chairs in which four people sat lost in thought. It was as common a scene as the waiting room at the dentist's office, until I looked more closely at the four.

An older woman with skin a shade of green sat next to a boy holding his hands over his ears and humming to himself. Across from the boy sat a beautiful blond woman in a long-sleeved black dress who had the most luxuriant eyelashes I had ever seen. Beside her sat a man with a hump on his back that was moving beneath his shirt.

I was staring at the scene, my mouth open, when Natalie dug an elbow into my side. "He's the one I saw from outside," she whispered, pointing to a tall, thin man working at a high desk in the corner of the room.

The man's skin was as white as copy paper. He was writing with a feathered pen. He wore a long black coat with a fussy high collar, and his boots rested on the crossbars of his chair, which was almost as tall as a lifeguard's station. The man lifted his face and looked right at me with something sad yet encouraging in his gray eyes. I had been ready to run from the bizarre office, but the man's gaze gave me a shot of bravery.

I stepped forward and knocked on the secretary's desk with a knuckle. The woman stopped typing, jerked her face up at me, and stared sharply through her glasses.

"I'd like to talk to somebody, a landlord or a maintenance person, about Eli Webster. If the printing on the door can be believed, this was his office before the building turned into a ruin. Someone must know something."

"And who are you again?" said the woman.

"I never said."

"This is Elizabeth Webster," said Natalie.

"Elizabeth Webster?" squawked the woman. She turned to the calendar and pecked at one of the filled blocks with a pointed red nail. "Why didn't you say so at the start? We've been waiting for you."

"Waiting?"

"For you. Yes, of course." She turned the page on the calendar and pecked at another filled block, and another. "You're late, but no mind. Have a seat, have a seat. I'll see if he is ready."

The secretary jumped up from her chair and waddled like a penguin into one of the doorways that opened to the waiting room.

Natalie took hold of my arm and pulled me toward two chairs beside the secretary's desk. We sat across from each other, Natalie next to the humming boy with his hands over his ears, me next to the beautiful woman with long lashes.

Natalie leaned forward. "This is sort of creepy."

"You think? Maybe we should go."

"Are you kidding? They must know something. You want to find your father, don't you?"

"Of course."

"Then there we are. Nice hair, huh?"

I turned to the blond woman who sat next to me. She looked straight ahead, with no emotion on her face. I noticed sprouts of blond hair popping out of her long sleeves and from the neckline of her dress, and then I noticed—Gad!— her eyelashes weren't eyelashes at all. They were growing out of her eyeballs.

The woman turned and smiled at me. I almost swallowed my tongue. In a confiding whisper the woman said, "My name's Sandy. I'm suing a witch."

"My name's Elizabeth," I whispered back. "I'm looking for my father."

"I hope you have better luck than I've had."

"Problems?"

"Our writ has dissolved in a bubbling cauldron."

"That doesn't sound good."

"With witches, anything can happen, as I've sadly learned. And all I wanted was better hair. It was so lank and lifeless."

"Not anymore!" I said, trying to be supportive.

"He'll see you now, dearie," said the secretary from outside one of the offices. "Now he'll see you."

When Natalie stood with me, the secretary pointed one

of those red fingernails right at her. "Not you, dearie. Not you. Just her."

I calmed Natalie with a hand motion.

Sandy with the hairy eyeballs nodded reassuringly at me. I squeezed out a nervous smile in return.

The secretary led me into a dusty office with two desks and a fireplace. Over the fireplace hung a gigantic painting of an old, fat lawyer with a comb-over and a jacket way too tight for him. A skull with a wild white wig sat on the shelf below the painting. One of the two desks was small, with a clean, empty top. The other was huge and covered with towers of opened books and disorganized papers. It took me a moment to realize there was an old man sitting behind the desk, obscured by the tilting piles.

"Ah, Avis," croaked the old man in a raspy voice. "Have you seen the Hensley Testament? It up and disappeared on me again."

"The Hensley Testament?" said the secretary.

"Yes, precisely. I'm in great need of the Hensley Testament."

The secretary skittered to the desk, grabbed a page off one of the high piles, and handed it to the old man. "Here."

"This?" The old man studied the document for a moment, moving it back and forth in front of his eyes. "Oh yes, of course this is it. See to it that you don't misplace it again, you forgetful old finch."

"Your appointment is here."

"Well, bring her in!"

"I already have."

"Where?" He leaned around a stack of books to gaze at

me. He was short and bald, with a round nose and great gray tufts of eyebrows. He looked more elf than lawyer. I suddenly smelled cookies. "Her? Can't be."

"Should I put her out?"

"No, no, put out the cat, but she can stay. Just get me the Hensley Testament, and be quick about it. This is an office, not a chicken-plucking party."

"I'll get on it. Right on it," said Avis, giving me an exasperated glance before fluttering out of the room and closing the door behind her.

"So, you're our Elizabeth?" said the old man. "Taller than I thought you'd be, but I suppose that's only to be expected, considering how late you are. Why, last time I saw you, you were knee-high to a leprechaun. I know that because a leprechaun was in the office on that very day. That's your desk over there. Might as well settle in. We have much work to do on the Hensley Testament. You are ready to begin, I assume?"

"To begin what?" I took a step back from the strange old man. "Are you sure you're talking about me?"

"How could I be mistaken about something like that? It was right in this office when your father first brought you in to see me. You played on my lap and I threw you into the air and you spit up right on my suit. He was so proud."

I looked at the old man and for a moment was sure that I had never seen him before, and then a startling realization reached inside and grabbed at my heart. It was in his jaw that looked so much like my father's jaw. It was in the squint of his eye that looked so much like my own.

"Grandpop?"

10

WEBSTER THE ELDER

It felt like a long-forgotten dream had just marched up and tweaked me on the nose.

I had grandparents already—plenty really. My mother's parents, the Weintraubs, were stern, but surprisingly fun. And the Scalis, Stephen's parents, were all warm and cozy. They tried to treat me like a real granddaughter, not a step-granddaughter, even though all that trying seemed like such hard work. The four were enough to check off the grandparent box, thank you—wanting anything more would be greedy.

I knew that my real father had parents, but I assumed they were dead or somewhere in Arizona. The truth was, with all the grandparents I had wandering around me, I really didn't give it much thought. But now, here I was, face-to-face with another grandfather, who was still, apparently, very much alive and not living in the desert.

In that moment I was flooded with memories of an old man in a dark suit doting over a little baby still in diapers. Was that me? Was that him? Was any of it real?

"Grandpop?"

"Your grandfather, Ebenezer Webster the third, at your service." He pushed himself out of his seat and staggered around the desk with the help of a cane. His legs were skinny and bowed, his frame was bent almost in half. "Who on earth did you think I was?"

"I don't know, the landlord, maybe?"

"I'm that, too, since I own the building. Have for decades. Bought it cheap, a real steal, and the upkeep is remarkably reasonable."

"But if you own it, why did you let it get so run-down like this?"

"Like what?"

I looked at him.

"Seems in reasonable shape to me," he said. "And the condition keeps the taxes low. Never underestimate the dangerous effect of taxes on digestion. So, let us get to work. I have piles for you to do. Oh, I'll keep you busy as a mule through the whole of your apprenticeship. But at the end of it, you'll be ready, I promise you. Just like your father was. And I was. Like all the Websters before us. Oh yes, I'll have you fit and ready."

"Ready for what?"

"To take your place before the bar."

"I'm going to be a bartender?"

He stared at me for a moment like I had just said something in Finnish. "I have to admit that the work occasionally builds up a thirst. In fact, I might be ready for a wee bit right now. Care to join me in a libation?"

"I'm in seventh grade."

"Perfect. I was drinking hard cider at the age of eight."

I shook my head as if to shake out a cobweb. Nothing made sense, and yet I could feel a joy bubbling through me.

"Grandpop?"

"Yes, my dear?"

"Where have you been all these years?"

"Why here, of course. All the time." He leaned forward on his cane, twisted his face toward me. "Waiting for you."

"Why didn't you ever come to see me?"

I thought I saw a sadness slip into his eyes, before he brushed away both the question and the emotion as if he were waving away a housefly. "Ask your mother if you want to know the truth. But this is all beside the point. There is work to be done. We have the Hensley Testament to deal with. Are you ready to begin your apprenticeship, young Elizabeth?"

"What about school?"

"What is school compared to learning a profession that will last you a lifetime? Or, truth be told, more than a lifetime? What can school give that would ever serve you better?"

"I'm not sure, but I think I'll stay in and find out."

"You're not here to sit at your desk?"

I shook my head.

"Then . . . I don't understand. Why in the blazes have you come?"

"I'm looking for my father."

"Oh, is that all."

"Is he here?"

"No, not today. And not often. Usually, he's out following the circuit. That's the path for the young ones, trailing the court as it makes its way about the country. I did it longer than most, but then I got into a spat with that moth-eaten judge and haven't been in court since. Oh, how I miss the open road: Mobile, Chicago, Duluth. The stories I could tell of Duluth. But the court is due back shortly, so don't despair. Is there a problem? Do you need the assistance of Webster and Son?"

"I don't know," I said. "What exactly is it that you do here?"

"Why, we're lawyers, of course."

"What kind of lawyers?"

"General practitioners of a sort, but it is the 'sort' that makes all the difference."

"It says on your door, 'Attorneys for the Damned.' "

"Indeed we are," he said. "We have the most unusual clientele."

"Like the people waiting outside?"

"All the poor misfortunates who have no place else to turn. But isn't that what being a lawyer is all about, helping those in desperate need? We, at Webster and Son, for almost two centuries now have helped our clients in their battles with the other world."

"What other world?"

"The world beyond, dear, what is sometimes called the supernatural—a term I always disliked. What could be more natural than angels and demons and devils and ghosts? That is the other world. And when that other world is troubling you, where can you go? Not to the police, surely. Not to a government agency. No, there is only one place to go."

"Where?"

"Here."

"Here?"

"Yes, to Webster and Son. Haven't you been listening? The story of how we came into this field is better left for a later time, but just know that we are here, all of us, to help the living in their trials with the dead and undead."

I thought on what he told me for a moment. It all seemed so impossible, so ridiculous, and yet it made an odd sort of sense. It would explain why Henry's ghost had muttered my name. It would explain why my father always seemed as if he had been beamed down from another planet.

"Wow," I said.

"Precisely. Wow." He punched feebly at the air. "And tell me, dear, isn't that why you've come looking for your father?"

"Yes, actually. There's this ghost—"

"A ghost?" he said, interrupting me midsentence. "Say no more. Ghosts are right up our alley." He banged his cane across the floor as he hobbled toward the door, flung it open, and called out, "Barnabas!"

The tall man in the frock coat was already standing in the doorway when my grandfather pulled open the door. Long-faced and pale, he stood calmly with his hands clasped behind his back.

"Sir," he said in a proper British accent.

"My granddaughter is having problems with a ghost."

"Indeed," said Barnabas, raising one eyebrow.

"You're being haunted, I assume," said my grandfather.

"Not me," I said. "A friend."

"Oh, a friend. Well, no family discount, then. We are lawyers, after all."

"He's just a kid."

"Then maybe something could be arranged. For you. This once. Though the rent must be paid, even to ourselves. And what would your friend have us do with this spirit? Would he have us hurl it into the depths of the underworld for all of eternity?"

"No, no," I said. "Nothing like that. I think my friend actually likes it."

"You don't say. Did you hear that, Barnabas?"

"I did indeed," said the tall, mournful man.

"He just wants to make it go away," I said.

"As simple as that, is it? Barnabas, get all the particulars from my granddaughter and then draft a complaint for an Action in Ejectment." When he said the word *ejectment* he thrust a finger into the air as if the very gesture was all that was required. "An Action in Ejectment"—that finger again—"is just the thing. What do you propose, Barnabas, to make sufficient service of process?"

"Is this a ghost you have seen yourself?" said Barnabas to me.

"Oh yes. And she rolled her head at me."

"Imagine that," said my grandfather. "Remarkable."

"I propose we use a stake made from the wood of an alder tree," said Barnabas.

"Precisely," said the old man. "The alder stake. Quite effective and indisputable in court. Now go along with Barnabas, Elizabeth, and give him the particulars. He'll tell you how to advise your friend. We'll let Barnabas handle the difficult bits. I would take this up myself, but right now I have much to do. The Hensley Testament cannot wait another second. Where is that blasted thing? Avis, you swallowtailed kite, you," he called through the door. "Where have you put the Hensley Testament?"

"This way," said Barnabas.

I began following as Barnabas led me out of the office but then hesitated a moment before I turned around to see my grandfather, aged and stooped and leaning heavily on his cane, staring at me.

I rushed back and gave him a hug that lifted his cane right off the floor.

"Grandpop," I said.

A LESSON
IN THE LAW

"**W**hat is an Action in Ejectment?" I asked the next night at dinner.

My stepfather, Stephen, froze in his seat, a fork-speared piece of baked chicken floating halfway to his mouth. He was a terrible actor, which is the only thing that made his acting enjoyable.

"Is something the matter, Stephen dear?" said my mother. "Do you need more gravy? Can I get you some peas?"

"Peas please," said Peter. "Please peas."

"Do you want more peas, Peter?"

"No, I just like saying it. Peas-peas-peas—"

"Puh-leeze," I said, stifling my irritation not at my brother but at my mother. I was still feeling the excitement of yesterday's adventure, but I was also just so mad at my mother. I tried not to show it, but it was hard.

"Peas," said Peter in a whisper.

"First I was surprised to hear our daughter speak," said Stephen. He placed the chicken back onto his plate. "And then what came out of her mouth was even more shocking. Action in Ejectment. I haven't heard that one since I studied for the bar exam. You might as well have asked about the Rule Against Perpetuities."

"What's the Rule Against Perpetuities?" I said.

"Heck if I remember. If it's not in the patent law, it's pretty much been flushed out of my brain. Where did you hear about ejectment?"

"It was in a book I was reading."

"Something by a Brontë, I'd bet. If I remember, you bring an Action in Ejectment to kick someone off your land, but I don't think anyone uses it nowadays. It's a common-law action, which means it's not based on a statute, just old-time practice from merry old England. No one really does too much under the common law anymore, since there's a written law for everything and written laws count for more."

"It's nice to see you taking an interest in Stephen's profession," said my mother.

"Ejectment is something you learn the first year of law school, get tested on in the bar exam, and then never deal with again. Sort of like legal ethics."

"Stephen!"

I narrowed my eyes at my mother. Ethics indeed. Over the entire course of my life she had been keeping the whole Webster & Son thing a secret from me. The time for a confrontation with my mother over that would come, but it was not tonight. If she knew I had visited my grandfather she would blow a fuse and I wouldn't be leaving the house again until I was in high school. So tonight was for keeping my secret and serving process with an alder stake upon a headless ghost, whatever that meant.

"What's service of process?" I said.

"Elizabeth, my lord, where did all this interest in the law come from?" said my mother.

"Both my dads are lawyers," I said. "I guess it's genetic."

I caught a smile breaking out on Stephen's face and it puzzled me for a moment until I figured it out. I guess I slipped.

"Service of process," said Stephen, "is a cornerstone of the law."

"Oh no," I said. "This sounds like a lecture."

"It's not enough to file a lawsuit with the court," said Stephen. "You also have to serve the complaint on the person you're suing. If you don't, the case could go on without that person even knowing about it, and that wouldn't be fair. There's a whole bunch of rules about how to do it, but usually you just hire someone to hand it to her. If she hides from you, you can sometimes nail it on her door."

"Doesn't that leave a hole?" said Peter.

"I suppose it would."

"Cool. Can I do the hammering for you?"

"Well, Peter, if we can't find Apple next time we try to sue it for patent infringement, I'll fly you out to California and you can nail the complaint on their big glass door."

"Crash," said Peter with a laugh.

"Exactly."

"More chicken, Elizabeth?" said my mother.

"No, thanks. Actually, I have to be going."

"It's a school night."

"Is it?"

"And I thought we'd start working on that quilt for the school fair."

"Whose idea was that?"

"You used to love quilting."

"When I was six."

"You were so cute when you were six."

"Yeah, what happened to me?" I said.

"Where are you off to?" said Stephen.

"To Henry's house."

"Henry Harrison? Again?"

"I don't know if I like that idea," said my mother. "You weren't acting quite normally when you came home from there the last time. And you were covered in grass stains and dirt like you had been rolling down the hill."

"It's a big hill," I said.

"Can I come, Lizzie?" said Peter. "Tyler has a hill behind his house and we roll down it until we get sick. But his hill is small."

"Maybe next time," I said. "We'll make a party of it."

"If you do, bring a bucket," said Stephen.

"Is something going on between you and this Harrison boy?" my mother asked.

"Yes. It's called linear equations. But don't worry, Natalie's coming along."

"What does Natalie know about linear equations?"

"Less than Henry, if that's possible," I said. "I figure if Natalie understands what I'm saying, then it should be able to slip through Henry Harrison's thick skull. And Natalie wants to see the house." I quickly stood from the table and gave my brother a kiss on the head, which he squirmed away from. "Bye."

"Did she just kiss her brother?" said Stephen as I was leaving the kitchen.

"I believe so," said my mother.

"Does she have a fever?"

"She must."

"Maybe aspirin would help."

"Or a cold compress."

I could still hear the chuckleheads chuckling about me as I grabbed my backpack and headed out the door.

THE COMPLAINT

"**H**ow do I look?" said Natalie as we made the long walk up the drive to the Harrison house. The monster's head was darker than the dusky sky about it, dark as a warning. "Are my sneakers sparkly enough?"

"They don't really fit with our evening plans," I said.

"You don't like them?"

I looked down. Even at night the red sequins glittered. "Actually, they're amazing."

"And what about the jacket? It's my favorite denim jacket. A little hippie-ish. A little hot rod–ish. I wanted to look just right."

"We're not going to the fall dance."

"I know that, because Henry Harrison would never go to the fall dance. But I feel like something big is going to happen tonight. Something earthshaking."

"Oh, something's going to happen all right. We're going to give a legal document to a headless ghost, and she won't be happy about it."

"But how romantic will that be, me and Henry Harrison and the shrieking moans of a headless spirit. Maybe I'll faint and he'll cradle me in his arms and cry out my name and when I open my eyes he'll be staring longingly at me."

"I can't believe you're looking forward to this evening."

"Of course I am. I mean you've already seen the ghost, and you've had this great meeting with your missing grandfather, and you got to spend gobs of time with that dreamboat with the funny collar. What was his name, Barney?"

"Barnabas."

"All I got to do was sit across from the lady with the hairy eyeballs."

"Sandy. The eyeball thing is a little gross, true, but you have to admit she has a great head of hair."

"She was giving me shampoo advice," said Natalie. "The key, she said, is rosemary and lavender."

It was a little shocking that Natalie didn't seem freaked out about her coming encounter with a ghost, but it wasn't only Natalie who was taking this whole supernatural thing in stride. In a way, it all seemed kind of normal for me, too. It was as if everything that had happened in the past few days was supposed to have happened. As if, maybe, the ghost who had mentioned my name to Henry Harrison had somehow known me better than I had known myself.

"I've been waiting," said Henry, who had answered the door at the first knock.

"Family dinner," I said. "I couldn't get out of it."

"Hi, Henry," said Natalie, smiling a little too brightly. "It's me, Natalie, remember? From the lunchroom? You thought I was her but I wasn't. I was me. Wasn't that funny?"

Henry looked at Natalie for a moment and then turned to me.

"She's my assistant," I said.

"How much does she know?"

"Everything."

"Everything?"

"That about sums it up," said Natalie.

"And you're not scared?"

"Sure I'm scared," said Natalie. "Like at a haunted house on Halloween. What would be the fun if I wasn't scared?"

"A haunted house is not so much fun when you're living in it," said Henry, stepping back so that a shadow covered his face. "Can we get started? My parents are at a school board meeting, and I want to get this over with before they come home."

We sat around the kitchen table. With an official flourish, I took a file out of my backpack and handed it to Natalie. For Henry's benefit I was pretending that I knew what I was doing. Who said I wasn't an actor?

"First," I said, following a script I had been given by Barnabas, "you have to sign a contract with my grandfather's law firm." I snapped my fingers and Natalie handed me the first document in the file.

"A law firm?"

"I know, it sounds batty, but that's the only way he can help you. You're going to sue the ghost."

"Sue it?"

"Sue it right out of the house. This just says that you're hiring the law firm of Webster and Son to represent you, and that you're willing to pay them what they charge."

"Pay?"

I brushed the hair away from my face. "Just your first-born son."

"What? You're kidding, right?"

"Yes, I'm kidding. My grandfather agreed to represent you as something he called 'pro bono.'"

"Who's Bono?"

"Isn't he the Irish guy with the glasses who's always talking about Africa?" said Natalie.

"The guy from U2?" said Henry.

"That's him, yeah," said Natalie.

"What does he have to do with anything?"

I looked at them, first Henry, then Natalie, then Henry again. "You two make quite a couple."

Natalie beamed.

"It means my grandfather is not charging you," I said, "as a favor to me."

"Thanks, Webster," said Henry. "My wallet appreciates that."

"Sign," I said.

I took a feather pen and a bottle of ink from my pack, unscrewed the top of the ink, and handed them to Henry. He looked at me as if I were handing him an armadillo.

"My grandfather is a bit old-fashioned," I said.

After a little hesitation, Henry took the feather pen, dipped the tip into the ink, and scratched his name across the bottom of the paper.

"Then we have the complaint we'll be filing with the court," I said, snapping my fingers again. Natalie handed me an irregularly shaped piece of stiff brown paper that was covered with fancy handwriting.

"What kind of paper is this?" he asked.

"It's called vellum," I said. "It's made from goatskin. The court is strict about its documents. We need you to read it carefully, make sure it's all correct, then sign it."

"In blood?"

"Ink will do. For now."

He stared at me nervously for a moment before turning to the document.

"It basically says that your family owns the house," I said, "and that the ghost haunting your bedroom has no right to trespass on your property, and that you want to eject the spirit from the premises."

"I have to tell you, Webster, I don't understand this whole thing. What good will a court be? She's a ghost."

"It's a different type of court. I don't really get it, either. But you want the ghost to leave you alone, right?"

"I think, yeah."

"Then read and sign."

He read through the complaint, dipped the feather pen in the ink, and signed where he was required to sign.

"And we have another complaint for you to sign for the files. It's the same as the other one, but on regular paper."

As he was signing that one, I snapped my fingers and Natalie gave me a third copy, this one on vellum, too. "One more and we'll be done."

"Who's this one for?" said Henry.

"The ghost," I said.

"Have you done this before?"

"No."

"You seem pretty good at it."

"I guess it's in my blood. But you're the one who has to give the complaint to your ghost."

"Me?"

"That's right."

"How?"

"We'll tell you. But first, sign."

Just as he finished signing, the doorbell rang. Henry was so startled he scrawled a line of ink off the document and onto the table.

"Who's that?"

"A friend."

When Henry pulled open the door, Barnabas was standing on the porch, tall and mournful. His long frock coat was black, his face was pale, his lips were dark, his hair was darker. A tangle of vines dripped from one hand, and clutched in the other was a two-foot-long wooden stake.

"Is everything executed as I instructed?" he said.

"Yes," I said.

"Good. And do you, young man, have anything of the deceased that I can use to summon her ghost?"

"Uh, no," said Henry. "Nothing."

"'Tis a shame," said Barnabas. "It makes everything a bit more difficult, but not impossible. So now, children, are we ready to raise the dead?"

THE ALDER STAKE

"*Audi haec verba, audi haec lamenta, daemonium a regno spirituali,*" recited Barnabas in his crisp British accent.

The rug of the solar system was rolled up and pushed to the wall in Henry's bedroom. The room was lit by a small candle in Natalie's hand and five candles flickering on each point of a large five-pointed star called a pentagram, which Barnabas had marked on the floor in chalk. Natalie and Barnabas stood in the far corners of the room. Henry and I stood together facing the pentagram. Henry gripped the alder stake in both hands like a baseball bat. Wrapped tightly around the stake, and bound with a vine that had been growing on the Harrisons' property, was the signed complaint.

In response to Barnabas's incantation, Natalie read from

a strip of parchment that Barnabas had given her. "Hear these words, hear these cries, spirit from the other side."

Barnabas let out another line of gibberish and Natalie read again from the parchment. "Come to us who call you late, cross to us through the elemental gate."

"What language is he speaking?" whispered Henry.

"Latin," I whispered back.

"What if the ghost doesn't know Latin?"

"I think it's a required course for the dead," I said.

Barnabas intoned ever more Latin, and each time Natalie recited from the parchment:

"Bound you shall be by the points of the star.

"Come to obey us and to do us no harm.

"Hear these words, hear these cries, spirit from the other side."

As Natalie finished, Barnabas let out a final howl of Latin that shook the trophies on the shelves. "*Dimitte me, ut mihi sepulcrum, O daemonium, te obsecro!*" The howl was so personal and full of grief that I grabbed hold of Henry's arm. There was something more than legal babbling behind that howl.

A breeze picked up and whipped around the room like a bouncy ball. It zoomed here and there until it blew out all the candles, plunging the room into darkness.

There was a cry of surprise, a gasp.

Someone called out, "Yikes alive."

Someone called out, "Who has a match?"

Someone shushed us to be quiet as there came the smell, soft and ripe, not of flowers now but of rotting flesh, foul and vinegary.

A pale light sizzled to life in the air above the pentagram. The light took off for the far corner of the room but something stopped it and the light burst into a cloud of sparks before dimming again. It zipped the other way and burst again into sparks.

It was trying to get out, to free itself, but it was locked within invisible walls rising from the shape marked in chalk. It tried again and again, and failed again and again, until from within the star rose a bitter moan.

Then bit by bit, starting with the eyes, she appeared. Young and whole, with that beauty mark beneath her eye, dressed and posed just as before, poodle skirt and all. She stared at Henry and smiled, scanned the rest of us in the room with the disdain of a cheerleader examining the chess club, and then turned her attention back to Henry.

"Go ahead now, Mistress Elizabeth," said Barnabas.

"Are you . . ." I said, shaking so hard I could barely get the words out. "Are you . . ."

"Speak up, Mistress Elizabeth," said Barnabas in a voice so calm it gave me the courage to say the words he had instructed me to say.

"Are you the spirit who haunts this house?"

The ghost ignored me as she continued staring at Henry.

"Now accept the silence as confirmation," said Barnabas.

"We accept your silence as a confirmation," I said, "and therefore we serve unto you this Action in Ejectment."

The ghost turned her head and sneered at me before trying again to dart outside the pentagram's bounds. Sparks flew as she failed and failed again. Then she calmed herself, smiled, and reached her arms toward Henry. She flicked her hair with a twitch of her pale transparent neck. A ghostly tongue emerged to lick see-through lips.

The girl, dead as she was, still had moves.

"Now," said Barnabas. "The stake."

I used my grip on Henry's arm to shove him toward the spirit. He hesitated. In the spirit's glow I could see him staring at her even as his hands tightened on the alder stake.

"It's dangerous to wait," said Barnabas. "Do it now."

Henry took a step forward. The ghost brightened her smile and rubbed her hands down her sides. Henry took another step forward and, without him knowing it, a sneaker landed on one of the pentagram's lines, smearing the chalk.

The ghost let out a vicious laugh and zipped through the gap, darting over Henry's head, whooshing around Barnabas, rising to the ceiling before dropping in front of Henry and wrapping her spectral arms around him.

And pulling him close.

And kissing him.

A head-turning, breath-sucking kiss.

As she kissed him she began to change, growing brighter, more substantial, as if she was stealing substance from Henry. Even as her hair fell to the ground in handfuls and her skin mottled and blistered until it fell off the bone, she became more dense, impossible now to see through.

And at the same time Henry, lit by the ghost's own glow, also began to change. His face, locked on to the ghost's skull, became gray. His solid torso started shaking. His body withered and turned misty. The alder stake fell from his fingers and rattled onto the floor as more of Henry Harrison flowed into the ghost's gaping mouth.

Natalie screamed.

"It's turned into a succubus," shouted Barnabas. "Stand back."

"What can we do?"

"Nothing. He must save himself."

"How?"

"An act of will. Master Henry has to want to be free of her."

But Henry didn't look like he wanted to be free of her. I remembered the way Henry had talked of the ghost as if she were a friend, or even something more. He had told me how he wanted so much to help her, and maybe part of him thought this was the way.

It could only end badly. I had signed on to this whole ghostly thing to help Henry, but it was turning wrong before my eyes. Barnabas was frozen in the corner, as if something was forbidding him from stepping in. And Natalie was still screaming, as if that would help. It was up to me. I had to do something, I needed to do something.

I didn't think it through—I wouldn't have moved a muscle if I had. Instead I picked up the fallen wooden pike and in one swift, savage motion jammed the stake into the heart of the ghost.

The sound that pierced the night was like the shriek of a cat that had swallowed a siren. Through the stake I felt the rush of something dark and swift pouring into my body. Something electric and foul and full of pain.

I let go with a shriek of my own. As I fell back, I could see that the stake was still stuck in the body of the ghost.

The ghost now unlocked her lips from Henry's and staggered backward into the pentagram, screeching madly. As her body convulsed, she lifted her skull off her neck. I thought she would roll it at me again, but what happened was even weirder.

A pair of ghostly lips appeared around her skeletal teeth and the lips started speaking. To me. She repeated herself three times. After a startled moment I realized what she was saying.

Save me, save him. Save me, save him. Save me, save him.

Then the ghost lifted the skull into the air and started spinning wildly. Her agonized moan rose and fell with each turn. Until, in a wild explosion of sparks and swoops of blue light, the spirit, detached skull and all, disappeared.

The alder stake fell whole and undamaged to the floor, along with a loose bundle of vines. The signed complaint, a single page of vellum, hung in midair—as if nailed into the emptiness—before it burst into flame and vanished.

"It is done," said Barnabas before flicking on the room's lights. "The Action in Ejectment has commenced."

When I could tear my gaze from where, just a few instants before, the ghost had spun off into some other dimension, I turned to check on Henry. Poor Henry. He was passed out on the ground, his head cradled on Natalie's lap.

"Oh, Henry," said Natalie. "Wake up, Henry."

NUTS

The first of the nightmares came that night.

This was after we had recovered from the high craziness of the alder stake. When Henry finally opened his eyes, his head was still cradled on Natalie's lap, and he could barely recall his name. He didn't remember anything that had happened once the candles had been blown out.

It was up to me to tell him that the ghost had come, that she had been served with the complaint, and that the lawsuit had begun.

"I feel like I've been drugged," said Henry. "Did anything else happen?"

"Not really," I said.

"Nothing other than a wild kiss and Lizzie's thrilling act of heroism," said Natalie.

"What kiss?" said Henry.

"Your kiss. You don't remember?"

"No."

"It was some kiss," said Natalie. "A real lip locker. You really don't remember?"

"Who kissed me? You?"

"Not me," said Natalie, giggling. "The ghost. If you want, I can show you how she did it."

Henry sat up right out of Natalie's arms. "You're kidding me."

"No."

He sat there thinking for a moment. "Did I like it?"

" 'Like' is not quite the right word, Master Henry," said Barnabas. "You were being consumed by it."

"Wow."

"And then Lizzie stuck the stake in the ghost's heart and saved the day," said Natalie. "Our brave Lizzie, the ghost slayer. They should make a video game about you."

"Stop," I said.

"Thanks, Webster," said Henry. "I wish I could remember. It sounds like quite the party."

"You should lie back down, Henry," said Natalie. "You need to rest."

"There's been enough excitement for the night," said Barnabas, raising his chin and an eyebrow at the same time. "I think it best for all of us if we let Master Henry sleep it off."

"That's an idea," said Henry with a yawn.

Outside the Harrison house, as Barnabas, Natalie, and I walked together down the long drive, Natalie did a little skip. "How great was that?" she said. "And it ended just like I imagined, didn't it, Lizzie?"

"Although you weren't the one swooning," I said.

"But he wondered if I had kissed him," said Natalie. "Doesn't that mean something? It has to mean something. I'm so glad I wore these shoes."

"We just had a near catastrophe and you're thinking about your shoes."

"Well, the ghost was pretty cool, I have to admit, in a mean-girl kind of way. And you were amazing, ripping that stick right into her heart. But Henry Harrison was lying down with his head in my lap, staring into my eyes. Do you know what that means?"

"No," I said.

"Neither do I, but I'm going to find out."

"Barnabas, is he going to be okay?"

"It appears so," said Barnabas. "But it was a good thing you acted when you did, Mistress Elizabeth."

I looked up at him, tilted my head. "Why didn't you act?"

Barnabas, his pale face glowing in the night, said, simply, "I'm not permitted."

"What does that mean?"

"It is enough to know that any direct contact I initiate with the spirit world could have disastrous consequences."

"She said something to me three times," I said. " 'Save me, save him.' What does that mean?"

"I couldn't say. Maybe Master Henry's fate is somehow connected with that of the ghost. We don't yet know, but all will be discovered at the trial. Now, Mistress Elizabeth, I am sorry this simple matter slipped out of hand, but I must be going."

We watched him stride away from us, off the driveway and straight down the hill before he disappeared into the darkness. There was a secret there, a story about Barnabas that I would find out someday. But tonight I was too tired to care. It felt like the ghost had drained half my energy through the stake I jammed into her heart.

"I have to get home," I said. "I'm exhausted."

"I'm not," said Natalie, skipping into a spin on the driveway. "I feel like I could dance the whole night through."

"Please, don't," I said. "Just the thought of all that dancing is making my knees shake."

And when I did finally reach home, I didn't so much turn in as collapse into my oh-so-comfy bed, fully clothed. I was dead asleep before the pillow hit my head.

Then I had the dream.

I am running low to the ground, darting here to there, back and forth, filled with terror. I push aside dead leaves with my nose as I run. Behind me I can feel it getting closer—the yellow hound that is chasing me.

I glance back, past my furry gray side, and see the dog gaining ground. Its mouth is open. Its long yellow teeth drip saliva. I veer hard to the left and lift my tail just enough so that the hound, as it snaps its jaws, takes a hunk of fur instead of flesh and bone.

A V-shaped split opens in front of me. I leap through
a gap between two tree trunks. I keep running, sprinting,
squealing. Ahead I see a boulder shaped like a gray sailing
ship. I dive into a narrow space between the ground and
the rock, safe for the moment. The moist dirt is cool on my
stomach, and the jagged rock presses against my back and
skull. I turn to face the woods and take a few quick breaths.

The black-and-yellow muzzle of the dog jams into the
gap.

The dog sniffs, pokes, bares its teeth. I back away until I
am deep enough below the rock so that even the dog's tongue
cannot reach me. Slowly the terror fades. The dog snaps its
jaws, growls in frustration. My breath evens out, my little
heart slows. Beneath the rock I feel safe, but I am wrong.

Something slithers behind me, something dark and
electric that raises my fur. I try to spin away, but the weight
of the rock presses down, holding me in place, and then a
double dose of pain shoots through my thigh and sends me
skittering out from under the rock. I am free for an instant,
shaking in pain, before the dog's jaws clamp down on my
head.

I try to scramble free. My arms flail, my legs shiver. The
dog shakes his head with me in its teeth. My bones rattle as
the dog tosses me into the air and catches me again. In the
spinning of the world around me I see, beneath the rock, a
triangular head sticking out, coppery, splotchy, its mouth
hissing open.

And then the dog's teeth are released and I am gently
pulled free. I try to twist and turn, to free myself from the
gentle hold, but my muscles aren't working. Even as my

heart beats wildly my muscles grow slack. Whatever is holding me is doing it gently, petting my side, rubbing my neck.

I am saved.

I feel drowsy and calm, until I am lifted toward a boy. He is large and hulking, with a scar on his upper lip and a flat nose. In the boy's hand is a cage.

The boy opens the cage and I am placed inside. The hand that was holding me pets my side before the door is shut. I try to turn to see who was petting me but my muscles are useless and I can see only the boy. My chest heaves and my heart churns faster and faster, like a little engine about to explode.

I woke with a start in my still-lit room, fully clothed and covered in sweat. My heart was racing.

I sat up and looked at my hands—human hands, thank goodness. It was just a nightmare, it was only a dream. Still, somehow, it was the realest, truest thing I had ever dreamed. And sitting in the brightness of my room, my safe purple room, I began to think it might have been less of a dream and more of a message . . . sent by a ghost.

But what the message was, or what I was supposed to do with it, I had not the slightest clue. Yet.

A NAME

When Henry Harrison decided to abandon his usual section of the lunchroom and eat with Natalie and me, it created a scene. The kids around us craned their necks to see what was going on, even as the eighth graders at his normal table tried and failed to look like they hadn't noticed.

"No one can understand why you're sitting with the lowly likes of us," I said.

"Who cares?" said Henry. "At our tables everybody knows everybody's business. It feels more private here. After last night, I could use a little privacy."

"We need to keep up the cover that we're all just friends," said Natalie. "Lizzie, laugh at something."

"Are you cracked?" I said.

"Everyone's looking. We should be having fun." Natalie

threw her head back and laughed loudly before dropping a hand on Henry's shoulder. "Good one."

"I still haven't recovered," said Henry. "I couldn't keep up with my lane this morning. The coach was on me all practice. The truth is, I'm not even sure what happened."

"We told you, remember?" said Natalie. "Lizzie stuck the stick into the ghost like you were supposed to."

"But I haven't been able to remember the other part."

"You mean the kiss."

"Yeah," said Henry, his voice slow. "The kiss."

"Are you okay?" I said.

"Why wouldn't I be?"

"Maybe because you were making out with a ghost."

"From what I could tell," said Natalie, "the ghost was making out with him."

"Same thing."

"Oh, Lizzie, you can be so naïve. That's not the same thing at all, trust me."

"Her name was Beatrice," said Henry. "Beatrice Long."

I was startled by Henry coming out with a name. It seemed so random and yet . . . "How do you know that?"

"I just do," he said. "I woke up and I knew."

"Like from a dream?"

"Maybe."

"Or through the kiss," said Natalie. "She spoke to you through her kiss. That is so romantic."

"You know," I said, "I had a creepy dream last night, too. I dreamed I was a—"

"Can I join you guys?"

I looked up and saw a tall eighth-grade girl standing behind Henry and holding a tray. Debbie Benner, captain of the tennis team, the best-dressed girl at Willing Middle School West, and—ta da!—Henry's girlfriend. She was haughty in the way some people can act without even knowing it. And she had left the eighth-grade tables to eat with us. *With us?*

Henry turned around, looked at her, and then turned back. "No," he said.

"Really? There's room."

"This is private," said Henry.

"Sorry," said Natalie with a little toss of her head.

"What are you guys talking about?" said Debbie.

"Math?" I said.

"I love math," said Debbie.

"Not now, Debbie," said Henry. There was a coldness in his voice. "Can't you just leave us alone?"

I watched as Debbie Benner's expression sagged and then hardened, before she spun away. I felt uncomfortable—I never liked to say no to anyone, certainly not about something as risky as where to sit at lunch. But Natalie was beaming, and Henry was reacting slowly, his eyes unfocused.

As I looked at Henry, then at my best friend, and then back at Henry, I grew worried. Natalie was gazing at Henry with stars in her eyes. And Henry, still dazed from the night before, was staring off toward the far corners of the lunchroom, as if seeking something that wasn't part of this world.

"What were you saying, Lizzie?" Natalie asked.

"Last night I dreamed I was a squirrel."

"How cute," said Natalie. "The crinkled nose, the big front teeth. Like the Fraydens."

"It wasn't cute. I was a squirrel being chased by a dog. And when I climbed under a rock I got bitten by a snake."

"Ouch," said Natalie.

"I jumped out of the rock and then the dog got me. He shook me in his teeth, and none of my muscles worked, and my heart was racing. Then someone saved me from the dog and petted me. I thought I was saved, until a boy appeared and stuck me in a cage."

"And then what?" said Henry.

"I don't know. I woke up."

"With an acorn in your teeth?" said Natalie.

"It sounds silly, I know, but it didn't seem silly when I was dreaming it."

Henry twisted his face. "Do you think we made a mistake?"

"What kind of mistake?" said Natalie. "Wrong ghost?"

"I mean, is this what happens in a normal legal case?" said Henry. "Life-sucking kisses and messed-up dreams?"

"If so," said Natalie, "I'm definitely going to law school."

"Maybe we're dealing with stuff we shouldn't be," said Henry.

"Do you want to stop?" I said, looking at him carefully. "You sound like you have doubts."

"We have to get rid of the ghost, but I don't want to hurt Beatrice."

"Why not?" said Natalie.

"I don't know, I just don't."

"It's wrong for her to haunt you," I said.

"Are we sure? Maybe Beatrice has a good reason. Maybe she needs our help."

"She's a ghost," said Natalie. "What kind of help could we give her? Clean sheets?"

Henry didn't respond, but there was something in his eyes. I glanced at Natalie to see if she noticed the danger in his expression, but Natalie was just seeing what she wanted to see, the handsome swimming star sitting at her table. I saw it clearly, though: Something had gone wrong, all wrong, and it was more than I could fix by myself.

"Natalie, can you cover for me after school?" I said. "Just say that we're studying together."

"Sure, why?"

"I don't want my mom to know, but I'm going back to talk with my grandfather."

16

THE GREAT ANCESTOR

I sent my mom a text that I was studying with Natalie before I turned off my phone. Then I caught a train into the city. Was my message to my mom a lie?

Maybe. Technically. If you want to be a stickler about it, but does anybody really want to be a stickler? *What are you going to be when you grow up, little Jenny? A stickler!* No, see, which just proves my point.

And it wasn't as if my mom had been dealing honestly with me during my entire life. I mean, she never told me about my grandfather. What was that about? And what else had she been hiding? Sometime soon I'd get to the bottom of everything between us, maybe treat my life as a word problem, turn everything she had never told me into an equation and slap a line on a graph to see where all the lies led.

But until then, I figured a little technical lie of my own was justified.

Still, when I walked past City Hall and felt the black-hatted Pilgrim on the tower staring down at me, I lowered my head and hurried on to the offices of Webster & Son.

"Barnabas told me everything that happened," my grandfather said.

The door to his office was closed for privacy, and I was sitting behind the little desk, which I guess had become my desk after all. My grandfather's shrunken figure was mostly hidden by stacks of books and papers on his desktop. The piles appeared to have grown since I'd been there last and they trembled, as if somehow alive.

"Shocking," he said, "and quite dangerous."

"Barnabas said something about a sucking bus?"

"A succubus. You must learn your terms. I'll get you a copy of *White's Legal Hornbook of Demons and Ghosts.* It's quite standard in the field. A succubus is a demon that draws power from a victim through a kiss or, ahem, other means. It can be quite dangerous. I dealt with a succubus in Delhi and I barely made it out alive, though as I remember it, she was quite the charmer. Have you ever been to Delhi?"

"No."

"Ah, the sights, the smells—"

"What about the succubus?"

"Oh, yes. From the description, I doubt our little ghost was a full-bore succubus."

"We think her name is Beatrice. Beatrice Long."

"Good. We have a title for our case at last. *Harrison v. Long.*"

"And I have the sneaking suspicion, Grandpop, that Harrison sort of has a crush on Long."

"That can happen, yes. I've seen it before, and it complicates things terribly. There was a time in Moline that . . . that . . . What was I saying?"

"We were talking about my friend. He's thinking of stopping the action."

"Oh no, he can't do that. Once it starts it must be completed. The consequences of stopping in the middle can be disastrous. Our ghost would have free rein, not just over the house but its inhabitants, too. Your friend Henry has no choice now but to continue the Action in Ejectment." Once again, he emphasized the final word with a point of his finger.

"So what do we do?"

"There is little we can do other than move boldly forward. That is always the ticket. It's up to your father now. He'll handle the entire proceeding."

"Not Barnabas?"

"Heavens, no. Barnabas has no standing before the bar. He is merely a clerk, not a barrister."

"What's a barrister?" said Elizabeth.

"A lawyer who handles cases in court. It is an old-fashioned British thing, but then, regretfully, so is our judge. It's all about robes and wigs and whatnot."

Ebenezer Webster pointed his cane at the shelf above the fireplace where the skull sat covered with what looked like a mop head.

"My wig. It's a bit moth-eaten, I must say. I haven't been in court since I had a run-in with Judge Jeffries years ago that almost left me . . . Well, enough about that prideful scoundrel. Your father's the one to handle the case. But it is not a complicated matter. He'll ask your Mr. Harrison some questions and he'll interrogate the ghost. Simple as that and it will be over. Just make sure your friend brings the deed to his house into court."

"How does he get that?"

"There must be one lying around. It's often stuffed in a kitchen drawer. And he must bring some grass from his property, a good-sized piece of sod."

"Sod?"

"Oh yes, sod. Quite necessary. An old custom to prove ownership. But other than that, it is all up to the barrister in charge, and that will be your father."

I hesitated for a moment, lowered my voice. "Does my father know I've been here?"

"I haven't yet been able to tell him, but I'm sure he'll be delighted." For some reason I felt my heart skip and then soar at the word *delighted*. "And why wouldn't he be?" continued my grandfather. "For decades and decades firstborn Webster males have all been part of the family business."

"But I'm not that."

"True, but you're the best we've got. I'm surprised your father never told you about how we came into this peculiar practice."

"He hasn't told me much about anything. As far as I knew, he was just a lawyer like any other lawyer."

"And your mother has kept quiet, too, of course. She's a

good one for keeping secrets, I'll give her that. Well, this must be rectified, and immediately. You have a right to know. An absolute right. It is your heritage, your birthright."

My grandfather rose and banged his cane on the floor as he made his way around the desk until he was standing, bent and bowlegged, before the fireplace. His chin was so low he was staring at me through his wild eyebrows.

"You've heard, of course," he said, "of Daniel Webster. Attorney, congressman, and the greatest orator of his day."

My grandfather slapped his cane on the wall next to the painting of the old lawyer, a big-chested man with fierce eyes and a sour mouth.

" 'Liberty and Union, now and forever, one and inseparable.' Daniel Webster proclaimed that thirty years before the Civil War. It was taught to schoolchildren all over the North, and was on the lips of all those who fought and died under Lincoln to end slavery and preserve our nation. That was Daniel Webster—and you, young lady, carry his blood."

"On me?"

"In your veins."

"I'm a descendant of Daniel Webster?"

"As close as exists after the death of his children. We are, you and I and your father, descendants of his father, Ebenezer, after whom I'm named, through Daniel's brother Ezekiel, also a lawyer. We are all of us Websters, and that puts us in a unique position."

"I don't understand," I said.

"Listen to the story of your legacy. Many years ago, well

before the Civil War, a farmer named Jabez Stone made a deal with the devil."

"Does that really happen? I mean, really?"

"Oh yes. Just look at the US Senate. Now, when the time came for Jabez Stone to deliver on his promise, he had second thoughts. Understandable, yes? Eternal hellfire is just so . . . eternal. So Jabez Stone contested the contract in the Court of Uncommon Pleas in a trial that was held in his own barn. *Scratch v. Stone*, it was called, Mr. Scratch being the devil's name in the case. And though Mr. Scratch had the contract and the law on his side, as well as the judge in his pocket and a jury rigged with the worst scoundrels in American history, Jabez Stone had brought something ever more powerful to the court: your ancestor, Daniel Webster.

"Now mark this: Though Daniel Webster had the devil himself as an adversary it wasn't a fair contest, for when Daniel Webster spoke, even the dead perked up and listened. Through his wits, his wiles, and his grandiloquence, he convinced the jury to find for Jabez Stone. Hurrah!"

"Wow."

"Yes. Wow, indeed. And after he won the case, Daniel Webster took hold of Mr. Scratch and with all his mortal strength wrestled out of him two concessions. First, he preserved for Jabez Stone his soul for all eternity. But, more crucially for us, he also gained for himself and his descendants a place before the bar of the Court of Uncommon Pleas until the end of time. It is before the Court of Uncommon Pleas that your father will try the case against the ghost of Beatrice Long."

"So, it's a family thing."

"Yes, of course. Webster and Son. What about that name don't you understand? It's not Webster and Someone We Hired off the Street. I am the current Webster. Your father is the current son. And you, my dear, are next in line, though it might require the firm to find itself a new name."

And there it was: the truth that had somehow been hovering before me since I first saw the ghost of Beatrice Long. To be next in line for something, anything, would be more than I had now. But to be next in line for this was . . . was . . . well, way cool. It was like I was becoming a manga character. All I needed were bigger eyes and a magical little animal friend. I felt a sudden wave of affection for my father, my wonderful father, who had been waiting all this time to give me this fabulous gift.

"Where is my father?" I said. "I need to talk to him."

"Of course you do. And besides, we can't do anything more about our ghost until he arrives. But I've already received word that old Judge Jeffries and his Court of Uncommon Pleas is on its way back to Philadelphia, and so your father is due at any time."

My grandfather took a pocket watch from his vest, flipped it open. A moth flew out before he flipped it shut again.

"He's due back any minute, actually. I wouldn't be surprised if—"

And right then, as if the moth had signaled my father's presence, there was a knock on the door.

"Well now," said my grandfather. "That must be him. Come in, boy," he called. "Come right in."

I stood and my heart seized twice as the door opened. First because I was expecting to see my father, my missing, wonderful father. And then because of who actually came walking through that doorway.

From the set of my mother's jaw, I knew she was not in the mood for milkshakes.

THE GROUNDLING

The woman standing in that office was no longer the concerned and kindly schoolteacher who had raised me. Her jaw jutted out. Her hands were balled at her hips. She was a comic-book superhero readying for battle. If she meant to scare the bejeezus out of me, it worked.

"I thought we had an agreement," said my mother.

"I'm sorry, Mom," I said, more than a little breathless at the sight of this astonishing creature, "but you don't understand. I needed to—"

"Not you," said my mother. "I'll deal with you and your impudence later. Right now I'm talking to your grandfather."

"A pleasure to see you, too, Melinda, after all these years," said my grandfather, a sly smile bending his lips. "And I've kept it, our agreement, as unfair as it might have been, kept it to its very bones."

"Yet here she is."

"She came on her own, my dear, without my bidding. The song of the blood is more powerful than we can know. The European eel swims three thousand miles to mate in the Sargasso Sea."

"Elizabeth might be slippery, but she is not an eel and I will not allow this," said my mother. "I know all too well the price."

"Indeed you do. But you've ignored the benefits, the way it fills the soul with purpose."

"She'll find some other way to fill her soul. Is Eli better off now that he's back at it? Wandering the country alone, without a family of his own, other than the spirits of his dead ancestors driving him forward like a mule."

"Whatever other family he had, you took from him, Melinda. And after all he did for you."

"All I ever wanted for him was what I wanted for myself—to be normal. And that is what I will insist on for her. But you know I've never kept him from his daughter—that's been his choice."

"He is on the circuit. There is much to be done."

"And you and he can do it, but not her. I forbid it."

"Mom, stop—"

"Quiet, Elizabeth."

"No, I won't be quiet," I said, speaking in a way I had never spoken to her before. "Don't talk about me like I'm not even here. I've been left out of enough already." I pointed at the portrait of Daniel Webster staring down at us from the wall. "This is my history."

"Is that what he told you?"

"I only told her the truth," said my grandfather.

"That ancient fable about Daniel Webster and Mr. Scratch? You are doing her no favors, Ebenezer."

"You don't understand," I said.

"Better than you might realize."

"But this is part of me, don't you see?"

"No, it is not part of you," said my mother. "I will not allow it to be a part of you. You and I will talk about this later. But for now, Ebenezer, know that my daughter won't be back. Her connection with your operation is severed. For good. And you tell Eli that I insist on speaking to him immediately."

"As you wish, Melinda," said my grandfather. "I never could stop you from doing what you chose, no matter how much trouble it caused you."

"Let's go, Elizabeth."

"Mom, this isn't—"

"Elizabeth!"

"Go on, Elizabeth," said my grandfather. "Go with your mother. As she would be sure to tell you, the Websters have always believed that nothing is more important than family."

My mother turned and stalked out. Before I followed, I ran to my grandfather and gave him a great, tight hug. I could feel his fragile bones beneath my arms.

"Stay strong," he said. "Stay a Webster."

I followed my mother out of my grandfather's office and into the waiting room. Every eye followed the two of us, my mother storming ahead and me trailing meekly behind. I looked at Barnabas on his high clerk's chair and he raised a single eyebrow in response. The giant in the brown suit

I had seen leaving the office on my first visit was sitting in the waiting chairs. He shook his head at me and muttered, "Nothin' to be done." Sitting beside the giant, Sandy, wearing a blue dress this time, raised a hairy hand in support. I tried to smile back.

When I passed Avis at her desk, the secretary said, "See you soon, dearie. See you soon."

"No you won't," said my mother on her way out the door.

The car ride home was cold and silent. My mother stared through the windshield as if searching for her superhero archenemy on the horizon. I wrapped my arms around my knees, let my hair fall over my face, and withdrew into myself like a turtle hiding in her shell.

"What do you have to say for yourself?" my mother finally asked.

I had nothing to say, at least not to her in her warrior mode, and not now with my emotions so raw.

"You had a doctor's appointment today," said my mother. "When I called Natalie's, her mother knew nothing of any plans. Then I thought of that Henry Harrison, and wondered if maybe you had gone there again. In the course of my conversation with Mrs. Harrison, she threw off a light comment about the house's ghost. And suddenly, all your legal questions at the dinner table made horrible sense. How could you have lied to me like that?"

Sometimes your only choices are to say everything or say nothing. Wondering about who had actually done all the lying in our pasts, and afraid of what I might blurt out through my anger, I decided to say nothing.

"You turn insolent and silent whenever you feel bad about yourself," said my mother, "so that might be a good sign. We can talk this over with your father if he ever shows his face. But as of now, you are not to go back to that office, do you understand?"

Oh, I understood all right. I began to mentally graph the facts my mother had never told me about myself, about my grandfather, about my father, about my heritage. There was a line shooting up and to the right in my graph—a line that arose from the point where the x-axis, the years of my life, and y-axis, my destiny as a Webster, met. The point of origin. I sensed something missing right there, at the origin, something that might explain everything, but that my mother was still keeping from me.

As I thought all this through, I remained silent as a stone. My silence spread to my mother, who stopped talking, too. By the end of the car ride there were no words between us, only anger and resentment as thick as smoke. How pleasant. Before we stopped in the driveway, my door was open and I was out of the car, heading for the house.

"Oh, and one more thing," my mother called out. "You're grounded."

Right, as if that could hold me back.

THE LOLLIPOP FACE

"**I**'m out," I told Henry and Natalie the next day.

There was the usual cafeteria gawking at Henry Harrison sitting at a table with two seventh graders, but not as much as before. The middle school lunchroom adapts faster than the flu. There were even other eighth graders scattered around tables with sixth and seventh graders, as if Henry had somehow, by sitting with us, started an epidemic.

"Out of what?" said Henry.

"I'm out of your case against the ghost of Beatrice Long."

"Forget it, Webster. You can't be out."

"But out I am," I said. "I'm grounded."

"Is that all?" His eyes calmed as he calculated. For someone like Henry Harrison, a swimming star with total sway over his folks, a grounding was a temporary thing that could be dodged with a smile and plea. "No biggie. What happened? Did you get an A-minus in math?"

"I think my mom would have preferred me being sent to remedial Geometry than finding me in my father's law office."

"How'd she find you there?" Natalie asked.

"Your mother didn't know we were supposed to be studying together."

"Oh, yeah, sorry about that." Natalie shrugged. "But she never knows where I am. If I told her something, that would have made her suspicious."

"And it didn't help that Henry's mother started blabbing to my mother about ghosts."

"She's become a bit obsessed," said Henry with a nod.

"And my mother always knows everything anyway," I said.

"She does, doesn't she?" said Natalie. "It's freaky. Remember that time we ran to the mall one Saturday morning without permission and found her there waiting for us?"

"I remember."

"And that time that—"

"You can't quit on us, Webster," said Henry. "What about Beatrice? She needs our help."

"So help her. She's your ghost, deal with it. But make sure you deal with it," I added, remembering the thing the ghost had said after I stuck a stake in her heart: *Save me, save him.*

"What am I supposed to do?" he whined. He looked like his lollipop had just been stolen.

The lollipop face annoyed me. Henry dragged me into

this and now he wanted to sit back and let me do all the work. I'd seen it before, in all the chuckleheads assigned to my math workgroup who spent the sessions punching each other in the shoulder while I did the problem sets. There are always kids who let other kids do the work while they get the credit. Enough of that.

"Figure it out," I snapped. "I've noticed you're very good at getting other people to carry your laundry for you, Henry Harrison. Maybe it's time you start carrying it for yourself."

"A little harsh there, Webster, don't you think?"

Just then Charlie Frayden approached the table. "I have your Coke, Mr. Harrison, sir," he said, bending low as he held out a red can of soda perched on a napkin. "Just like you asked."

"Thank you, Charlie," said Henry, taking the soda as if being served cans of Coke was as natural as breathing.

"And there's some change."

"Keep it," said Henry.

"Thank you much, sir," said Charlie as he backed away. "That's very kind of you, sir."

I looked at Charlie, then back at Henry as he popped the top of the can and took a long swallow.

"You're ridiculous," I said.

"How do you know the Fraydens?" Natalie asked.

"I saw you guys sitting with Charlie and his brother," said Henry, "and so I said hello to them in the hall. They seem nice."

"You're talking about the Fraydens?" said Natalie.

"Sure. And you know, one thing led to another."

"And now Charlie's buying sodas for you," I said.

"They're trying to get me to join debate club," said Henry. "Actually, you should join, Webster. You'd be good at it."

"I bet Charlie told you to say that," I said.

"True," he said before taking another sip.

"Don't worry about being grounded, Lizzie," said Natalie. "You can climb out onto the tree by your window, scurry down, and you'll be free as a bird."

"But that's just it, I don't want to be free," I said.

I had thought about it all night, wondering what I was really searching for in this whole ghostly episode. And when I realized the answer was my father, I grew angry. Why should I have to search for my father? Why wasn't he searching for me? Maybe it was time to make myself easy to find. So I decided that I would accept my grounding. I would go to school and come straight home and stay up in my room until it was time to go to school again. And that would be my life until my father came and rescued me. Was that childish? Why, yes it was, thank you.

"I'm not going anywhere," I said, "until I talk with my father."

"I can't do this without you, Webster."

"Sure you can. Natalie knows where my father's office is. She can take you there to get set up for the trial."

"If you insist," said Natalie, a little cat smile breaking out on her lips. "We can take the train this afternoon, or Monday if that's better. And there's the best gelato shop right at—"

"And once you get there, Barnabas will tell you what to

do," I said. "And my father will show up and try the case. You don't need me anymore."

Henry thought about it for a moment, his face turning glum. "Maybe I'll just forget about it."

I leaned toward him, lowered my voice. "Is that what you want to do?"

"I don't know. Maybe. I've been having second thoughts."

"You like it when she shows."

"Sort of."

"And you'll miss her when she's gone."

"Maybe, yeah."

"But you said she was sad and needs your help. How is not helping her helping her?"

"I don't know. Stop it. What are you, a lawyer now?"

"Only by blood," I said, before leaning back.

"Charlie's right, you should be in debate club," said Henry. "And you're right, too. I do want her to stay. I don't know why, but I do. And I also know I need her to go. But most of all I just want to help her. I want her to be happy, like her happiness is the most important thing in my life. What is that all about? What is happening to me?"

I looked at Natalie, my eyes wide, and she had the same expression as she looked back at me. Something had gotten into Henry and we both sensed what it was.

"This whole haunted-by-a-ghost thing is too much for me," he said. "Every moment I feel like I'm on the edge of puking. You can't abandon me in my time of need, Webster."

I felt the urge to help rise in my gut, but then the image of Charlie Frayden hand-delivering that soda—as if it was just too much for Henry Harrison to walk twelve steps to the machine and slide in the quarters on his own—pushed it down again.

"Sure I can," I said, "and I have. You're on your own, Henry. But you don't have a choice anymore. My grandfather said now that the case has been started, if you just let it go, then for the rest of your life that ghost will own you."

"Can this get any worse?" he whined.

"Yes, actually," I said. "So stop complaining about your upset tummy and get going. You'll need a deed for your property and some sod from your land to try the case. Good luck, I'll be rooting for you."

And that was it, the end. Story's over, folks. Put down the book, kill a few video werewolves, binge-watch a series or two, move along, there's nothing more to see here.

Because I was finished with the whole ghost-of-Beatrice-Long thing. Let Natalie flirt with Henry while he flirted with his ghost. I was out.

I stayed in that night, and the rest of the weekend. And I didn't eat lunch with Natalie or Henry on the following Monday, either. I could see them sitting next to each other, their heads leaning close, talking quietly, but I sat at a different table with the Fraydens. I kept my chin down and my hair over my eyes while I swirled the gunk on my plate and listened to tales of the debate team's tragedies and triumphs. Joy. And when I came home I ate a silent dinner with the Scalis before running up to my room and doing my homework and then losing myself in a copy of *Vampire Knight*.

I hadn't spoken to my mother since she had plucked me

from the offices of Webster & Son. I was in silent mode. But, really, what was there to say? All I intended to do was wait for my father to tell me how delighted he was to see me. Wait for my father to tell me all the secrets he had kept from me. Wait for my father to swoop me into his arms and tell me how much he loved me. Wait for my father, my father, wait.

Yeah, it hit me soon enough that I would be waiting a long time. Fine. I resigned myself to being like this for however long it took. Middle school, high school, old-age home, whatever.

And then I had another dream.

19

EGGS

I am coiled in a crevice beneath the huge gray rock, and I am hungry. So hungry I would eat my foot if I had one.

The last meal that slid down my throat is no more than a pile of fur sitting in a puddle in a corner of my burrow and there has been nothing but spiders since, and so I am hungry. There will be food deeper within the woods, somewhere beyond the V-shaped tree, but the pain in my long copper body keeps me close to my rock. I have wounds that still fester, bones that are snapped, and the yellow dog that attacked me is still out there somewhere. Every movement now is a struggle and so I lie here, curled and broken and hungry. So hungry.

And then, in a flick of my tongue, I pick up the scent of a bird. Something close. I lick the air as if the smell itself could *satisfy my hunger. Slowly, quietly, I unfurl from my coil and slither painfully forward.*

When I reach the mouth of my hole beneath the rock, the scent coats my tongue. Delicious and full of bird stink. I peek out, slowly. There is a nest built against the side of the rock. The nest is silver, and woven so lightly I can see the eggs inside, small and baby blue. I prefer something live and squirming—a tender little bird would be perfect—but my hunger is calling out to me. I look up for a parent bird protecting its nest, but there is nothing overhead, nothing on either side. A parent will return if I don't move quickly. Something whispers caution about the silver nest, but the bird scent is so fresh and my hunger shouts. There is a hole up one of the sides of the nest. I lift my head above the ground, dart into the hole, and hiss.

When I finally pull all of my injured body inside, I nuzzle one of the eggs with my nose and then open my jaws wide, wider, wider still. The delicious egg slips into my throat. And then the next. And then the next. When my jaws are closed again, I turn to go back through the hole, but my body with the eggs inside is too thick and so I begin to crush the eggs with—

Slam!

My head spins and I see the yellow dog. He bangs his muzzle against the nest and bangs it again before growling and showing his teeth. I jerk back painfully into the nest and hiss a warning at him as he slams the nest once more. I can feel my heart beat like a drum, but I am safe within the nest. The dog snarls, but I am safe. I want to laugh but all that comes out is a hiss.

Then, beside the dog, appear the legs of two humans.

I raise my head and see the boy, the familiar boy, large and with a flat nose. The boy lifts up the nest and shakes it, sending my injured body sliding this way, sliding that way. The other person, whose face I can't see, places a hand under the cage and gently rubs at my belly. I hiss at the boy, and just as I spin to take a bite out of the hand gently rubbing my belly—

Something tore me from my sleep.

I lay there in my bed, my heart racing, my throat full. Once again, I'd had a dream that was more vivid than a dream.

Then I heard it, the thing that had woken me from the nightmare. A tap-tap. I thought of ignoring it—the last thing I wanted to deal with right now was some flat-faced demon knocking on my window. But when it came again, I sat up and took a look.

Natalie, sitting on the tree branch outside my window, tapping a fingernail onto the glass.

I scampered to the window and flung it open. "What are you doing?"

"We need to talk."

"Now?"

"Oh yes," said Natalie. "Right now."

When we were sitting face-to-face and cross-legged on my bed, with the lights low and our voices lower, Natalie got right down to it.

"I went to your father's office today."

"With Henry?"

"Henry couldn't decide whether to go or not. Ever since that kiss he's become boneless, like a filleted fish. Our handsome Henry Harrison has become a sautéed trout. It's like he's wiping sliced almonds from his eyes. It's embarrassing."

"So you went alone?"

"Somebody had to. Am I crazy to think that he might be sick in love with Beatrice's ghost?"

"No."

"All that 'I just want to help her.' And all that 'Her happiness is the most important thing in my life.' I don't know, it's like so, so . . ."

"Pathetic?"

"Inspiring."

"Wait, what?"

"Think about it, Lizzie. There he was, the jock of Willing Middle School West, cruising around like he owned the world. I mean, what wouldn't I have given for a smile from him. But then he gets sick in love and now he cares about a ghost more than he cares about himself. It makes all that stuff that mattered before seem like so much fluff."

"Natalie, are you, like, okay?"

"Better than ever, Lizzie. Look at me."

I did—look at her, I mean. Her eyes were bright and she was almost glowing. What was that all about? And then I realized.

Beatrice, Beatrice.

Beatrice Long had showed me this bizarre family history I had no idea about. Then there was Henry, finally looking out for someone other than himself. And now here was Natalie, caring about the case more than her next pair of shoes. A single ghost can really shake things up.

"I decided," said Natalie, "that if you weren't going to help Henry, and he wasn't going to help himself, I was going to have to do something. Selfless of me, no?"

"Yes," I said, and meaning it.

"So anyway, I went to the office just to find out what I should do. And let me tell you, it was just as weird as before. Even weirder."

"Spill."

"Well, that owly secretary made me wait for Barney."

"Barnabas."

"Whatever. And while I was waiting I ended up sitting next to the guy with the hump. Remember him? And get this, he started talking to me."

"The man?"

"The hump."

"You're making this up."

"No, it actually called me sister. 'How's it going, sister?' it said through the shirt, and then it told a joke. 'What's the best way to hide a hump?' it said. The man had to apologize. He told me the bump on his back starts telling bad jokes when it gets inflamed from too much smoke. And I could smell tobacco on his breath."

"The man's?"

"The hump's."

"Stop it."

"It's true. I couldn't make this up."

"Did you get an answer?"

"*Camel*flage. Yeah, I know. Not bad for a hump. But when I got a chance to speak with Barney, he told me the trial is tomorrow at eight o'clock, sharp."

"That late?"

"Apparently. In City Hall. Barney said we can all meet up in the courtyard at seven forty-five."

"Not me."

"C'mon, Lizzie. Henry has to be there and he won't go without you."

"I told you I'm grounded."

"And you can't get out of it? I bet you didn't even try."

"You're right."

"Listen," she said before lowering her voice. "You said you were waiting for your father. Barney told me something else that might interest you."

"I'm not sure I want to hear it."

"He said your father sometimes goes to the other side."

"The other side of what?"

"I don't know, that's just what he said. But your father supposedly goes there to save people who are trapped. It's very dangerous, and only the bravest lawyers do it because once they're on the other side there's no telling what could happen. Maybe that's why he hasn't been around."

"That's crazy," I said. "That makes no sense." But even as I said it I feared it wasn't so crazy, and it made all kinds of sense. Because the story of people being trapped on the other side might explain all kinds of mysteries, including the mystery of the origin on my graph.

"You'll have to ask your grandfather for the details," said Natalie. "He'll know what's going on better than I do.

But they do expect your father at the trial. If you want to see him, you'll have to go."

"I can't."

"Yes, you can. If you wanted to, you could make it happen. Don't we have to see this through, Lizzie? For Henry's sake, at least. He's in love with a ghost. How's that going to work out well?"

And as was usually the case, my dear friend Natalie had a point.

20

THE DOORKEEPER

A whipping wind pushed us across the City Hall courtyard, as if it were being blown at us by the black-hatted
Pilgrim himself. I had begun to really hate that guy. But we
held our ground, Natalie and Henry and I, as we waited for
my father to appear and lead us to the courtroom.

Natalie was yammering on, full of excitement. Henry,
carrying a bundle wrapped in brown paper, was silent
and nervous. And as for me, well, the courtyard, right in
the middle of City Hall, used to be where criminals were
brought in buses with caged windows to be tried in the
city's courts. I felt like one of them, having slipped like a
thief out of our house and down the block, where Natalie
and Henry had waited to walk with me to the train. But
at least I hadn't left without bringing an envelope into my
little brother's room.

Peter was lying on his bed, legs crossed, reading a comic book.

"I need you to give this to Mom when she gets back from her meeting," I said.

He took the envelope from me and looked it over, back and front. "Why can't you give it to her yourself?"

"Because I have to go out."

"But you can't go out. You're grounded." He said the last word as if were written in big, glowing letters. "That's what 'grounded' means."

"Just give it to her, all right?"

He put down the comic book and sat up on his knees. "If you have to go out, why don't you just put some pillows in your bed and pretend you're sleeping so she won't know you're gone. That's what I do."

I looked at him.

"Or what I would do," he said, "if ever I got grounded and had someplace to go. I'll help you do it. You have to fluff them up just right. And we can use a football for your head. At least then you'd have a chance of surviving the night. Otherwise—"

"Peter," I said. "Please."

He shook his head at me like I was the biggest dope. "I'll give her the envelope."

"Thanks," I said. "You might want to get out of there before she reads the note inside."

He spread his arms wide and made an exploding sound.

"Exactly," I said.

Dear Mom,

I have promised to help Henry with a serious ghosting issue. It wouldn't be right to abandon him in his time of need. You, more than anyone, can understand that, I'm sure. Dad will be there, too, and I very much need to see him and talk to him. There is a lot I have to ask him about his past and my future. I hope you understand why I need to do this.

I love you.

Elizabeth

There it was, the flat truth of where I was going and why. I wasn't going to lie to my mother anymore. I figured at least one of us should be honest with the other.

"Where is he?" said Henry, looking around the deserted City Hall courtyard.

"He's only my father," I said. "How should I know?"

"Am I dressed okay?" Natalie was wearing platforms and a faux-fur getup. "This whole court thing has thrown me for a loop. I don't want to stand out, but I want to make an impression."

"Oh, you'll make an impression," I said.

"Do you think we could find the courtroom ourselves?" said Henry.

"And then what?" I said. "What can we do without a lawyer? I should have known that my father wouldn't show. He never shows when he's supposed to."

"None of this is good," said Henry. "What do we do?"

"What I've been doing for years," I said. "We wait."

We didn't have to wait long, though it wasn't my father who came hurrying through the southern gate for us. Barnabas rushed into the courtyard, dressed in a formal black coat with many buttons and a white cloth tied about his throat. A wild bundle of bound scrolls was stuffed beneath his arm.

"Where's my father?" I said to him.

"We don't know. We've been waiting for him at the office. *Harrison v. Long* is on the docket, so he absolutely knows he must show up."

"What's a docket?" Henry asked.

"A listing of cases to be heard in court, Master Henry. Every lawyer knows if his case is on the docket. Maybe your father is in the courtroom already, Mistress Elizabeth. One can only hope. Come, come, we mustn't keep the judge waiting."

Barnabas hurried past us. We looked at each other uncertainly before following.

We trailed him into the east arch of the courtyard and down a stone stairway that ended in a hallway fenced off for construction. Barnabas gripped the edge of the metal fence and pulled it back, leaving a gap wide enough for us all to slip through. On the other side of the fence, he headed for a door that opened to his push and led us into a basement maze of rough-cut stone.

Left, right, left. We were seemingly going around in circles, or squares. I tried to keep track of our path in case I needed to take it back again without him, but it was impossible to remember the tangle of turns. All I could do was follow the split tail of Barnabas's long black frock coat, as Natalie and Henry followed me.

Finally, we reached a locked doorway. From his coat pocket, Barnabas pulled out a long metal key with what looked like a human tooth stuck to the end. He slipped the key into the door's old lock and spun it twice. With a frightening creak the door slid open.

"Hurry, hurry, hurry," he said as he held the door for us.

"What are we going to do if my father's not there?"

"Let's not think of such things," said Barnabas. "Your father is usually quite reliable."

"Are we talking about the same man?"

"Come now, Mistress Elizabeth. Sometimes the court makes you wait for hours and sometimes it is quite prompt, especially when you least want it to be."

On the other side of the door was the start of a narrow, circular stairway, lit by torches sticking out of the walls. I looked up and the flames seemed to rise forever. City Hall is only five stories tall, except for the tower, so that must have been where we were. As soon as Barnabas closed the door again, he charged up the stairway. After a moment's hesitation the three of us started climbing.

Up and up, around and around, up and around, the only sounds the taps of our shoes, the rush of our breaths, the tom-tom beats of our hearts. Gusts of wind from outside slipped through unseen openings, darting and diving around us as we climbed. It smelled of damp and age and of something sweet, too.

"This is like being on a stair climber," I said.

"Think what it's doing to your thighs," said Natalie.

It seemed like we were going up forever, climbing higher than the tower itself. Finally we reached a landing just big enough for the four of us to stand together.

In front of us now was a great wooden door with iron hinges and a brass knocker shaped like a gavel. Barnabas slammed the gavel onto the door, once, twice, and then quickly a third time. The thwacks rang in the circular stairwell.

A horizontal plank at the top of the door swung open and the large bulbous face of a man appeared in the gap. Unless the man was standing on a ladder, he was very very tall.

"Barnabas," croaked the man.

"Ivanov," said Barnabas.

"Case?"

"*Harrison v. Long*," said Barnabas.

"Counsel?"

"Eli Webster."

The man leaned forward so his massive forehead pushed through the gap. He looked over our little group and shook his head. "And where is Mr. Webster, may I ask?" he said.

"On the way," said Barnabas.

"He best hurry," said the man. "Your case is high on the list, and it doesn't pay to be late, not for Judge Jeffries. They don't call him the rehanging judge for nothing."

"Of which Mr. Webster is very well aware," said Barnabas.

The man's head disappeared, the plank was replaced, and a moment later the door opened wide. Barnabas rushed forward and the three of us followed. As we passed through the doorway I looked to the side. There stood the doorkeeper, in a navy-blue uniform with brass buttons, his massive head sitting on a body no bigger than a guitar. Beside him was a stepladder.

"Always good to see you, Barnabas."

"You too, Ivanov," said Barnabas.

"Now hurry on, the rest of you," the doorkeeper said. "And welcome to the Court of Uncommon Pleas."

THE COURT OF
UNCOMMON PLEAS

It smelled like licorice. And that was the least odd thing
about the Court of Uncommon Pleas.

Barnabas led us into a circular room that spanned the
width of the tower. Wooden benches, like pews in a church,
were crowded with people sitting as silently as stones.
Barnabas deposited us onto one of the rear benches and
then rushed forward to talk to a woman at the front of
the courtroom. The woman was basketball-player tall, with
hunched shoulders and green skin. Iron bolts stuck out of
either side of her neck.

As Barnabas talked, and the green woman scrawled into
a large leather-bound book, I took in the scene around me.

The room was quite serious-looking and trimmed in
gold. White columns held up a ceiling dome with little flying babies painted across the heavens. I looked closer. The

little painted babies were alive, floating around that dome with their wings flapping, twittering to each other in voices loud enough to be heard.

On the first bench, a line of white-powdered wigs rested on a line of stiff heads. The wig wearers all wore black robes. In front of the wigs was a high, ornate desk for the judge. Two tables sat before the judge's desk, right next to a section of the courtroom surrounded by a wooden railing that held twelve seats—a box for a jury, I assumed. To the left, hanging from a chain, was a birdcage of sorts, big enough for an ostrich. And on the wall behind the judge's desk was a five-pointed star, just like the star Barnabas had chalked on the floor of Henry's bedroom. At the center of the star was the mounted head of a ram, with great curled horns. The ram's jaw moved as if it was chewing on a tough piece of vine, and its eyes shifted back and forth as if it was keeping track of the goings-on in the strange courtroom.

"Can you believe this place?" said Natalie a little too loudly. "And what's that smell? Like black Twizzlers. I don't know why we had to climb so high, since it's more like a courtroom from the bottom of—"

Before she could say anything more, a man in front turned around and shushed her. Generally, you couldn't shush Natalie quiet, that was one of her charms—go ahead and try—but the man had only one eye in the middle of his forehead, and that seemed to do the trick.

As soon as he turned around again, we saw Barnabas hurrying back to us.

"Is my father here?" I whispered to him when he sat down next to me.

"Not yet."

"Is he usually late to court?"

"It has been known to happen."

Before he could say more, the ram on the wall lifted his chin and bellowed a trumpet blast that ricocheted around the courtroom. Then he called out in a loud, neighing voice, "All rise."

Everybody in the courtroom stood quickly, as if afraid to be caught not standing by the ram's glossy eyes. The room went silent, even the babies on the ceiling stopped their twittering.

"Oyez, oyez, oyez," the ram called out. "The Court of Uncommon Pleas, sitting now in the land of Penn's Dominion, is hereby called to order, with the Right Honorable George Jeffries, First Baron Jeffries of Wem, presiding. All persons having business before this court are ordered to draw near and give their attention or give their necks. May the Lord Demon save this honorable court."

A burst of smoke appeared behind the judge's desk, and a man emerged from within the cloud, coughing and waving away the smoke. He wore a red robe with a black stripe down the middle, his scraggly white hair hung past his shoulders, and his eyes were blood-red marbles. He stared out at us, his nose twitching in disgust.

"Be seated," he said, between waves and coughs.

Just that quickly, we all sat.

The judge aimed his red eyes at those of us in the back benches. "Be brief in your pleadings or a price will be paid," said the judge, his voice old and thick, like he was still choking on the smoke. "We have a long night and I hear the call for bloody retribution. Any emergency motions? First call, last call, come forward and be heard or be forever silent. As there are apparently no emergency motions, the court clerk shall call our initial case."

"*Samael v. Corcoran*," shouted the tall green woman in a garbled voice.

A bright light flashed in the hanging cage and a man appeared, his eyes red-rimmed with terror. He was too tall for the cage. He had to bend at the waist to stand, and he grasped the bars with a frantic desperation. Two of the men wearing wigs and robes in the front row stood and took places at the tables in front of the judge. Just that quickly a trial broke out in the courtroom.

"What's going on?" I whispered to Barnabas.

"Our Mr. Corcoran was caught using the wrong incantation."

"What does that mean?"

"It means he used a book he didn't understand, to waken a spirit he didn't want to waken, and now he is dealing with the consequences."

"What's going to happen to him?"

"Nothing good. Judge Jeffries has little tolerance for error."

"He seems British."

"He is, or was, however you choose to consider the long dead."

"Then why is he in America?"

"Well, it is an odd story. The church he was haunting in London was moved, stone by stone, to someplace in Missouri as a tribute to Winston Churchill. Unfortunately, the ghost of the hanging judge was brought along with the stones."

The Cyclops turned around again and looked at Barnabas, who put a finger to his lips and nodded. We sat and watched the rest of the trial in silence as poor Mr. Corcoran was roasted by the court, literally, with fire and everything. Natalie was wide-eyed, enjoying the show— she'd have been eating popcorn if it were on sale. Henry grew increasingly nervous. For my part, I kept glancing at the entrance—waiting, as usual, for my father. How many times had I hoped to see him only to be disappointed? You'd think I would have learned by now.

The judge banged his gavel and the cage holding Mr. Corcoran, with all kinds of squeaks and creaks, began to drop slowly, moving lower and lower until it slipped through a hole in the floor and disappeared. A moment later the cage rose again, with all the same squeaks and creaks, only now it was empty.

"The clerk will call the next case," said the judge. "We don't have all night. Or maybe we do, but that doesn't mean we must waste it."

The tall green woman called out in her garbled voice: "*Harrison v. Long.*"

My nerves, already stretched thin, started vibrating. What happened next was the oddest thing—the out-and-out most extraordinary thing—and something that would change my life forever.

THE BARRISTER

Four of us stood at a table in the front of the courtroom. Henry, Natalie, and I shivered like freshly shaven lambs, and then there was Barnabas. The judge stared down with distaste, as if he had just eaten a rotten fig.

I turned to the row of wig-wearing barristers, hoping against hope to see my father among them, in his robe, beneath a white mop head, ready to come to our aid. But all I saw were strangers, staring at us with gazes cold as Popsicles.

One of the wig wearers stood and took his place at the other table. Tall and pudgy, he tossed us a smile that looked insanely pleased with itself.

"Josiah Goodheart at your service, sir," he said in a raspy, rhythmic voice with a southern twist. "I'll be representing the defendant, Beatrice Long, a Class Three animated spirit."

"Goodheart?" whispered Barnabas. "Why is he representing poor, dead Beatrice? He is Redwing's counsel."

"Redwing?" I whispered back.

"Quiet in the court," said the judge, glaring at us with those solid-red eyes. As the judge stared, the ram on the wall, still chewing, snickered. "Mr. Goodheart," continued the judge, "as always it is a pleasure to have you before us. And is your client present?"

"I can summon her, Your Lordship."

"Then do so, Mr. Goodheart. Time is wasting on us all."

Josiah Goodheart uttered a few words beneath his breath and waved his hands a bit like he was being swarmed by gnats. Suddenly I felt the telltale breeze swirl around us, along with the scent of flowers. In the next instant the space beside the barrister glittered with light as Beatrice Long, in her tight sweater and poodle skirt, made her ghostly appearance at the table.

"Very good," said the judge. "We'll be with you shortly, my dear."

The ghost moved her lips, and though no sound came out, the judge nodded.

"Yes, yes, of course. Your counsel will explain it all. Now, is the plaintiff here? A Mr. Harrison?"

Natalie gave Henry an elbow in the ribs. Henry, who was staring with his mouth open while his ghost fluttered her fingers at him, turned to the judge. "Uh, yeah. I'm here. Yes. Henry Harrison, sir."

"Ah, so you know who you are," said the judge. "That is always a good first step. Now, where is your counsel? No one can stand before the Court of Uncommon Pleas without proper counsel."

"I, uh, I don't know?" said Henry.

"You don't know? How is that possible? You don't know. I've never heard of such a thing. Is this man's lawyer in the courtroom? Come on, speak up."

At this, Barnabas said, "If I may, Your Lordship."

"I know you, Barnabas Bothemly," said the judge with a shake of his head. "You clerk at the disreputable firm of Webster and Son. But you are not permitted to stand as counsel for this young man. So who will?"

"Mr. Harrison's lawyer is Eli Webster," said Barnabas, "who appears to have been detained."

"If I may interject right here, Your Honor," said Josiah Goodheart. "Mr. Webster is indeed detained, I say quite detained. But what bearing should that have on the case at hand? According to the rules of this court, your very rules, the plaintiff still needs counsel."

"Yes, he does," said the judge. "Yes indeed. Or there will be consequences."

"What do you mean, 'detained'?" I said to Goodheart with his white wig and diabolical smile. I knew I should have kept quiet, but I didn't like the sound of that word, *detained*, and what it might mean for my father.

"And who are you, young lady?" said the judge.

"I'm, uh . . . I'm, uh . . ."

"Out with it, girl."

"I'm Elizabeth Webster. Eli Webster is my father."

"Ah, so, another Webster. You Websters are like a

plague. And believe me, I know of the plague. But you have no standing to speak here. I don't even know why you're standing here in the first place. Sit down."

I dropped into a chair by the table.

"And keep your mouth closed for the rest of the proceedings," said the judge, "or we'll have to close it for you. You might find it difficult to eat with a muzzle of iron where your lips should be. Now if there be no barrister on your behalf, Mr. Harrison, then you must suffer the consequences. That is the way we do it here, and the way we do it here is the way it has always been done. And consequences, as I like to say in my courtroom, are consequential."

The judge picked up his gavel and raised it in the air.

"In the matter of *Harrison v. Long*," he said, "an Action in Ejectment of a Class Three animated spirit, the court rules that—"

A voice sounded out from the back of the courtroom, a rough, familiar croak of a voice. "Not so fast, you old pepper pot."

Judge Jeffries jerked his head up, sniffed at the air, squinted into the distance. "Who is that brazen . . . ah, it's you, is it? I should have known."

I turned and saw my grandfather, and my heart leaped. He would handle the judge. He would save Henry and my detained father. My grandfather would be the hero of the day.

The old man, bent almost in two, banged his cane on the floor as he moved forward.

"How dare you show your face again in my courtroom, Ebenezer Webster," said the judge. "After the matter of

Tinsley v. Van Helsing, which was an absolute scandal, you were forever banned for contempt, for a contemptuous contempt, I must add, and you accepted the punishment willingly, so I'll hear no appeal to that judgment now. Nothing you say can change the facts that this boy, this Harrison, has no rightful counsel and that you are forbidden from filling that role."

"Don't worry your foppish little head," said my grandfather as he continued toward the front of the courtroom. "I would sooner roast on a spit than argue before you."

"That can be arranged."

"I'm not here to lawyer for Mr. Harrison. I have come instead to introduce before the bar of this court the attorney who will try this case. Someone you haven't yet bullied into submission, someone who will do us all credit."

"Well, get on with it, then," said the judge. "The sooner it is done the sooner I can be free of your noxious presence. What barrister have you brought before me and where are his credentials?"

"I bring you," said my grandfather, "Elizabeth Webster."

"Who, her?" said the judge.

"Who, me?" I said, standing.

"Yes, her," said my grandfather with all the force he could manage. And then, turning to me with a voice soft with sympathy: "Yes, you."

"No, Grandpop," I said, not understanding what was going on, only knowing that it could not possibly be what I feared it might be.

"Quiet," said my grandfather, softly, so that only I could hear. "Our Mr. Harrison is in grave danger. Remember what Beatrice told you. 'Save me, save him.' We have no choice here."

"Have you gone mad?" said the judge. "This Elizabeth Webster is just a sprite. Has she any education in the legal arts? Has she finished her apprenticeship? Has she passed her exams? The answer to all these questions is clear. She has done none of it. Additionally, she has no robe. How could she dare appear before me without a robe? Not to mention that she is a girl. In all my years on the bench, I have never stooped to listen to the hysterical ravings of a female barrister, and I don't intend to begin now."

"What?" I said, startled into anger. "That's just rude."

"You are out of order, Miss Webster. You too, Ebenezer Webster. Enough nonsense. It is time for judgment." The judge lifted his gavel once again. "In the matter of *Harrison v. Long*, I rule—"

"Even if all of what you say is true," said my grandfather, once again interrupting the judge and provoking a hard stare from his red eyes, "none of it matters a whit. She is a Webster and need not follow your rules. She has been granted rights by a higher authority than you. Go ask Scratch himself if you must."

A gasp ran through the room. The judge recoiled. The little flying babies on the ceiling all covered their eyes.

"Though I would be careful waking him," said my grandfather. "He tends to be grumpy early in the millennium."

"Yes, there may have been a promise, if I remember my history," said the judge. "But where are her credentials? I need do nothing without credentials."

"You want credentials?" said my grandfather, pulling a

brown scroll out of his jacket pocket. The scroll was bound by a red ribbon. "Here are her credentials."

He handed the scroll up to the judge, who looked down suspiciously before he untied the ribbon and straightened the scroll into a long piece of vellum, aged and absolutely blank.

"You mock me for the last time, Ebenezer Webster," said the judge. "This is even more contemptible than your contempt."

"All she need do is mark it with her proof and then you will be bound by our grant," said my grandfather.

"I suppose, yes," said the judge, "and then the proof, as they say, will be in the groaty pudding. So, it will be done. Come, girl, and mark this skin."

"You want me to sign it?" I said.

"Don't be ridiculous," said the judge. "Your right is all about the blood, and that is what you must mark it with. We'll see if you be imposter or real enough to fulfill the vow. Do it quickly, girl, or I'll hold you in contempt along with that old fool who claims to be your grandfather."

"Go ahead," said Barnabas as he slipped a small pocket-knife from his vest and pulled it open. The edge of the blade glinted. "Be brave."

Now you tell me: What was I supposed to do? If ever there was a club I didn't want to join, this court was it. At the same time, who would step up for Henry? Who would step up for my detained father? Should I trust my grandfather and do this thing, or should I trust my instincts and race like a startled rabbit out of there? I was torn and uncertain.

But there sat Judge Jeffries high on the bench, the rehanging judge, looking at me with those horrible red eyes, hoping I would fail somehow so he wouldn't have to listen to the hysterical ravings of a girl. Maybe it was time to rave on.

"Fine," I said, grabbing the knife out of Barnabas's hand.

I stepped up to the bench and jabbed my forefinger with the point of the knife. A drop of blood beaded on my skin. I smeared the blood on the blank piece of vellum, and the red streak disappeared—as if it had been swallowed by the goatskin.

I stepped back. Judge Jeffries stared for a moment at the vellum.

"Aha," he said. "Nothing, exactly as I expected." He showed the blank document to the whole of the courtroom. "This will be the last straw for you, Ebenezer Webster. This is beyond contempt, this is an outright fraud on the—"

He stopped talking as printing began to appear on the vellum, careful and ornate, as if being drawn by an invisible artist. The lines became words, and the words slowly filled the whole of the goatskin.

The judge's mouth turned down. He handed the document to the tall green clerk, who held it open before the head of the great ram. The ram stopped chewing long enough to read it to the courtroom.

" 'To all persons to whom this writing may come,' " bellowed the ram. " 'Greetings.' " He went on to read a detailed history of the promise given to Daniel Webster by the Lord Demon of the Underworld. Then he read out my name and granted me the degree of Juris Doctor. Finally, he gave me the right to represent the damned before the Court of Uncommon Pleas through the whole of my life, and then through the whole of my afterlife, to the end of time, or to the day of judgment, whichever came first.

There was a moment of stunned silence in the courtroom before a great cheer went up from the spectators. A cheer for *me*. Imagine that. Sparks fell from the domed ceiling as the little flying babies waved fiery wands like the sparklers we wave during the Fourth of July.

Natalie jumped up and down. Henry patted my back. Barnabas, still long-faced and mournful, reached out to shake my hand. Josiah Goodheart at the other table gave me a nod and a toothy smile as the barristers in their wigs rose to their feet and clapped their hands, hurrahing. Even the ghost of Beatrice Long was clapping, as if she had intended this moment to happen all along.

Best of all, my grandfather looked at me with tears in his eyes and gave me a hug. "That's my girl," he said. "Welcome to the team. Welcome. Welcome."

It felt, all of it, true. Like a part of me I didn't know existed had been exposed to the world and that I, Elizabeth Webster, was worth cheering for. Explain that if you can. I couldn't. But still, all I wanted to do was jump around like a fool and celebrate.

"Order!" yelled Judge Jeffries with a bang-bang of his gavel. "Order in my court. Quiet down or I'll put all of you in chains and hang you by your ankles from the rafters. This is a courtroom, not a barnyard. Order, I say."

The celebration quieted. I tried to stifle my smile.

"Now, Miss Webster," said the judge.

"Yes, sir."

"Congratulations, I suppose, are in order," he said in a sour tone. "You may make merry over your elevation on your own time, but this is my time and I shan't have it wasted. Take back your credentials and answer me this. In the matter of *Harrison v. Long*, are you ready to proceed?"

I took the scroll from the clerk and then looked at Barnabas, who nodded at me.

"Yes, I suppose."

"Well, then do, Miss Webster. Call your first witness."

THE ACTION
IN EJECTMENT

We've all watched enough television to know how the whole trial thing works, right? Some guy sits in the chair, you ask questions, he answers them, and you win. Pretty simple. Sure, it might have been my first case as a barrister standing before the Court of Uncommon Pleas, but I had the blood of Daniel Webster in my veins. And I had Barnabas whispering in my ear the whole time, making sure I asked what I needed to ask. What could go wrong?

You tell me.

We called Natalie to the stand. While she sat in the witness chair, the tall, green-faced clerk approached her with halting, stiff-legged steps. The clerk held a red satin pillow on which sat a skull covered in gold. The ram ordered Natalie to place one hand on the top of the skull's head and raise the other.

The golden skull shivered to life. "Do you, Natalie Delgado," it said in a voice with a very proper British accent, "swear on my severed royal head to tell the truth, the whole truth, and nothing but the truth, or be tossed into the dark realm of the Puritan king slayer Oliver Cromwell, where no dancing, no prancing, no fun at all is to be permitted now and through all eternity?"

"The skull seems a little bitter," I whispered to Barnabas.

"With reason," whispered Barnabas back. "It is the skull of Charles the First, and Cromwell took off his head."

"Lots of missing heads in the spirit world."

"In our world, too, if you look closely enough."

The judge leaned over his bench and stared at Natalie. "Say 'I do,' child."

"I do," said Natalie. And so it began.

I asked Natalie questions about what she saw the night we served Beatrice Long with the alder stake. We even put the stake, which Barnabas had brought, into evidence. Then Henry sat in the chair and swore to tell the truth on the skull before I asked him about what he saw on those nights when Beatrice Long appeared. After that, Barnabas made sure I asked about the deed.

"Who owns that house?" I asked.

"My mom and dad," said Henry.

"Do you have, like, a deed or something?"

"Yes. A deed. Here." He pulled a piece of paper out of his pocket. "I found this."

Barnabas whispered in my ear.

"I move the deed into evidence as plaintiff's Exhibit Two," I said.

"No objection here, Judge," said Josiah Goodheart.

"Fine, it is in evidence," said the judge.

Barnabas whispered again in my ear.

"And did you bring something else with you, Henry?" I asked.

He lifted the brown paper package that had been sitting on his lap. "You told me to bring some of the ground from my property."

"Good. Now I think what you have to do is open the package and pound the dirt with your fist and then . . ."

Barnabas whispered in my ear.

"Are you sure?" I said.

Barnabas nodded.

"And then say three times as you hit it, 'I eject you from my property.'"

"Really?"

"Yes. I think," I said. "Is that right, Judge?"

"It's a formality, but vital. Just do it and get this over with."

Henry unwrapped the parcel, showing a square piece of dirt with grass growing out of it. He looked at the ghost, who was pouting back at him. I could see Henry hesitate.

"Do it," I said.

Henry pounded the sod three times, pausing to speak between each strike. "I eject you from my property. I eject you from my property. I eject you from my property."

Each time Henry hit the dirt, the ghost of Beatrice Long moaned. And each time he said he ejected her, she brightened and brightened. The third time Henry repeated the statement, the ghost of Beatrice Long burst into flames.

I thought that was the end of it. I had won my first case as a lawyer. Easy peasy. Maybe I had found something I was actually good at.

But when the ghostly flame went out, Beatrice Long was floating beside Josiah Goodheart, just as she had been before.

Barnabas whispered in my ear. "The plaintiff rests," I said.

And that's when it all went to . . . well, where do you think?

As soon as I sat down, Josiah Goodheart stood and with his jazzy, raspy voice called the ghost of Beatrice Long to the stand. She glided over the table and sat demurely in the witness chair, her ghostly hands flattening the ghostly creases in her ghostly poodle skirt. She smiled sweetly at Judge Jeffries, whose red eyes fluttered as he smiled back.

I turned and caught Henry waving coyly at her.

"What are you doing?" I whispered to him.

"Just being friendly."

"Stop flirting. You just ejected her from your house."

"But that doesn't mean we still can't be friends."

Beatrice swore silently on the king's golden head. Then Josiah Goodheart stuck his thumbs into his armpits so that his fingers pointed up, wiggling, and asked the ghost a series of questions. Her name. Her age. Date of death. Last known address. The questions were all clear, and the ghost mouthed her answers as if she was talking quite plainly to the court.

But there was a slight problem.

"Your Honor," I said. "I can't hear a thing."

"You'll be missing the meat of it, then, I suppose," he said.

"How can I represent Henry if I can't hear what she's saying?"

"Not well," he said. "Not well at all. Did you bring an interpreter for a Class Three animated spirit?"

"Uh, no."

"Well then, what could you expect?"

I looked at Barnabas, who shrugged. I turned around and saw my grandfather in the back of the courtroom nodding his head, as if this was exactly as it should be.

"Now, you heard the testimony here today, Miss Long, so let me ask outright," said Josiah Goodheart. "Are you haunting the Harrison house?"

An answer I couldn't hear.

"And why on earth would you be doing such a thing?"

She spoke for a long moment and I caught not a word.

"I see, yes. That is only to be expected. Now, when did you and your family live in Mr. Harrison's house?

"Not so very long ago in the scheme of things, not so long ago at all. And you know that he has tried to eject you. What, pray tell, is your defense?

"Mercy. How did such a thing happen?

"I speak for all in this courtroom when I say that what happened to you is a tragedy, an absolute tragedy. And now you are only asking to be made whole again, isn't that correct?

"What could be more reasonable on this good green

earth? And if it doesn't happen, how long do you intend to stay at the Harrison house, waking Mr. Harrison in the middle of the night and visiting like you do?

"That long?

"Indeed. Now let me ask you this, you poor unfortunate thing. Is there anything that would prompt you to stop your haunting?

"Simply that?

"You are being quite reasonable, I must say. Who among us would expect anything less? I have no more questions of this witness, Your Lordship," said Josiah Goodheart, with a gallant sweep of his hand.

"Any questions, Miss Webster?" said the judge.

"How can I ask a question if I can't hear any of her answers?"

"Loudly, I would suppose. Do you have any questions for the witness, yes or no?"

"Just one," I said. "Beatrice, who told you to mention my name to Henry?"

She looked at me, the ghost of Beatrice Long, and mouthed something that, against all odds, I thought I understood and that scared me witless. Or maybe I should say more witless than I was.

"Any more questions?" said the judge.

"Uh, no," I said.

"The defense rests," said Josiah Goodheart.

"Excellent," said the judge. "So we have completed our proceeding. Let me take a moment to carefully consider the evidence and the law of the case." The judge closed his eyes for the shortest moment possible—a blink, if that. "I've considered long enough."

I gave Henry a smile with far more confidence than I felt. I guess I was learning all the lawyerly skills pretty quickly. Next thing you'd know I'd be padding my bill.

"It is merely common sense, and common courtesy," said the judge, "that a deceased has the right to be buried with its full complement of flesh and bone. Now, the testimony is clear, and not contradicted, that Beatrice Long was buried without her head. Miss Long claims she is haunting the house where she lived at the time of her death until she is once again made whole, which is her inalienable right under the Uncommon Law. Who among us would not exercise that very same right? My duty here is clear. In the matter of *Harrison v. Long*, an Action in Ejectment, I find in favor of the defendant, Beatrice Long, until her head is found and a proper burial can be completed."

The judge's words cut through me like a squeaking clarinet. We had lost, *I* had lost. My first case was a disaster, another failure in front of a live audience.

A murmur went through the courtroom. The flying babies on the ceiling twittered gaily. I turned to look at Henry, who was gazing at his ghost. Did he look pleased? What a mess.

As Henry gazed, the ghost of Beatrice Long rose from her spot beside Josiah Goodheart. She zipped here and there, spun around the ceiling with a celebratory groan, and landed in front of Henry. She smiled at him, wrapped her ghostly arms around his neck, and locked her ghostly lips on to his. But this time, in the middle of the kiss, Beatrice exploded into sparks. Henry wobbled backward and fell into his chair.

"I suppose, yes, that settles that," said Judge Jeffries. "Case dismissed. And, Miss Webster?"

I pulled myself out of my misery and looked up.

"Next time you appear before me, come in a proper robe and be far better prepared in matters of fact and law, or don't come at all. Though, I suppose, what more could this court expect from a Webster?"

The ram's head snorted and stuck out its black-stained tongue at me. The judge slammed his gavel. "Next case."

An Unwelcome Visitor

"Where's my father?" I asked Barnabas. We had passed by Ivanov, standing tall once more on his ladder, and started on our way down the long flights of stairs in the City Hall tower. "And what did that grinning Goodheart mean when he said my father was detained?"

"One can't be sure," said Barnabas.

"We can be sure it isn't good," said my grandfather, banging at the steps with his cane as he creaked after us. "Not good at all."

As we climbed down, Natalie and Henry Harrison followed. Henry, still dazed by the ghostly kiss, moved slowly, as if through water. Natalie held Henry by the arm and carefully led him step-by-step. You'd think this would have been one of the greatest moments in Natalie's life, helping a helpless Henry Harrison down the stairs, but when I looked up at her, she had the expression of an exasperated nanny.

"I was quite surprised that Barrister Goodheart was involved in a simple Action in Ejectment in the first place," said Barnabas, snapping my attention back to his conversation with my grandfather. "Normally the primary counsel for Redwing wouldn't intervene in such a minor case."

"Who is Redwing?" I said.

"One of the muck-a-mucks on the other side," said my grandfather. "A difficult character, a scurrilous character. This is not good, Barnabas. We must get on this right away."

"Yes, sir."

"This might involve your Isabel."

"Indeed, sir."

"The case of Beatrice Long could be a bigger fish than first we thought," said my grandfather. "We have much to do, Elizabeth."

"We do?"

"Oh yes."

But even as he said it, I was thinking maybe not.

After we reached the bottom of the stairway, we marched this way and that through the stone corridors in the belly of the old building until we finally reached the City Hall courtyard. It was barely lit and empty at this time of night, each of the four entrances blocked by a great iron gate that had been swung closed and locked.

"I'm sorry, Henry," I said as we huddled in the middle of the courtyard. "I'm sorry I screwed up the trial. I'm sorry I screwed up everything. It would have been better for you if I had never seen the ghost at all."

Henry looked back with dazed eyes and nodded as if I were simply blowing bubbles in a pool.

"I thought you were amazing in there, Lizzie," said Natalie. "And that courtroom was a gas. Did you see the judge's eyes? Yikes alive! And didn't it smell like licorice?"

"Yes, it did," I said. "Why is that?"

"Because he chews it incessantly," said my grandfather.

"Who, the judge?"

"The ram," he said.

"How cool was he? How cool was everything! And look at you now, Lizzie. Elizabeth Webster, attorney-at-law."

"Attorney-at-failure," I said. "Attorney-at-losing."

"Nonsense," said my grandfather with a knock of his cane on the courtyard stones.

"Even the little flying babies were laughing at me," I said.

"They were, yes, those fledgling fools," said my grandfather, "but what do they know? I thought you were excellent, actually, for your first time. What say you, Barnabas?"

"You did fine, Mistress Elizabeth, considering."

"Considering that I lost? Considering that Josiah Goodheart skewered me like a shish kebab?"

"Of course you lost," said my grandfather. "There was no way you could win. You had neither the facts nor the law on your side. Even your great ancestor Daniel Webster would have had a hard time winning this case in front of that red-eyed scalawag. You'll get them next time."

"There's not going to be a next time," I said. "I'm sorry,

but I only did this to see if I could help Henry. I didn't, I couldn't. In fact, I've only made things worse. I failed at lawyering like I pretty much fail at everything. Have you ever heard me play the clarinet?"

"I'm sure it is delightful."

"Not even to a mouse. I'm not much of a Webster."

"You are very much a Webster," said my grandfather. "And we Websters get up when we're knocked down and rap our canes on the door of opportunity."

"No cane," I said. "No door. Just done." I gazed around at the gated-in courtyard. It looked just then like a prison. "I'm ready to go home."

"Don't think it's the blood that makes you a lawyer," said my grandfather. "Yes, it gave you your credentials— the deal with old Scratch took care of that—but the lawyer part must be earned. You still have much to learn, but you learned some of it today. It is not only whether you win or lose, Elizabeth, but what you gain from the contest."

"I notice people only say things like that when they lose," I said.

"Your grandfather might be right, Webster," said Henry, his voice slow as syrup. "All along I felt that Beatrice needed my help in some way, and now I know that she does."

"She's just going to keep haunting you and haunting you," I said. "Forever."

"Unless we find her head," said Henry.

"Exactly," said my grandfather. "That is what we learned today, that was our crucial gain. To stop the haunting, all Henry need do is find the head of Beatrice Long. Quite simple, actually. Pick it up, drop it into her grave, and give her the peace of mind she so richly deserves."

"How is Henry going to find her head?" I said.

"Well, it starts, like everything else in this life," said my grandfather, "with the trying. Are you young people ready to try?"

"I am," said Henry. "I don't really have a choice."

"I'm in, too," said Natalie. "Absolutely. Once you start these things, you have to finish them or there's no point."

"But how can we possibly find a head from so many years ago?" I asked. "I'm sure the police searched and searched and found nothing."

"Sometimes old crimes give up their secrets more easily than fresh ones," said my grandfather. "And you have an advantage the police didn't have."

"What's that?"

"We have Beatrice," said Henry. "She'll guide us, I know she will."

"You'll help us, won't you, Lizzie?" said Natalie.

As I looked at Henry and Natalie, who were staring at me with hope on their faces, I felt my posture slump. I had never realized how tiring it was to play at being something I wasn't. My father was in trouble. Henry was in trouble. They both needed the help of a real attorney. Whatever I was, that wasn't me.

"I can't, I'm sorry," I said. "And even if I agreed to help, it wouldn't matter. I told my mother the truth of where I was going tonight. Once I get home I won't be allowed to leave the house again until I'm thirty. Which is good, because all I can do is mess things up for everybody. You saw what I did in there."

"You were terrific," said Natalie.

"I lost," I said. "You'll be better off without me."

I shook my head and turned away from their disappointed faces, and that was when I saw it, the thing climbing like a spider through the circular gap between the locked iron gate and the top of the stone arch at the west entrance. A great, dark, monstrous thing.

And it was calling my name.

THE ANIMATE

It was giant and inhuman and four times my size. It dropped onto the courtyard with a clang, before rising to its full height and walking toward us with the noisy wrench of metal. Scritch, clank.

"*Elizabeth Webster,*" it shouted. Scritch, clank. "*Elizabeth Webster.*" The voice was a harmony of horror, three mismatched voices calling out my name all at once. "*Elizabeth Webster.*"

The short pants, the stiff metal jacket with lines of buttons, and the tall round hat clued me in to what this thing was. The bronze sculpture of the Pilgrim high on the City Hall tower had come alive—to find me.

"*Elizabeth Webster.*" Scritch, clank.

Its footsteps rang with the sound of bronze striking stone. At first it walked, then it trotted, and then it ran at me, brandishing a metal scroll, readying to smack me like a baseball into the next life.

"*Elizabeth Webster. Elizabeth Webster.*" Scritch, clank. "*Elizabeth Webster.*"

I was too shocked to move. I stood stock-still in horror. I was already anticipating the crack of metal against my skull, when someone jumped between me and the giant black statue.

"Begone, foul creature," shouted Barnabas, waving his pale hands at the beast. "Begone."

The great bronze Pilgrim slid to a stop, sparks rising from its bronze buckled shoes as they scraped the stone of the courtyard. The scroll was still raised, ready to deal a deadly blow, but it would fall now upon Barnabas and not me.

"No, Barnabas," I shouted.

My grandfather grabbed my arm. "Leave him be, Elizabeth. Barnabas can more than take care of himself with a dastardly animate like that."

"If you seek to harm young Elizabeth you'll need to destroy me first," shouted Barnabas. "And as you well know, that won't be so easy to do."

The great bronze Pilgrim reached down and grabbed Barnabas by the shoulder of his frock coat, lifting him into the air until their faces were close. The Pilgrim snarled, showing bronze teeth big as tombstones, and then turned his head to face me.

"*Step into that courtroom again, Elizabeth Webster,*" it said, "*and you will see me a second time. It will take more than Barnabas Bothemly to stop me then.*"

The Pilgrim tossed Barnabas at me like he was a piece of trash. Barnabas slid sprawling and facedown just to my right. The Pilgrim sneered once more, then turned around and scratch-clanked back toward the locked west entrance before climbing over the iron gate and out of the courtyard.

It took me a long moment to chase my racing heart and catch my breath before I joined the huddle around Barnabas. He lay there motionless, still facedown, splat, on the stone floor of the courtyard. He had sacrificed himself for me. And what was I willing to sacrifice to help Henry, to find my father, to do anything good in this world? My eyes welled with tears. I put a hand on Barnabas's shoulder and felt a quiver of muscle through his coat.

"Barnabas?" I said.

"He'll be fine," said my grandfather. "It will take more than that monstrosity to put a dent in our Barnabas."

"That's easy for you to say."

"No, Mistress Elizabeth," said Barnabas. With a groan he turned over and then rose into a sitting position on the courtyard paving. "Your grandfather is correct." He moved one arm and then the next. The joints in his shoulders clicked but otherwise he seemed unhurt, and his face was miraculously free of any scrape or bruise. "Regretfully, I remain alive and well."

"What was that creature?" said Henry.

"An animate," said my grandfather. "A dead thing brought to life by an unearthly power. But more interesting than what it is, is why it was sent. Fear."

"You got that right," I said. "I'm still shaking. I've never been so afraid in my life."

"You have it mixed around, Mistress Elizabeth," said Barnabas. "It is not the fear in you that is most relevant here. It is the fear *of* you. Someone or something fears you mightily, or an animate would not have been sent with your name on its lips."

"Me?"

"You."

"Why?"

"Because you're a Webster," said my grandfather. "And you now have a license to practice before the Court of Uncommon Pleas, which gives you power. Have no doubt that this case has become something far bigger than the mere ejectment of a ghost. Old Scratch himself would never send such a creature, not against a Webster. So it is some other fallen angel out to do its dirty work in our dimension. Fates hang in the balance, and they all seem to depend on you, Elizabeth."

"What did Beatrice say when you asked who told her to mention your name to Henry?" said Natalie.

"I think she said a lawyer told her, and then she called me Lizzie Face. That's what my father calls me."

"Ah yes," said my grandfather. "Things are becoming ever clearer."

" 'Save me, save him,' " said Barnabas. "That's what the ghost said when we served process with the alder stake. 'Save me, save him.' We thought the 'him' was young Henry, but maybe the ghost was talking about your father, Mistress Elizabeth."

"Your father needs your help, Lizzie," said Natalie.

"But what can I do?"

"Be a Webster," said my grandfather. "The Websters are lawyers, so that is what you must be. As lawyers, we have the power, and more importantly the duty, to help the beleaguered and raise the misfortunate. That is what strikes fear in the heart of evil. It is up to you to move forward in those never-ending tasks, and the ghost of Beatrice Long has illuminated your path."

"You absolutely must help us find that head, Lizzie," said Natalie. "You must."

"Not too much pressure," I said.

"I know you're scared," said Henry Harrison. "We're all scared, but Natalie and I could really use your help. What do you say, Webster? Are you in?"

What could I say? My insides were still quivering, my failure in court still stung, and there was a fallen angel from the other side who was animating a twenty-foot hunk of metal so it could rip out my guts. And then of course there was my mother. All of this was enough to send me scurrying home to hide in my room until everything passed, including maybe my youth.

And yet there was Henry Harrison, pulled out of his self-absorption through a love for a girl long dead. And there was my grandfather, with an absurd belief in me just because I was his granddaughter. And there was Barnabas, who had just placed himself between me and the Pilgrim, ready to pay any price to protect me. It was hard to figure the right thing to do.

Then I looked at Natalie and it came to me as quickly as

that. In her eyes I saw nothing but faith in me and a courage that shamed. I had underestimated her all this time. Maybe I had been underestimating myself, too.

"Okay," I said. "I'm in until the end. Let's find that head and save my father."

"That a girl," said my grandfather.

"Very good, Mistress Elizabeth," said Barnabas before rising to his feet and wiping the dust from his now-ripped pants with his long, pale hands. "I will be of whatever assistance I can."

"We'll get on it tomorrow," I said. "But first can you get me out of this locked courtyard? It's time to go home and face the music."

"Waltz?" said my grandfather.

"More like a funeral march."

"Mozart?"

"Mom."

At the south entrance, Barnabas pulled one of the gateposts out of the ground. The raised post allowed him to swing open a piece of the lower portion of the gate, creating a small gap. We all ducked to get outside, all except my grandfather, who was short enough and bent enough to make it through the gap with his normal tap of the cane. We said our good-byes before Barnabas and my grandfather headed to the office and Natalie, Henry, and I made our way around City Hall to the train station.

On the ride out of the city, the three of us plotted our next moves. We had a story to discover and a head to find, and we had to do it quickly. As we talked, Natalie and Henry seemed to treat me differently—more seriously—because of what had happened to me in that courtroom. But then I began to think that maybe they weren't treating me any differently at all—maybe I just felt differently about myself, and that made all the difference.

It was a peculiar sensation, feeling good about myself for once, and it lasted the whole ride out of Philadelphia and into Willing Township. In fact, it lasted until the moment I walked into the kitchen of our house and saw my mother sitting at the table, her hands crossed over my note, staring at me with eyes iced in anger.

26

BOARDING SCHOOL

"Sit down, Elizabeth," said my mother, her voice flat and cold. The kitchen was all in shadow except for a cone of light from the fixture over the table where she sat.

"Maybe I should stand," I said. There was an anger flowing from her that seemed to wrap around my throat, something as alive and as real as Beatrice's ghost.

"Sit," she said.

I slumped into a chair as if my mother's anger had grabbed me by the collar and flung me down.

"I've been thinking all evening of what I should do about our problem."

"So that's what I am, a problem to be solved?"

"Well, aren't you? Didn't I tell you that regarding Webster and Son there is no debate? I will not allow you to have any involvement with that firm. I know things you don't know.

And if I must do something drastic to get you away from the world in which your father operates, I will. I know of a boarding school in Massachusetts where you would fit in wonderfully."

"I suppose it's filled with misguided freaks just like me," I said.

"You're not a freak."

"Just misguided."

"Yes."

"And that's your answer. Shuffle me off to boarding school so I can no longer infect your new family with my Websterism."

"Maybe we'll go up this weekend and take a visit."

"Don't you want to know where I was tonight?" I said. "Don't you want to know what happened?"

"It's enough that you are back and safe, at least this time. I can imagine the rest."

"I'm sure you can."

"What does that mean?" snapped my mother. "And what did you mean in your letter when you said that I, more than anyone, can understand your desire to help that boy?"

There was so much about my mother I didn't know, more than I could ever have imagined before I first stepped into my father's office. I stared at her for a long moment. They say the eyes are the windows to the soul, but in my mother's eyes the shades were drawn.

"Dad's missing," I said.

"He's been missing from your life for years. What's new about that?"

"I think he's in trouble."

"He has been in trouble since the day I met him."

"How did you two meet?"

My mother flinched, as if a wasp were coming near. "It's not important now."

"I've been asking for years, and all you do is smile," I said. "Maybe now it's time for some truth."

"You're asking me for the truth? Don't you find that ironic?"

"I kept what I was doing a secret because I knew how you'd react. I'm sorry for that. I left the note with Peter so you would know that I won't lie to you anymore. But I'm not the only one who's been hiding things. You kept my father's business, his office, and my grandfather from me. My grandfather!"

"I would have eventually told you everything."

"When, Mom? How old would I have to be to learn the truth about myself?"

"This isn't about you."

"I heard that Dad is a hero. I heard that he goes to the other side to save people."

"The other side of what?" she said. "You don't even know."

"That's the point. I don't know. But you do." And that's when I went fishing with a little worm that had been crawling around my brain. "How did Dad save you, Mom?"

She shook her head, but the startled look on her face gave her away. "I won't talk about this now."

"Why not? Isn't that as big a part of my history as the divorce and Stephen and Petey? Don't I have the right to know?"

"Sometime, maybe. But not now, not when you are in the middle of all of it. Later, when you are away and have a better perspective."

"When I'm in my boarding school."

"Maybe then, yes."

I reached into my bag, took out my newly won credentials, and slid the scroll across the table. She stared at it for a moment as if it were a snake writhing in front of her, before she untied the ribbon and rolled it open. I thought she'd be impressed by the fancy legal language and careful calligraphy. I thought she'd see me in a new light. I thought she'd be proud of me for once.

Instead, she burst into tears.

And as if her tears were infectious, I started crying, too.

We cried together for a bit, until we stopped, too embarrassed to look at each other. But somehow, the anger of the moment had vanished. She was my mother, not a warrior princess. And I was her daughter, not a barrister before the Court of Uncommon Pleas. And there we were again, in the months right after the divorce, when my mother and I sat together at the kitchen table and pretended that we weren't alone and lonely and scared. I understood now what Henry meant about not wanting to grow up. If I could have gone back to that time when I was so close to my mother, when I felt so lost yet still so safe in her arms, I would have, like a shot.

And just remembering made it clear there was no way I was going to some stupid boarding school in Massachusetts.

"It's just that I don't want this for you," she said.

"I don't know if I want it for me, either," I said. "It was a little crazy in that courtroom, let me tell you. But for now, I need to help Henry, and maybe Dad, too. I think Dad's imprisoned somewhere on the other side."

"And you have to be the one to save him?"

"Who else? Is that what you taught me, to sit back and let someone else do the hard work?"

"You don't know the cost."

"But I'll find out. On my own. And when it's time to decide whether to keep doing this law stuff or not, I'll let you tell me all the reasons to say no."

"You won't," my mother said. "You'll be swept up in it like your father was swept up in it."

"I won't. I promise, at least not before letting you tell me everything. You can tell me then how you and Dad met. And you can also tell me all the reasons I shouldn't follow in his footsteps."

"That's a long talk."

"We'll go out for ice cream."

"I do like ice cream," said my mother, wiping at her damp eyes.

"But right now," I said, "I have to take care of this thing with Henry's ghost. And I think Dad sent me a message of what I need to do to save him, too. But I can't do it if I'm fighting with you the whole time."

"Is there anything I could say to change your mind?"

"No."

She looked at me like she was looking at me for the first time. She was looking at me like Henry and Natalie had looked at me on the train. "Maybe I can help," she said finally. "I'd like to help."

"If I need you, I will tell you. I promise."

"Okay," she said. "So what is it you have to do to save everyone?"

"I have to find a dead girl's missing head."

"Oh," said my mother, the briefest smile flitting like a sparrow across her lips. "Only that."

Old News

After a session of bizarro night court with a talking ram, a raging Pilgrim, and a red-eyed judge, things were a little weird the following day. I felt kind of nervous around Natalie and Henry, and I sensed they were just as nervous around me. Sometimes, when you go through something so intense, it's hard to slip back into normal life.

At lunch, Henry was camped out at an eighth-grade table, leaning back in his chair and laughing with his buddies while Natalie and I sat quietly together, barely glancing at each other. Across from us, the Frayden twins were talking on and on and, yeah, on.

"You should have seen the debate competition yesterday," said Charlie. "Doug had this one girl near to tears."

"I did, yes I did," said Doug.

"Whenever she made a point, he had the same comeback."

"Indubitably," said Doug.

"She didn't know how to respond."

"Indubitably."

"It just got into her head. He said it over and over, and every time he said it you could see her cringe."

"Indubitably."

"Eventually she just sat down and put her head in her hands."

"That seems about right," I said. "What were you debating about?"

"International politics or something," said Charlie. "It doesn't matter. The point is to win the argument."

"Don't," Natalie said, pointing a finger at Doug.

"Don't what?" said Doug.

"Say that word."

"I wasn't going to say it," whined Doug. "I wouldn't do something like that to you, Natalie. I just wouldn't."

"Indubitably," said Charlie, and they laughed and laughed. Then the twins looked up and their laughter died in their throats. Henry was standing behind us.

"Hey, Webster," said Henry. "I'm, uh, still having some trouble with the math. I wondered if we could work tonight?"

"Maybe we can meet up at the public library," said Natalie.

"You're helping Henry with math, too?" said Charlie.

"Sure, why not? I have skills."

"Indubitably," said Doug. "But not math skills."

"The library works," I said. "There's something I wanted to look up anyway."

"We like the library, Henry," said Charlie. "In fact, we were thinking of going there tonight, weren't we, Doug?"

"Were we?"

"We were going to work on our math, too."

"Oh, yeah. Math," said Doug.

"I don't think that's a good idea," I said.

"Oh, it's a splendid idea," said Charlie. "And maybe, while you're working, we can bring you guys sodas from the Wawa down the road. What do you say about that, Henry, I mean Mr. Harrison, sir?"

Henry looked at one Frayden and then the other Frayden and then back to the first. "Do you guys know if they have old county newspapers at the library?"

"They have microfilm!" said Charlie, as if he had just pulled a rabbit out of his hat. "It goes back like a hundred years. Doug and I did a report on the Vietnam War once."

"That didn't go so well," said Doug.

"The report?" said Natalie.

"The war."

"Think you guys could help us look something up?" said Henry.

"Sure we can," said Charlie. "What about?"

"Just some historical research," said Henry. "About a murder."

"Murder?" said Doug. "How intriguing. Anyone we know?"

"Not yet," I said. "But give it time."

"What are we supposed to do with this?" said Natalie, after Charlie dropped a red brick of a thing on the long wooden table at the Willing Township Public Library.

"It's an old information device," I said.

"But there are no buttons," said Natalie.

"Funny," said Charlie. "That's funny."

"Not that funny," I said.

At first, we had tried to find what we could about Beatrice online. The web archives of the local newspapers went back only so far. When we plugged in "Beatrice Long" we found her on a list of murder cases that remained unsolved. Along with her name we found the date of her death, almost fifty years ago to the day.

"This is the newspaper index for the year that you asked for," said Charlie as he tapped the cover of the thick red book. "The articles you want will be listed inside."

"And then?"

"Write down what you want to see and then we go to the microfilm."

Natalie and I paged through the book and discovered that Beatrice Long had her own entry. We jotted down the dates and pages of the articles. Doug found the drawer with the relevant roll of microfilm and wound the roll, about the size of a grapefruit, into a rickety machine with a big screen. It was sort of fun, doing this by hand without the computer, like we were archaeologists digging in the Egyptian desert for some long-lost city.

When Doug switched on the reader, the front of a newspaper appeared unfocused on the screen. He fiddled with the lens while I read out the first date we needed, and then he started spinning through the roll. Suddenly there it was, an article dated a few days after Halloween, talking about our very own ghost.

WILLING GIRL MISSING
by Delores Baird

The Willing Police have reported that Beatrice Long, of 213 Orchard Lane, has gone missing. Miss Long, fifteen, the daughter of Forrest and Sandra Long, is a freshman at Willing High and a junior varsity cheerleader. Miss Long is five feet three inches tall with curly red hair. She was last seen Saturday at a Halloween party. Miss Long was wearing a fifties costume, with a pink sweater and a poodle skirt. Anyone with any information is asked to contact Officer Derek Johansson of the Willing Police Department.

"Hey," said Charlie, "isn't that your address, Henry?"

"How do you know my address?" said Henry.

"We just learned it in passing," said Doug. "Nothing to worry about."

"What are you doing?" said Charlie. "Researching your house for a history assignment?"

"Yes," said Henry. "That's it exactly."

"Cool," said Charlie. "The only interesting history in our house is when Doug found that wasps' nest in the attic."

"Ouch," said Doug.

"His face blew up like a beach ball," said Charlie.

"What's next?" said Natalie.

I started reading out the dates and Doug forwarded the film. The following group of articles repeated the facts as the search for the missing girl grew ever more desperate. There were leads going nowhere. There was a five-thousand-dollar reward, then a ten-thousand-dollar reward. There were rumors that a boy had broken up with Beatrice and the girl, upset, had fled to California. While reading the articles of the continuing search, I couldn't help but hope, along with the Long family, that Beatrice would be found alive and well, eating a hot dog on the Santa Monica pier. But I knew what was up, I had seen her ghost. And then on the microfilm came the confirmation.

BODY OF GIRL DISCOVERED
by Delores Baird

The body of a young woman was found yesterday afternoon along a deserted section of Whistler's Creek by a hiker and his dog. Police were called immediately and a search commenced for evidence in the area that includes sections of both Willing and Upper Pattson Townships. Police will not confirm the identity of the deceased, but sources say they believe it may be the body of Beatrice Long, the Willing Township girl who went missing just over two weeks ago from a Halloween party. The condition of the body has made identification difficult, but the clothes on the young woman match the costume Miss Long was wearing. Police have labeled the case a homicide and have already questioned a suspect. Also questioned about her disappearance was a classmate of Miss Long, Anil Singh. A police department spokesman stated the department will provide more information as soon as it becomes available.

"That's interesting," said Charlie. "Very interesting. Mr. Singh knew her."

"Who's that?" I said.

"Anil Singh owns a tech company on City Line Avenue," said Doug. "Singh Electronics. Charlie and I did an internship there."

"It wasn't really an internship," said Charlie. "It was a couple of weekends with the computer club. Community outreach, you know. They gave us some programming tasks to work on, but the stuff was pretty basic."

"It wasn't BASIC," said Doug, "it was Python."

A pack of hyenas broke out in laughter right there in the library. I glanced up at Henry, who had invited them. He shrugged.

"Our teacher set it up," said Charlie. "It should look good on the old résumé."

"You can never have too much on the old résumé, right, Henry?" said Doug.

"It depends," said Henry. "I think there are some things that Grimes won't put on his."

"Can we get back to work here?" said Natalie, which was as un-Natalie a thing as she had ever said.

I gave her a look before reading out the following date. Doug whirled the film spool and then stopped at another article. We were, all five of us, quiet as mice as we read.

BEATRICE LONG, 15

by Delores Baird

Beatrice Long, a Willing High freshman, was buried today by her parents, Forrest and Sandra Long of 213 Orchard Lane, at a ceremony at Mount Lebanon Cemetery in Willing Township. Miss Long, who had gone missing on Halloween night, was found by a hiker and his dog one week ago at a secluded spot by Whistler's Creek. Police have labeled her death a homicide.

Friends and family remembered Miss Long as a friendly, outgoing girl who loved animals and was a loyal friend to many. Miss Long had been a junior varsity cheerleader and was a member of the Social Action Club. "Beatrice was just so pretty and sweet," said her sister, Roberta, a junior at Willing High. "She loved the outdoors and was a friend to everyone. For this to happen to anyone is a tragedy, for it to happen to my sister breaks our hearts. When they find who did this, we'll all make sure justice is served."

Also at the funeral was Anil Singh, a classmate of Miss Long's who has been questioned by the police. An altercation at the funeral between Roberta Long and Mr. Singh was broken up by Officer Derek Johansson, who was attending the funeral on behalf of the police department. No charges were brought as a result of the incident.

The family has said that donations in lieu of flowers may be made to the Willing Conservancy.

"You know what?" said Henry. "Just reading about funerals makes me thirsty. Hey, Charlie, didn't you say something about getting us sodas at the Wawa?"

"Yes, sir, Mr. Harrison, sir," said Charlie. "Coke?"

"Sure," said Henry, "Anything for you guys?"

"I'm fine," I said.

"Seltzer," said Natalie.

"Right away," said Doug.

"And why don't you guys get something for yourselves, too," said Henry, dragging a few bills out of his wallet and handing them to Charlie.

"Why, thank you, sir," said Charlie. "That's very kind of you, sir."

When the Fraydens left on their soda run, Natalie turned to Henry and me and said with wide eyes and a low voice, "Of course identification was difficult. She was missing her head."

"It didn't say that," I said.

"No, the cops were being polite, but that's what was going on," said Natalie. "Read between the lines. The condition of the body making identification difficult. Using the clothes to ID her. Well, they had to, didn't they, because there was no head."

"Did the killer take her head so they couldn't identify the body?" I said.

"He's not so smart if he did," said Henry. "The clothes were a dead giveaway. And what about fingerprints and stuff like that? No, taking the head was about something else."

"That's a frightening thought," said Natalie, rubbing a hand across her neck.

"Do you think the killer threw it in the creek?" I said.

"Do heads float?" said Natalie.

We all thought on that for a while without coming up with an answer.

"But if it was in the creek and it wasn't found," said Henry, "then it would have dissolved or been eaten by fish long ago. Beatrice wouldn't have sent us searching if the head didn't still exist. I know it."

"But you don't know where it is."

"Maybe she doesn't, either," said Natalie. "That's why she's haunting Henry, to find out. We need to talk to the sister."

"We need to talk to Anil Singh," said Henry.

"We need to get them in a boxing ring," said Natalie, "and let them go at it."

"What's the use?" I said. "The police have already gone over this again and again, and they found nothing."

"What did your grandfather say?" said Henry. "That sometimes old crimes give up their secrets more easily than new ones. That might be true here. We have to try."

"Of course we have to try," said Natalie. "We're detectives."

I looked at Natalie, with her bright eyes, and knew she was right. This was part of it, my new role as attorney for the damned. It wasn't enough just to show up in court and win or lose depending on the whims of some undead judge. It was also about doing whatever needed doing to help the client. My father understood—that was why he was caught on the other side. The client now was Henry, and he needed my help, and playing detective was the only way to give him what he needed.

"Okay, so we're detectives. What do we do?"

"The first thing we do," said Natalie, "is get ourselves trench coats and hats."

"Then, I suppose," said Henry, "what we do next is ask some questions."

"And I know just where to start," said Natalie.

28

THE WHISTLE

"**I** don't understand," said Roberta Hamilton as Natalie, Henry, and I sat in her living room and tried to balance teacups on our laps. An older woman with big forearms, Beatrice Long's sister leaned back on her chair and eyed us suspiciously. "Why exactly are you here again?"

"It's for a school report," said Natalie, repeating the cover story thought up by Charlie Frayden, of all people. The one thing we couldn't say was some crazy tale about a headless ghost and a ruling by a long-deceased rehanging judge regarding how we go about getting rid of the thing. I mean, we were in the middle of it and we could barely believe it ourselves. "We have to write the story of our houses for history, and when our friend Henry started researching his own house, he learned about what happened to your sister."

"What happened," said Roberta, "was a murder."

"We loved that house," said Sandra Long, Roberta and Beatrice's mother, who was also sitting with us. "We had such joy in that house, until . . ."

"I can imagine staying there would have been difficult," I said.

"We had no choice but to move on."

"So, we thought that it might be interesting to learn about what happened to your daughter," said Natalie. "Maybe even find some answers that have been missing."

"Wouldn't that be something?" said Mrs. Long. "Wouldn't that be remarkable?"

"We thought so," said Natalie with a bright smile.

Even though it was Roberta we had come to visit, it was Mrs. Long who, standing with a walker behind her daughter in the half-opened doorway, had invited us in. And it was Mrs. Long who insisted we stay for tea. Our ghost's mother was a thin, tired woman with pale blue eyes. She was too old for me to figure out how old she was, but she was old, like really old. And she seemed so sad, though out of that sadness she smiled kindly at us, almost as if she knew us. Almost as if she had been expecting us all along.

"I'm not sure we want to dredge up old memories for a history paper," said Roberta. "They're very painful."

"I understand," said Henry.

It hadn't been easy to track down Beatrice's sister. She changed her name when she had married, but we found someone online who knew someone who remembered the whole story and where Roberta lived now. Henry had a car account to help him get to his swim practices, so the day after our visit to the library, we caught a ride right from school. Unfortunately, we hadn't gotten around to getting the trench coats.

"They never found her killer," said Roberta. "The case went cold and then they turned their backs. It still hurts."

"The police tried," said Mrs. Long. "They worked very hard, dear, you know that. There was that one officer who kept coming around, asking all kinds of questions."

"Was that Officer Johansson, who was in the news reports?" asked Natalie.

"Yes, that was his name," said Mrs. Long.

"Not that he found anything," said Roberta.

"One of his sons was a special friend of Beatrice's, so he took a keen interest," said Mrs. Long. "But he said he wasn't even sure it was a murder."

"He was wrong," said Roberta. "Of course Beatrice was murdered."

"The officer said the case was confusing," said Mrs. Long. "The condition of her body when they found her indicated she was murdered, yes, but the cause of death wasn't clear."

"None of this needs to go into the young man's paper," said Roberta.

"In the newspaper article about the funeral," said Natalie, "there was a mention of some sort of confrontation between you and . . . what was his name?"

"Singh," said Roberta. "Anil Singh. I didn't think it was right that he was there. He disagreed. And then maybe I tried to make my point a little more forcefully than I should have."

"Why shouldn't he have been there?" said Henry.

"I don't really remember. It was so long ago."

"No it wasn't," said Mrs. Long. "It feels like yesterday. I bought her the skirt from a thrift shop for her Halloween costume that year. I helped her dress for the party. She even wore an old pair of my saddle shoes. She looked so nice all dressed up, instead of her usual ripped jeans and T-shirts. We shared stories and lipstick as she got ready to go and then she was gone. You know it killed my husband, the heartbreak of it."

"That's enough, Mother," said Roberta.

"They should know," said Mrs. Long. "Losing your child is the kind of tragedy from which you never recover."

"Did you suspect Anil Singh of something?" said Natalie.

Roberta glared for a bit, as if Natalie was prying. I was surprised, too. Natalie seemed to be taking to her new role as detective with a little too much enthusiasm. But she asked with such courage and assurance that, after a moment, Roberta replied as if she had no choice.

"Anil was smart, and handsome, and he played varsity soccer," she said. "He was the most popular boy in the school. All along we knew he was going to Harvard. Beatrice was pretty and young, but he was out of her league. He shouldn't have been going out with her in the first place."

I saw it then, a still-living resentment aimed at the younger, prettier sister. And it seemed as if Roberta was also jealous of all the attention Beatrice continued to receive because of her death. Talk about ghosts. It kept getting sadder and sadder, the whole Beatrice Long story.

"Anil was too full of himself," continued Roberta. "He

didn't take care of her like he needed to. That's what I was upset about."

"How didn't he take care of her?" said Natalie.

"He was a boy. He acted like a boy."

I glanced at Henry, who nodded along with the answer as if it were somehow too obvious to need an explanation.

"Now he's rich," said Roberta. "He comes to the reunions with that big smile. I had to stop going myself. To see him so content with everything in his life made me sick to my stomach."

"More tea?" said Mrs. Long.

I began to beg off, intending to say, *No, thank you, we need to be going,* but Natalie interrupted me before I could get out the second word.

"Yes, please, that would be lovely."

"How nice," said Mrs. Long.

"And are there any more cookies?"

"Of course, dear. They're store bought, I'm afraid, but Roberta can open another box when she refills the pot. And while you're here, maybe you'd like to look at her things."

"Mother, I don't think that—"

"We'd love to," said Natalie. "That would be so great. For Henry's paper, I mean. Thank you."

I looked at Henry, who was staring at Natalie as if her hair had just turned purple. Who was this girl full of questions and a ravenous hunger for tea and cookies? I turned to Natalie and she winked at me.

A few moments later there was a fresh pot of tea, a plate of cookies, and a cardboard box, square and closed, sitting on the coffee table between us.

"I had to pack up her room when we moved out of the house," said Mrs. Long. "My husband couldn't bear it, so I did it alone. I only boxed what I thought she would have wanted me to keep. I used to sift through the things, as if there would be some clue in there, but I don't do it much anymore."

We all stared at the box. It seemed sacred sitting there, like a crypt. And yes, it was just about the size of a head.

"Well, go on," said Mrs. Long. "Don't be shy."

Even as we leaned forward, I couldn't help but wonder what would have been in my box. My black canvas Converse All Stars, my copy of *The Math Book*, my scrolled-up credentials? I grew depressed just thinking about it.

And then Natalie opened the box's flaps.

All of it was aged, all of it from a different time. There was a browned Willing High cheerleader sweatshirt and a maroon-and-white pom-pom. There were little records with big holes in the middle: "Lady Madonna" by the Beatles, "Jumping Jack Flash" by the Rolling Stones, something called "Bad Moon Rising" by Credence Clearwater Revival. There was a yellowed paperback copy of *Rosemary's Baby*. There were little stuffed animals. There was a pair of black suede high heels. As we searched through the box, Henry looked soulfully at each item, not like he was seeing it for the first time, but like he was remembering it instead.

Something odd in a clear plastic holder caught my eye. When I reached for the holder—

¡Snap!

I jerked my hand away from the spark and rubbed my fingers to dull the pain. Inside the plastic holder was a skull, small and flat, with almost human-looking molars on the sides and four front teeth. The spark—and the size of the gap between the molars and the front teeth, a gap that would perfectly fit an acorn—clued me in to whose head this was. I picked up the holder and examined the little skull closely. Alas, poor squirrel of my dream, I knew it well. But how had Beatrice gotten hold of it?

"Do you know what this is?" I said, holding up the plastic holder.

"I don't, no," said Mrs. Long. "But Beatrice loved animals. She volunteered at the zoo, and sometimes she would go into the woods, find injured birds, and bring them home. I can still see her feeding sugar water to her little patients with a dropper."

"And what's this?" said Natalie, lifting a metal whistle that was attached to a long silver chain.

"Well, now, look at that," said Mrs. Long. "It was a cheerleading thing."

"I didn't know cheerleaders used whistles," said Natalie. "I might have to join after all."

"Oh, Beatrice loved being a cheerleader," said Mrs. Long. "She was so proud when she made the junior varsity as a freshman. Most of the rest were already sophomores. Would you like it, dear?"

"The whistle?" said Natalie.

"Yes."

"Really?"

"No, we couldn't," I said. "These are your memories of your daughter."

"They're just reminders," said Mrs. Long. "And I need

them less and less. It's like every day Beatrice and my husband visit. That's why I don't go through these things much anymore. It would mean so much to me, and to Roberta, and even to Beatrice, I'm sure, if they got used again. Take it, please."

"Okay," said Natalie, "if you insist."

"In your paper, young man," said Mrs. Long to Henry, "please make sure to say that she was a darling girl with an open heart."

"I will, ma'am," said Henry.

"And you also must say that with all the love she showed to animals, and people, too, what happened to her was a crime against nature."

PAPER CHASE

"What got into you?" I said to Natalie as we waited for the car to take us back to Willing Township. "You were like some movie detective the way you went after Beatrice's sister."

"I was just asking questions. That's what we went for, isn't it?"

"But you were so relentless, and then you asked for more tea, as if you were some English lady." I gave my voice a high-pitched British accent. "*More tea, please. It's time for tea.*"

"Don't you ever watch television, Lizzie? The detective always asks for coffee or tea or something. That way she can't be rushed out before she asks all her questions. As long as she's drinking her tea they have to keep talking."

"It seemed to work," said Henry.

"But then you went and took the whistle?" I said. "That didn't seem very nice. I mean, it means more to Mrs. Long than it could ever mean to you."

"Well, I might try out for cheerleading in the spring," said Natalie, "so it could come in handy. And look how shiny it is. And it says 'Thunderer' on it, which is pretty cool for a dead girl's whistle."

"Natalie?"

"And remember when Barnabas came to Henry's house and asked us if we had anything of Beatrice's to summon her ghost with, and we didn't?"

"I remember," said Henry.

"Now we do."

"Wow," said Henry. "Do you think it will work?"

"I don't know," said Natalie, lifting the whistle to her mouth. "Maybe I'll try."

"Don't!" I yelled.

"I was just teasing," said Natalie.

"Not a good idea," said Henry. "Beatrice doesn't like being teased."

I looked at Natalie, whose eyes widened along with mine. We waited for Henry to laugh at his joke, but there was no laughter.

"Well, if you want to hear something creepy, I have creepy," I said. "That little skull in the box? I think it was the skull of the squirrel in my dream."

"That is creepy," said Natalie. "Good and creepy."

"That sounds like a candy name," said Henry.

"*Good and Creepy*," said Natalie in an announcer's voice. "*For the ghoul in all of us.*"

"There were two people in both my dreams," I said. "I only saw the face of a boy. The other person must have been Beatrice."

"Who was the boy?" said Henry.

"I don't know, but I'd bet he had something to do with what happened to her."

"So what do we do now?" said Henry.

"I think it's time we talk to Beatrice's old boyfriend, Anil Singh," said Natalie as she took out her phone and started tapping. "Oh, lucky us. His office is on the way home and we still have time before they close."

Singh Electronics was on the fifth floor of a big glass office building in a section of Willing Township filled with big glass office buildings. We had to check in at the security desk in the lobby, sign our names in the register, and pin little name tags on our shirts before we went up in the elevators.

"Yes?" said the office receptionist, who smiled brightly at us. "Can I help you?"

"We're looking for Mr. Singh," said Natalie, who had apparently become our lead investigator.

"Do you have an appointment?"

"No," said Natalie. "But we're Willing Middle School West students working for the school newspaper, and we have some questions for one of our most successful alumni."

I took a step back. Where did that lie come from? We had created a beautiful monster.

"I'm sorry, Mr. Singh is quite busy today," said the secretary. "Is there anything specific you wanted to ask?"

"We're doing an article on a former classmate of his," said Natalie. "Beatrice Long."

The receptionist wrote the name down on a pad.

"She died while still in high school," said Natalie. She looked left, looked right, lowered her voice. "Murder, they say. We just wanted to clear up some issues with Mr. Singh before we printed our article."

"Have a seat, please," said the receptionist, "and I'll see if he can spare the time."

We sat in the waiting room, ignoring the magazines. Natalie and I played with our phones. Henry leaned back, putting his arms behind his head.

"I didn't know I was a reporter for the school newspaper," said Henry. "Maybe Charlie's right about the old résumé. Tomorrow we should pretend to do community service."

I glanced up at the receptionist and noticed her trying not to stare at us as she spoke with hushed tones into the phone.

"Is she looking at us funny?" I said quietly. "And I don't mean oh-look-how-cute-they-are funny, more like what-are-they-doing-here funny."

"A little paranoid, Webster?" said Henry.

"I guess so," I said before standing and heading to her desk.

The receptionist looked up and immediately put her hand over the phone. "Yes?"

"Is Mr. Singh going to be able to see us or should we come back later? We can come back, no problem."

"No, you should definitely stay," she said. "They're looking for him now. He must be in a meeting. They told me to ask you to wait."

" 'They'?"

"Mr. Singh's assistant. She's trying now to locate him."

"Okay," I said, but when I sat back down I saw the same nervous glance, the same hushed conversation.

"What's going on?" said Natalie.

"I don't know, but something's not right. It's like she's keeping tabs on us."

"You're seeing things, Webster," said Henry.

"Maybe, but it seemed as if the second Natalie mentioned Beatrice's name everything changed," I said. "I think we should get out of here."

"You want to just up and leave?"

"Yes I do."

"Maybe I should blow the whistle," said Natalie.

"Let's just go, please."

As we all got up, the receptionist looked startled. "It will only be a few more minutes."

"We have to get back home," said Natalie. "We'll call later for an appointment."

"You really should stay." And just as she said that, the door to the inner offices opened and out they came. Two big guys in tight sport coats.

Security.

The receptionist pointed at us.

And that was when we started to run.

NABBED

We dashed out of there before security could get hold of us. We stopped at the elevator just long enough to press the button before we saw the security guys bang out of the office door, and then we sprinted to the stairwell.

Down and around and down again, more leaping than stepping, two flights, three flights. We didn't even know why we were running—we hadn't done anything wrong, had we?—but still we ran. There was something in the whole setup that gave us the creeps and had us racing madly. And it was sort of fun, too.

Until we burst out the door to the lobby, ready to tear past the security desk, and were stopped by a cop. A real cop in full uniform.

"Yikes alive!" said Natalie.

The cop was smiling, but his right hand rested calmly on his gun. Behind him were the beefy security guys from the fifth floor, huffing and puffing. My brother, Peter, would have laughed, but I wasn't laughing.

"Ms. Webster, Ms. Delgado, Mr. Harrison," said the cop.

"What's this about?" I said, taking a brave step forward. "You can't stop us. We didn't do anything wrong."

"That might be true," said the cop, "but the three of you are still going to have to come with me. Chief's orders."

Next thing we knew we were in the back seat of a police cruiser with a metal screen between the three of us and the cop in front as we drove through the darkening streets of Willing Township. Natalie was on one side of me, looking around, seeming to be enjoying the ride. Henry was on the other side, his confidence lost as he contemplated what an arrest could do to his swimming career. And me, I was in the center, wondering how our attempts to help a ghost had gone so wrong. Why had Anil Singh called the cops on us? Why was there still so much fear about a girl who had died so long ago? What had we gotten ourselves into?

Things grew even more alarming when the police officer drove us to the township building and calmly led us in the back door and up the stairs to an imposing office at the end of the hall.

Do you know the name of your chief of police? I surely didn't. But the name on the office door of the chief of police of Willing Township was still somehow not a surprise.

Johansson.

That's right, the same name as our Officer Derek Johansson, the lead investigator of Beatrice Long's murder.

The door opened. Chief Johansson stared at us from behind his desk. And something in his eyes told me our creepy missing-head case had just taken a turn.

THE CHIEF

We were shoved into the office and pushed down, each of us, into one of three chairs facing the desk. Chief Johansson sat like a block of granite behind his desk.

He was tall and wide, with a blond crew cut and a fake smile. He clasped his hands together like he was keeping himself from reaching out and slapping us silly. How many times had a teacher sat like that when a class had been a bit too noisy? How many times had my mother sat like that at the dinner table after I blurted out something she didn't want to hear?

"Thank you for coming down and visiting with us this evening," said the chief.

"Did we have much choice?" I said.

"No," said the chief. He was old, but not old enough to

have been a police officer way back in Beatrice's day. The other Officer Johansson mentioned in the articles must have been his father. "How are you doing, Henry? We were all proud of your swims at the state finals. Give my regards to your father."

"Sure thing, sir," said Henry, so eager to please he had become almost Frayden-like. It was embarrassing.

"Now, I received a call that you three are dredging up a long-past tragedy," said the chief. "Normally, we encourage historical research by our students—Willing Township has a fascinating history dating back to the days of William Penn. But when digging into the past can torment some of our citizens, we take a less tolerant view. I think the Longs have suffered enough. Don't you agree, Miss Webster?"

"It's a sad story," I said. My arms were crossed, my hair hung over my eyes. This was my usual position in response to the whole hands-clasped-on-the-desk thing. I would have refused to eat my vegetables if there were any in front of me to push away.

"Your mother teaches in the high school, isn't that right, Miss Webster?"

"Yes."

"Good for her. I'm sure she enjoys the job."

Was that a threat? It smelled like a threat.

"Now, I know that you live in the house that used to belong to the Longs, Henry," said the chief, "and that might have sparked your interest. But interest itself isn't reason enough to force people to relive the most difficult time in their lives."

"Mrs. Long didn't seem so upset about it," said Natalie.

"You're the one who stole the whistle, isn't that right, Miss Delgado?"

"I didn't steal anything," said Natalie. "It was a gift."

"I checked with your history teachers. It seems there is no research assignment like the one you told Mrs. Long and her daughter about. You lied. There is something in the law called theft by deception."

"Are we under arrest?" I said.

"Not yet," said the chief. "But there's still time. Once I heard from Mrs. Long's daughter, I assumed that Anil Singh might be next on your list. I asked his office to contact me if you came by so we could have this chat. What are you three really up to?"

"We're just curious about what happened to Beatrice," said Henry.

"Beatrice? You act like you know her."

"She was only a little bit older than us when she was killed," I said. "A Willing High freshman trying to make her way in the world. We feel like we do know her."

"Except you don't, you see. She died long before you were born."

"But you knew her, didn't you?" I said.

He pulled back, surprised. "Why would you say that?"

"Just something we heard."

"I knew her a bit, yes, but Beatrice was quite a few years older than me. I only knew that she was a very sweet girl."

"We just want to find out what happened to her," said Henry.

"Somebody should," I muttered under my breath.

"Don't be impertinent, young lady," he said sharply.

"Just wanting to know is not a good enough reason, not when you're causing pain. It's time you three put this whole thing to rest. It's time to leave the Long family alone. Let me tell you about the way a community works."

The start of his lecture was a cue for me to tune out. Why adults think long speeches are the way to convince kids of anything is beyond me. Candy works better, always, but the chief evidently got the wrong memo. While he blathered on, I looked around the office. On the walls and bookshelves was a flag, a college diploma, framed citations, plaques, and personal photographs, among them an old family portrait that snagged my attention as if it was a hook and I was a flounder.

A man, a woman, two boys, all looking into the camera with serious expressions. The man had on a police uniform. The woman's face was lined and tired. And then there were the boys—one young, the other much older, taller, with a flat nose and a split upper lip.

I recognized him with a dread that slipped down my neck and seeped into my bones like liquid nitrogen.

Yes, of course, it was the boy in my dreams, the one who captured me when I was first a squirrel and then a snake. It was the older Johansson brother who had been Beatrice's friend.

"Is that your father in the police uniform?" I asked, interrupting Chief Johansson's boring little speech and pointing at the picture.

The chief stopped talking (yay!) and turned his head to follow my pointing finger. "Yes, that's right."

"Derek Johansson, the officer who investigated Beatrice's murder?"

"He was one of the investigators on the case. He put in forty years on the force. He died just a few years ago."

"And who's that, the boy on the right?" I said.

"That's my brother, Vance," said the chief, and at that moment the atmosphere in the office changed, as if the dread I had felt upon seeing the picture had spilled out to cover us all in a foul mist.

"He looks sad," I said.

"He had a difficult childhood."

"Where is he now?"

"That is none of your business," snapped the chief. "Now, to get back to our business here, I brought you in to tell you that your research project concerning Beatrice Long is over."

"Is that an order?" said Natalie.

"Absolutely," said the chief. "Disobey at your own risk."

"What does that mean?" said Henry.

"You don't want to find out," said the chief as he pressed a button on his desk. The office door opened and two cops in uniform, a man and a woman, their guns holstered, came in and stood on either side of the doorway. One of them was the officer who had driven us to this building, shaking his head at us as if he had just caught us egging a neighbor's house.

"Right now," said the chief, "you three are guilty of trespass and theft. I'm willing to overlook—"

"Where's her head?" I said, interrupting him again.

He turned to me. There was something dark and frightened in his eyes.

"Beatrice's head," I said. "Where is it?"

"Where did you hear anything about a missing head?"

"The articles in the paper."

"The articles mentioned nothing specific about the condition of her body. My father made sure of that."

"The articles said identification was difficult," said Natalie, giving me a warning look. "We just assumed the head was missing."

"As opposed to a hundred more likely possibilities? No, only the killer knew exactly what was done to Beatrice Long's body. Only the killer, the police, and now you. What have you gotten yourselves into?"

What indeed?

"We brought you in to give you a kindly warning," said the chief. "I was going to let you three leave after the talk. But now I think we're going to have to take you down to processing as we consider our options. Officers, will you please escort these three to the cells."

"The cells?" said Henry.

"Let's hold them in lockup while I make some calls to determine if the Long family is going to press charges."

"The cells?"

"Please stand," said the cop who had driven us. As he said it he took a couple sets of handcuffs off his belt.

"You can't be—"

"And put your hands behind your backs."

We looked at each other, Natalie, Henry, and I, and tried to act as if it was no big deal, but I'm sure my face betrayed me. It felt as if my life was veering off whatever course it might have finally and heroically assumed. Instead of becoming a lawyer for the damned, I was headed to the cells.

I knew what that meant: monochrome tattoos and stolen cigarettes and fights in the cafeteria. Later, I would spout slang out of the side of my mouth and tell stories about the big house. *Spoons, you've got to steal the spoons. The one thing in the slammer you can never have enough of is spoons.* I was letting my worst fears swirl inside my head when I heard a commotion outside the office door.

"No, no indeed," came a familiar voice. "I will not wait. I intend to go right on in without delay, and any attempt to stop me will be duly noted for the lawsuit we will be filing forthwith."

We all turned to see what was happening as, with suit on and tie tight and briefcase in hand, my father entered Chief Johansson's office.

THE ROCK STAR

It was my stepfather, actually, who stepped through the chief's door—Stephen Scali, attorney-at-law, specializing in patents and trademarks and such.

"Stephen?" I said.

"Be quiet, Elizabeth," said my stepfather. "Not another word from any of you. I'll do all the speaking from here on in. Why have you abducted these children, Chief Johansson? Why are you questioning them without their attorneys or parents present? What in tarnation is going on?"

Natalie and I looked at each other. *Tarnation?*

"It's good to see you outside of a Board of Commissioners meeting, Stephen," said the chief.

"I expect not," said my stepfather.

"We have ourselves an issue here."

"You may have an issue, but these young students have

rights. And now they have an attorney. If you ever want to talk to them again, get in touch with me and I'll arrange something consistent with their constitutional privileges. Is that understood?"

"You shouldn't be meddling in this, Stephen."

"I'm a lawyer. Meddling is what I do."

"We're just having a discussion. You're blowing this all out of proportion."

"I think you've done that already, or am I not seeing this correctly? Aren't these children being detained? Isn't that officer holding handcuffs? I seem to have gotten here in the nick of time—and not just for their sakes, but for yours, too. Imagine the hullabaloo that would have ensued if anything more serious had happened."

Natalie and I looked at each other again. *Hullabaloo?*

"It's just procedure," said the cop with the handcuffs.

"You can tell that to the judge. Are these three children free to leave with me? If yes, then we'll be going, thank you. If not, then I'll be heading off to federal court and filing an emergency petition for a writ of habeas corpus."

"Calm down, Stephen. Maybe we should talk alone."

"Let me take these children home now, and once they are safe in their bedrooms with their stuffed animals and their mothers, then you and I can chat all you want."

Natalie smiled widely at me and mouthed the words *stuffed animals*. I shrugged.

"But if you decide to keep them a minute longer, then the talk we'll be having will be in a deposition, under oath, and it won't be so cordial. Your decision, Chief."

There was a moment when the chief, unsure of what to do,

looked at his uniformed officers. I looked just at Stephen. I couldn't have been more flabbergasted if he had been standing there with long black hair and a leather jacket, playing an electric guitar with fireworks shooting out its neck.

Or more proud.

It wasn't until we were out of the township building that I noticed the tremble in my stepfather's hand or the way his eyes darted from side to side like two nervous fish. He had been solid as a tree trunk inside Chief Johansson's office, but now he was shaky as a leaf in a windstorm.

"Stephen?" I said. "Are you all right?"

"Keep walking," he said with tight lips. "If they're looking out the window, everything should be as calm as a Sunday stroll."

"But we don't take Sunday strolls," I said.

"I think we should start, don't you? It would be a nice family thing. The bright sun, the fresh air. Nature."

"But I hate nature."

"We'll begin this weekend."

"It was way cool how you laid it on that cop, Mr. Scali," said Natalie. "You were like . . . like . . ."

"A rock star?" I said.

"Yes, that's it," said Natalie. "A rock star."

"Thank you, Natalie, though I don't think I have the hair for it. But I must say, I never stormed into a police chief's office and threatened his job before. We don't do such things in patent law."

"What does a patent lawyer do?" said Henry.

"We protect intellectual property, Henry, and intellectual property is the cornerstone of the American economy.

Did you know that provisions for the protection of intellectual property were placed directly into the United States Constitution as a—"

"How did you know we were there?" I said, interrupting what I knew would be the most boring lecture in the history of mankind.

"Natalie's mother."

"And how did she know?"

"Well," said Natalie, "to be honest, I might have texted her."

"You texted your mother? I thought you didn't get along with your mother. All you do is complain about her."

"But we were in trouble," said Natalie. "And she's my mother. Who else was I going to text?"

"And she immediately called your mother, Lizzie, who gave me a call," said Stephen. "The point is, Natalie, that you got in touch with a responsible adult and your mother saved the day. Well done on everybody's part."

As Natalie beamed, I took a look at Stephen. He was still nervous—his eyes were still a pair of darting minnows—and he looked just then like anything other than a hero, but he had come through just when things had turned major-league creepy inside Chief Johansson's office. And the thing was, as soon as I recognized his voice, I knew that he would.

After we dropped off Henry and Natalie at their houses, I asked Stephen a question on our way home. "When we were in that office you threatened Chief Johansson with some sort of lawyer word."

"Habeas corpus," said Stephen, saying the words with a deep important voice. "The great writ."

"It sounds like a magic spell." I waved my hands in the air. *"Habeas corpus."*

"It is a little magical, I must say," said my stepfather. "If someone is being held in a prison, a habeas corpus petition requires the prisoner be brought before the court and forces whoever is doing the imprisoning to show why the prisoner is being locked up. It came into being something like seven hundred years ago when kings would routinely imprison whomever they wanted. That doesn't seem quite fair, does it?"

"No," I said.

"So they created the writ of habeas corpus to be a check on the power of the king. It has become the cornerstone of a free society."

"There seem to be a lot of cornerstones floating around."

"Are you making fun of me?"

"No. Well, yes. But not really. Thank you for doing what you did."

"Family, right?

"Sure, yeah, whatever."

"Elizabeth, I might only be your stepfather, but you've always been nothing less than my daughter. When I married your mother I knew you were part of the package, and I accepted that and everything it meant."

"We all have our crosses to bear."

"Yes, we do, but then you turned out to be you."

"Yeah, well, sorry about that."

"No, you don't get it. You turned out to be you, which is more than I could ever have hoped for. More funny, more surly and sarcastic, more smart, more loving to your brother—"

"Stop it," I said, not sure if I was talking to him, with all his tender dad talk, or the tears that were welling. Maybe it was a natural reaction to the tension of the moment in the chief's office, but maybe it was something else, too. Maybe what happened to me when I became a barrister in the Court of Uncommon Pleas didn't just happen to me. Maybe it happened to everyone. Change one person, change the world.

"Okay, you're right," said Stephen. "I'll stop the sappy talk. Your mother told me you were looking into some murder that happened before you were born."

"She told you that?"

"We're married, Elizabeth. We tell each other things."

Not everything, I thought.

"So," he said, "what did you find that caught the interest of our chief of police?"

"Nothing, really. From the newspaper articles, we learned there was some kind of fight between the victim's sister and the old boyfriend. We already talked to the sister and were trying to talk to the old boyfriend when the police grabbed us. Something was going on back then, and I think the chief's brother might have been involved, or even the chief himself."

"Really? The chief? When did this murder happen?"

"Fifty years ago."

"How old was he then? Nine or so?"

"Something like that."

"A likely suspect, if the murder was committed with

baseball cards and bubble gum. And what do you know about the brother?"

"Not a thing. But we don't know where else to look."

"You mentioned some articles in the paper."

"Yeah, we looked them up on microfilm."

"You can sue a newspaper for something called libel if it prints stuff that's untrue, which means newspapers try to print only what they can prove."

"Another cornerstone?"

"When the law is falling on your head, it all feels like a cornerstone."

I laughed. "So?"

"Well," he said, "it means newspaper editors are always saying, 'We can't put this in, we can't put that in.'"

"So you think we should talk to the reporter?" I said. "And find out if there was anything she discovered that her editor wouldn't let her print?"

"It might not be a total waste. But finding her after all these years won't be so easy."

"We'll find her," I said. "We'll put Natalie on it. It turns out she's a total bloodhound."

A SIMPLE
LOVE STORY

My grandfather was somewhere behind the piles of paper and stacks of legal books that teetered on his desk when Avis announced my presence.

"Elizabeth has come back to us," she squawked. "Your granddaughter has returned."

"Of course she's returned," came my grandfather's voice. "She is part of the firm now. We need to change the sign on the door. Find a new name. Maybe Webster and Son and Son's Daughter. It has a ring, no?"

"No," said Avis. "No ring."

"Seat her at the desk, you grumpy grouse, and get back to work. And where is the Wedderburn petition? I've been waiting all day for the Wedderburn petition."

"It's been here the entire time," said Avis, before snatching a document from one of the piles and holding it out.

An aged hand reached through the piles and grabbed the document. "It's about time you found this thing. Wedderburn has just molted. He is ravenous. He needs to feed. Now leave us be."

Avis glanced my way and shook her head in two quick twists, left, then right, before skittering out of the office.

"And close the door!" shouted my grandfather.

The door slammed shut.

"That woman," said my grandfather as I heard a chair scrape backward. "We get more done in the winter when she heads south than we do while she's here."

The bang of his cane on the floor let me know he was coming my way. Bang, bang. And then from behind the mountainous piles on his desk he appeared, his back bent, his wild white eyebrows masking his eyes, the Wedderburn petition in his hand.

"Fact-check this for me, will you?" he said as he waved the document at me. "See to it quickly, before Wedderburn starts snacking on necks again. The last time that happened, it took the nation years to recover. That, of course, was the great molt of 1929 and the results, as you can imagine, were calamitous. After the petition is fact-checked and citations are added, it needs to be filed."

"I don't know how to do any of that," I said.

"Then learn." The cane rapped the floor. "You are now a barrister before the Court of Uncommon Pleas. That is a position of grave responsibility. Ask Barnabas for help, if need be. He knows how to do everything."

"Grandpop," I said. "Can I ask you something?"

"Of course, but be quick about it. Wedderburn is uncommonly hungry at this time of the year."

"If Barnabas knows how to do everything, why isn't he a lawyer himself?"

"He was, many years ago, but is no longer permitted to stand before the court. Now he is a simple clerk, an indentured servant of the firm."

"What did he do wrong?"

"It's not what he did, my sweet, it's what was done to him."

"When Barnabas saved me from that statue in City Hall, he acted as if the monster couldn't hurt him."

"You have a good eye, Elizabeth, a Webster's eye. That is all true, yes. It's a terrible story, quite unfortunate, really." He tapped his cane on the floor twice. Bang, bang. "So now, let's get to work. Wedderburn awaits."

"Aren't you going to tell me the story?"

"Why would I do that?"

"Because I want to hear it?"

"You want to hear his story? How extraordinary. Well, I suppose Wedderburn can wait a few minutes. I'll have Avis ship him a couple of ferrets from her pantry, that should keep him fed for a while longer. Now sit."

I took a seat behind the little desk as my grandfather, tapping his cane hard upon the floor, made his way to the great portrait of Daniel Webster atop the fireplace. He straightened up as best he could. One hand leaned on the cane, the other patted his breast as if he were about to give a speech to the masses.

"It all began," said my grandfather grandly, "when Barnabas passed into the other world."

"What does that mean, to pass into the other world?"

"For that you need to hear the entirety of the story. Buckle up your shoes, Elizabeth, the ride is about to get wee bit rough."

There was once a lawyer, practicing in a county called Sussex, on the southern coast of Britain. This was in Victorian England, the era of the Brontë sisters and Ebenezer Scrooge. Our lawyer, tall, handsome, and brooding, perfectly fit his times. He was much admired by the women of the town where he lived, but he kept his distance, preferring solitude to formal dress balls. Walking alone along the high chalk cliffs of the shoreline in his boots and tailcoat, his hands clasped behind him as the wind whipped through his long, dark hair, he would gaze out at the sea, as if seeking a ship on the horizon. This, of course, was our Barnabas, the second, and therefore penniless, son of Lord Bothemly, late of East Anglia.

One afternoon, a young woman named Isabel hesitantly entered Barnabas's office. Isabel's family had married her off while still in her teens to a rich old scoundrel named Cutbush, who showed only brutality to his young bride. Isabel had no idea what to do or to whom to turn, and so she came to Barnabas seeking her freedom. In those days, while it was a rather simple matter for a man to divorce his wife, it was much more difficult for a woman to divorce her husband. And even worse, Isabel had no money of her own and thus would be unable to pay the lawyer any fees. It was a hopeless enterprise, but Barnabas, seeing the pain in the woman's eyes, and understanding his duties as an attorney, agreed to take the case.

The course of law in England ran quite slowly in those years, and for many months Barnabas and Isabel worked together on the case. To get her divorce, Isabel had to prove both that Cutbush had cheated and that he had treated her cruelly. In the course of their work, Barnabas grew to admire Isabel's quickness of mind and the detached way she dealt with the most horrific matters of her married life. He once told her she had the soul of a lawyer, which, to Barnabas, was the highest of compliments. And Isabel grew to admire not just Barnabas's technical mastery of the law but also the streak of idealism that lay beneath it. In their time together, as these things tend to happen, the two fell deeply in love. Even so, Barnabas refused to act on his emotions, or even to so much as acknowledge them, while Isabel was still a client. There were rules against such things. There still are.

The proceedings in the case of *Cutbush v. Cutbush* were lengthy and bitter. It was unclear until the very end how the judge would rule. When the divorce was conditionally granted, it took another six months for it to become final and absolute, and in this period both lawyer and client avoided one another. If the wife committed adultery in the six-month period the divorce would be voided. But after the six months, Isabel was officially divorced from Cutbush. Upon hearing the news from her counsel, she stiffly discharged him from her employ.

The very next moment they fell into each other's arms.

The happiness that flowed into both their lives gave them each a golden glow that was noted all across the county. Not since Romeo and Juliet was a love so pure and heartfelt, said the townsfolk. Together the couple walked along the coastline, Barnabas no longer looking across the sea as if for some long-delayed ship, but instead into Isabel's dark brown eyes. There he found, for the first time in his life, true happiness. And for Isabel, being with Barnabas was like being reborn into a magical world wrapped in love.

One afternoon, on a blustery day, as the waves crashed menacingly upon the great rocks beneath the tall, pale cliffs, the lawyer fell to a knee and begged Isabel for her hand in marriage. She gave it wholeheartedly. Together they strolled arm in arm back to the village, their future promising nothing but joy and love, when, from behind a tree, Cutbush appeared and shot Barnabas right in his heart.

Dead is as dead does, and Barnabas was now dead.

Isabel was inconsolable. She refused to speak at the funeral, or at the subsequent murder trial, or even at Cutbush's hanging. She stayed mute as misery gripped tight her wounded heart. She spent hours walking alone across the same high, rocky cliffs Barnabas had paced, standing tall and angular, staring out at the sea as if searching for her beloved in the waves. It was during one of these walks that an old woman with a black shawl came passing by and instructed Isabel, without a word of explanation, to follow her. Isabel did.

The old woman lived in a shack on the edge of a dark wood. She indicated for Isabel to sit at a rickety old table. The old woman sat across from her.

"You are grieving, my child," said the old woman.

Isabel nodded.

"Your betrothed has been taken to the other side and you miss him terribly."

Isabel nodded again.

"What if I told you," said the old woman, "that I could send you to him, and in so doing allow you to return your betrothed to this side of the great divide, to once again walk across these bleak yet lovely cliffs?"

For the first time since the tragedy, Isabel spoke. "I'd do anything."

"Think, my lovely girl. Anything? The sacrifice could be greater than you can imagine."

"Anything," said Isabel.

The old woman leaned forward and kissed Isabel on the forehead before rising. She brewed a special tea and chanted over the bubbling liquid as she dashed in herbs and berries and squirmy little creatures. When she was finished, she ladled some of the potion into a flowered cup and placed it before the shaking girl.

"They say you two were like Romeo and Juliet," said the old woman. "It is time to prove it."

Isabel drank her bitter tea, and quick as that she vanished from the earth.

THE DEMON'S CURSE

"**W**here did she go?" I asked, in the middle of my grandfather's story.

"Where do you think?" said my grandfather with a wink.

My eyes opened embarrassingly wide and I whispered, "The other world?"

"Precisely," said my grandfather. "It is time you know what you are dealing with as a member of this firm. Our lives are like a voyage by train, and this world is but one of the many stops on the journey. For some the stop is short and painful, for others it is long and joyous, but for all of us, the time comes when we must step back onto that train and head for the next station. That station is the other world."

"Have you been there?" I asked.

"I have not yet had the pleasure—or the misfortune,

depending. It is a difficult thing to go back and forth, it takes much from you, and I was not made of such stern stuff. One glass of milk and I am flatulent for days. Imagine what a voyage like that would do to my system. It was left to my father and my son to make that journey."

"My father? He goes back and forth?"

"There are courts there, too, my dear. Lawyers are needed. Since Old Scratch's promise to your great ancestor, there has always been a Webster on the other side, defending the damned. Usually they are deceased themselves, but sometimes they must make the unsettling journey from this side to do their work. Every soul departing from that train is judged before heading to its rightful place, and even the worst of the scalawags deserve representation. How's your Italian?"

"Not so good," I said. "I can order a pepperoni pizza, but that's about it."

"Pity, because a fellow named Dante had a pretty good take on what it is like over there, and like most things it is better in the original. There are many levels and many seas and many islands, and somewhere in that world is a spot for each of us to inhabit, until it is time for us to get on that train again. The courts on the other side determine what that spot is and, as with all courts, mistakes are made and injustices arise. It is those injustices that cause the disturbances in this world. One can't solve them only on this side of the wall, my dear. One must have representation on the other side, too. And that is the noble work that your father does."

"Is it dangerous?"

"The travel is, yes, like flying on a plane through a hurricane with a cargo of monkeys, I am told. But even more dangerous are the guardians of the lower depths, fallen angels who rule their fiefdoms like cruel kings. And the cruelest of those is a fallen angel known as Abezethibou. As he plummeted from above, some of his fellow angels grabbed hold of a wing to stop his fall. The wing tore off, causing his other wing to turn the color of blood."

"Ouch," I said.

"Ouch indeed," said my grandfather. "Nothing stings like a torn wing, just ask Avis. Now, those condemned to live under the demon's hand call him Redwing. And it was Redwing who sent the old witch to those rocky cliffs to fetch our Isabel."

Redwing had gained dominion over Cutbush after the murderer had been dispatched to the other side through a noose. The hanged man, bitter and demented, blamed his crime and all his misfortune on the she-wolf Isabel, who, he claimed, deceived him with her soft voice and quiet manner.

Cutbush spent so much time going on about Isabel that Redwing naturally grew curious. So he peered through the lens of fate from that world into this and spotted Isabel walking along the rocky cliffs of Sussex with her regal posture and mournful silence. The fallen angel was so taken by the vision, he decided then and there that he must possess her. And so he dispatched a witch to intercept the young woman's path. The old woman brewed her foul concoction and Isabel, without ever dying, was sent directly to the other world.

But the law of this world and the next states that one cannot be taken unwillingly to the other side before death. Isabel would soon have to be returned to the world of the living. So Redwing, in order to possess that which he desired, induced Barnabas to climb down from the higher levels with the promise of seeing once again his betrothed. When Isabel arrived at Redwing's domain in the other world there was a moment of joy when she and Barnabas embraced. But that moment lasted only as long as Redwing permitted before the fallen angel came between them.

He appeared in his unadulterated form, a fearsome demon with hooves for feet and claws for hands and one red wing rising from his broad back. His horns were as red as his wing and glowed like embers. His tail writhed, and his voice . . . his voice was like the crackling blaze of doom.

With that voice, Redwing offered Isabel, out of the goodness of his fire-crusted heart, the opportunity to send Barnabas back to our world. To resurrect her lover by taking his place. While Isabel was more than willing, Barnabas refused to allow it. Isabel was inclined to respect his wishes, until Redwing explained, patiently and with a note of kindness in his voice, the painful situation the two lovers faced.

Often the betrothed-but-never-married were sent to different levels of this many-layered world, he said, and even after centuries of searching most would never see their loved one again. But Redwing swore that if Isabel agreed to stay with the fallen angel in Barnabas's place, and Barnabas promised to refrain from interacting with any figure from the spirit world, then when Barnabas returned to this world, Redwing would ensure that he and Isabel would be together for all eternity.

The offer felt wrong—evil, even. Barnabas urged Isabel to refuse, to return to her life and find someone new. But Isabel, hoping against hope for a future together with her one great love, agreed to the terms. In a flash, Barnabas was returned to our own world, and Isabel's fate was left in the clawed hands of the demon Redwing.

When Barnabas found himself back in our world, he was naked and adrift in the sea off the coast of Sussex. He determined to drown himself immediately to get back to Isabel. He swam down as deep as he could go and breathed in the sea. As his lungs filled with the frigid salt water, he felt the life ebb out of him, yet he awoke once again in the same turbulent waters. He tried a second and then a third time, failing and failing again to die. As he swam to the shore he let the waves crash him upon the rocky coast, but when he climbed onto the rocks, he observed that not only was he still alive, but his pale skin was unmarked.

And that was when he knew. Redwing, to keep his grip on Isabel, had made Barnabas immortal.

When he returned to the town, clothed in burlap from feed bags he had stolen along the way, no one recognized him. When, properly dressed, he tried to take his place before the bar of the court where he had practiced, he was thrown out of the courthouse. Everyone knew that Barnabas was dead and no imposter would be allowed to stand for him.

After years of roaming the landscape as a vagabond,

trying and failing to kill himself over and over, he heard tell of a firm of lawyers in the New World who made a practice of representing the damned. Certain that no one qualified more than he, Barnabas hired on as the lowest-level seaman on a cargo ship heading to America.

"That is the saddest story I've ever heard," I said. "And so romantic."

"It is the cliffs," said my grandfather. "Even I would be a striking figure on the cliffs. Imagine me there, leaning forward on my cane, peering out at the sea, the wind ruffling my eyebrows. Who could resist? That good man Barnabas has been with us now ever since he arrived on these shores."

"Is my father representing him?"

"Yes indeed, and he represents Isabel, too. The story is a travesty of justice that must be reversed. Barnabas now, being of neither this world nor the next, is ineligible to stand himself before the Court of Uncommon Pleas, but he is a crackerjack clerk, and in exchange for his work the firm of Webster and Son has been litigating this case against Redwing for over a century. Even your great ancestor Daniel Webster took a shot at it after he died. The case has taken twists and turns, yes indeed—your father has inherited it from my father, who inherited it himself—but we are getting close. In fact, your father was pressing what he believed would be the winning argument to the court on the other side when he failed to return as expected."

"And you believe this Redwing is responsible."

"He must be," said my grandfather. "And now, somehow, your father is communicating with us through the spirit of Beatrice Long. 'Save me, save him.' Your father is undoubtedly the 'him.' We must find her head, Elizabeth. We simply must. Are we getting any closer?"

"I don't know," I said. "We're at least getting people all in a twist, which is sort of fun."

"That's always a grand first step. Nothing gets done without plucking a few feathers from the poultry. Keep on working. Every day that passes increases the risk to your father. But first, before you do anything, you must take care of the Wedderburn petition."

"Yes, Grandpop, I know. Wedderburn must be fed."

"Precisely," he said.

A Necessary Requirement

I carried the Wedderburn petition out of my grandfather's office and headed to Barnabas's tall writing desk to ask for his help. He leaned over a scroll and carefully scratched out words with his feather pen. His long pale face seemed to glow as if lit by the document laid out before him.

I had become comfortable enough with Barnabas that I could crack jokes with him, not that he ever smiled at any of them, but now I hesitated. He was no longer merely an odd-looking man with kind eyes and long pale hands, he was a man with a tragic past. For me, he would never look the same again, and I was proud that my father was trying to help him.

I looked around the office, at Avis behind her desk and at the odd assortment of clients waiting in their chairs for time with my grandfather—Sandy with the wild blond hair, the giant in his brown suit, hump-man—and all of them looked different. I couldn't help but wonder at the tragedies that brought them to my father's office. And I began to think of the Frayden twins, Charlie and Doug, in the cafeteria. I had always been so preoccupied with my own insecurities that I hadn't been able to imagine what, or who, might have been tormenting the two of—

I caught myself mid-thought. Really, Lizzie? What was I doing worrying about the Fraydens' emotions? That was a little creepy. If the ceremony where I received my credentials had indeed changed me, maybe it wasn't for the better.

"Mistress Elizabeth," said Barnabas when he raised his attention from the document on his desktop and saw me. "Is there something I can do for you?"

"My grandfather gave me the Wedderburn petition."

"Ah, yes," said Barnabas. "The Wedderburn petition."

"I'm supposed to do all kinds of stuff to it and then take it to the judge."

"I'm sure you are," he said. "But I think you can dispense with those tasks for the time being."

"My grandfather said I had to get to it right away. He made it sound really important."

"I'm sure he did," said Barnabas kindly, "but he gave that same petition to me last week. The petition has already been fact-checked and filled with citations and filed with the clerk. The judge should rule momentarily. Your grandfather is a brilliant attorney and has forgotten more about the law than most ever learn, but lately the quantity he has forgotten seems to grow each and every day."

I looked at the document in my hand. "Is that a problem?"

"Oh no, not at all. He has your father and Avis and me and now you to help him. He is such a brilliant resource, not just in legal knowledge but in his spirit and outsized humanity. It is an honor for all of us to help him in any way we can."

I looked at the papers in my hand. "My afternoon seems to have freed up."

"How goes the search for our ghost's head?"

"It's going. Maybe out to sea, but it's going all right. So, I was thinking—"

"Splendid," said Barnabas. "Perhaps I should alert the heralds."

"Barnabas," I said, "did you just make a joke?"

"Certainly not," said Barnabas. "The heralds like to celebrate even the smallest victories."

"I think that was a joke."

"I can't disabuse you of your fantasies. Now, about that thinking you were doing."

"Well," I said, "if my father is being detained on the other side, why don't we just file something with the court? Maybe that habeas corpse thing my stepfather told me about."

"Ah, habeas corpus," said Barnabas. "The great writ. Very good, Mistress Elizabeth. You are picking up things quite smartly. Habeas corpus would be the way to go."

"Then let's do it."

"We would have filed it already, except there is a problem. In order to file such a petition in the Court of Uncommon Pleas, we need to know first where your father is being held. The other side is vast, and Judge Jeffries has made it abundantly clear that it is not enough just to point and say someone is being unfairly held over there. For the judge to order the prisoner brought to his court to determine the legality of a detention, we must have a precise location."

"So as soon as we find out where he is we can file the habeas thing?"

"Yes. We need the location in order to bring him physically into court. Now, in a normal law case, we are allowed to get information from the other side. It is called discovery, and we're permitted to look at documents and ask questions face-to-face in a procedure called a deposition."

"My stepfather mentioned that when he got us out of the police station. So let's do a deposition."

"We would, Mistress Elizabeth, but to compel such a thing, we at least need to know to whom we should ask our questions. Your father could be held only with permission of the ruler of the realm where he is being detained, so that is whom we need to depose, but without a location we don't know who that might be."

"Then how do we find the location?"

"Aye, there's the rub."

"Rub?"

"The difficulty. It is a bowling term. Have you ever played at lawn bowling?"

"No."

"Well, you haven't missed much. We have sent word to our clerks on the other side and they are scouring all the landscapes. When they find your father, they will send us the information we need to begin. But as I said, the other side is vast, and the hiding places are many, and as of yet our emissaries have had no luck. And so we must wait."

"I'm not good at waiting," I said.

Barnabas looked at me and a great sadness welled in his eyes, a sadness that I now believed I could understand.

"Neither am I," he said, "but sometimes we have no other choice."

Just then my grandfather barged out of his office, banging the floor with his cane. "What about 'The Magnificent Websters'? Talk about a firm name with pizzazz! And you know, I always wanted to join the circus. I was born for the flying trapeze. What say you, Elizabeth? Barnabas? The Magnificent Websters. Brilliant, no?"

"No," we both said at the same time.

36

THE COLLECTION

"Beatrice Long?" said Delores Baird, seated in a blue armchair, her white hair knotted at the back of her neck, her back straight and her ankles crossed. Henry and Natalie and I were sitting around her with notebooks on our laps. "That's a name from the past. I haven't heard anyone mention Beatrice Long in at least a day and a half."

I didn't realize that she was joking until the slightest of smiles creased her lips.

"Who's been talking about Beatrice?" said Natalie, as if someone had been gossiping about a friend behind her back.

"Oh, don't worry yourselves about it," said the old woman. "I certainly won't. What can I do for you now?"

"We have some questions about the murder," said Henry.

"There are some out there, to be sure," said Delores. "Too many to count."

Once Natalie had dug up her location, Delores Baird, who had written the newspaper articles about Beatrice Long's murder, agreed to meet us in the lobby of her nursing home. It was the Saturday after our run-in with the chief. I had expected rows of rocking chairs and bowls of mashed peas and people shouting into each other's hearing aids. But we were sitting in a beautiful building with nice furniture and old people crossing the lobby with determined steps. Some of those steps were steadied by metal walkers, true, but it still seemed like a cozy place. I wondered just then where my grandfather lived. I had never asked. I had never visited. I had never brought him a plate of home-baked cookies, not that I knew how to make them.

"We are doing a school project," lied Natalie so easily it was almost breathtaking. "Henry lives in Beatrice's old house and the assignment was to discover the secret history of our homes."

Delores sniffed the air, as if there was some foul scent. "That's not rightly so, at least not according to Chief Johansson," she said. "According to Chief Johansson the three of you are simply looking into the past to stir up old waters."

"Chief Johansson already talked to you?" I said, feeling like a soccer ball with the air leaking out. The chief was running interference. He wasn't going to let us learn what we needed to learn to help Beatrice or save my father.

"Oh yes, he came by personally," said Delores Baird.

"He said he had already warned you three in the strictest terms about asking these questions. Is that correct?"

"Sort of," I admitted.

"And yet here you are. Imagine that. The chief has advised me in the very same terms not to cooperate with you in any way, shape, or form. He was quite adamant."

"I guess that's that," said Henry, closing the notebook on his lap. "We're sorry to have bothered you."

"No bother," said Delores. "In fact, it does my heart good to see you disregarding the good chief's advice."

"Really?" said Natalie.

"Oh, sweetie, when I was still reporting, if I let every public official with a puffed-out chest push me around, I never would have written a word worth reading. All they want you to do is publish their press releases, but that wasn't my job. My job was to stir up those waters. You never know what you'll find. Sometimes the most illuminating things rise up from the muck. Not that they always let me keep on stirring."

"Was there something about Beatrice's murder they didn't want you to stir up?" I asked.

"Oh, that's a story and a half," said Delores. "I found something about the case that sparked my curiosity, all right. It wasn't definitive, but it was surely worth some more digging. My editor disagreed and spiked the investigation dead."

"Why?"

"I was never sure, but my guess was that our Chief Johansson's father asked the editor to shut me down. That was apparently enough."

"What did you learn about Beatrice that you were trying to investigate?" Henry asked.

"It's funny how you all talk about her as if you knew her. I like that. That's the way it has to feel when you're reporting, the good and the bad. You have to remember that names are not just names, if you understand me. Flesh and blood deserve our best efforts at the truth."

I leaned forward. "We read your articles, and there seemed to be stuff going on between Beatrice's sister, Roberta, and Beatrice's boyfriend, Anil Singh."

"Good catch," said Delores. "Something was going on with them, yes, and it was hard to figure out what. The sister was angry at the boyfriend, and the boyfriend was so terribly upset."

"It sounded like Roberta blamed Anil for what happened."

"It seemed like that, yes. But I spoke to a girl who told a different story. When I tried to confirm it, neither Anil Singh nor Beatrice's sister would do so on the record, but they didn't deny it, either. And it matched up with what else I had learned. Apparently, the older sister was jealous of the younger sister's boyfriend. She liked Mr. Singh, too. And so, at a Halloween party, she pulled him into the woods to tell him her feelings. Sisters can be like that sometimes. Things evolved, as they can, and that's when Beatrice found them."

"Oh, man," said Natalie. "I hate when that happens."

"What did Beatrice do?" I said.

"She was young," said Delores. "She was hurt. She felt betrayed by both of them and so she did the only thing she could think of doing. She ran away from the party, away from her sister and her boyfriend, into the woods. My source told me Anil tried to go after her, but the sister held him back. He had to knock her down to get away. She had a bruise on her face at the funeral, which I didn't write about, but which I noticed and which confirmed the story."

I thought about Beatrice's sister, complaining that Anil Singh hadn't taken care of Beatrice like he should have, and how she must have thought the very same thing about herself. That's a heavy load of bricks to carry all those years.

"Where was the party?" I said. "Do you remember?"

"No, dear, I'm sorry."

"Did Anil ever find Beatrice?" Natalie asked.

"Not according to what I heard. She ran, he chased, she disappeared. And two weeks later they found her body, poor thing."

"And then the editor killed your investigation," I said, nodding.

"Oh no, dear. I chose to leave be that part of the story. I told what I learned to the police and kept all my notes, in case it became relevant later. But we didn't follow up the story of the sister and the boyfriend because it would have raised a false assumption—that the boyfriend was involved, when there was nothing else that pointed to him. It seemed unfair. The story was more a piece of high school gossip than something newsworthy. That's not why I became a reporter."

"But you said your editor spiked your investigation," said Henry.

"Not that part of it."

"So what part?" said Henry.

"I thought there was something that deserved looking into more deeply. It turned out that shortly after Beatrice's body was discovered, a young man from the area was involuntarily committed to a state hospital for the mentally ill."

"An insane asylum?" said Henry.

"They don't call it that anymore—they didn't even call it that back then—but yes, that's where he was sent. The poor boy. There was a judge's order sending him to the high-security ward and keeping him hospitalized indefinitely. He was still a minor, so his name wasn't disclosed on the record, but we caught wind of it."

"I bet I know who it was," I said.

"I'd be surprised if you do, dear."

"Vance Johansson, the chief's big brother."

Delores looked at me, tilted her head. "Aren't you something. Aren't you just the slyest piece of something. And how did you know that?"

"A lucky guess?"

"I doubt that very much. Now, there wouldn't be a notable connection between the two events, except for the timing. The boy went into the hospital right as I got word there was a suspect in the case. And, it turned out that Beatrice had been especially kind to Vance Johansson, who was a troubled boy. They explored the woods together, took care of injured wildlife they found, that sort of thing. They had been close since grade school. She was sort of his protector with the other children."

"That's sweet," I said.

"Yes, it is. From what I discovered, Beatrice was an extraordinarily kind young woman."

"But why wouldn't the editor want you to look into a connection with Vance?" said Natalie. "It seems like it might explain what had happened, don't you think?"

"It might have. But there is politics in everything. I thought it was interesting that the police weren't following up on any leads that might have led to the chief's son. So I started raising some questions. But the chief asked my editor to stop my investigation, as did the mayor. I was told in no uncertain terms to back off. I complained about it, yes, all the way up to the publisher, not that it did any good. But that editor, he didn't like me going over his head like that. He took me right off the Beatrice Long case, right off the police beat, and sent me to cover a bunch of other stories: tax issues, a lawsuit against the county, a sewage problem at a school. These were issues, he said, better suited to a woman reporter."

"Wow," I said. "That's low. What did you say to that?"

"I said, 'I quit,' is what I said. And I did."

"You were like a superhero," said Natalie, "fighting for truth and justice."

"Nothing like that, more of a Lois Lane. I was just a reporter who believed reporting mattered. I worked the crime beat for the *Philadelphia Inquirer* twenty years after that and loved every day of it. That's why it does my heart good to see the pack of you ignoring the warnings, trying to get to the truth of things, for whatever reason. Any of you working for the school newspaper?"

"Not yet," said Natalie. "Henry swims and Lizzie does

math, but you might have sold me. I wouldn't mind expos-
ing all the dark truths at Willing Middle School West,
scouring the detention hall for the real story."

"There you go. Be sure to listen. People will tell you so
much if you really listen. And remember that emotions are
the key to a good story. I still remember the grief when they
found Beatrice by the creek."

"Without a head," said Natalie.

"Why do you say that?" said Delores, startled. "I didn't
report that."

"We just figured, from reading between the lines," I said.

"Be careful. Try not to assume too much. I wrote exactly
what they told me to write about the condition of the body
and nothing more. But I must say, that's interesting, if true.
Very interesting."

"Why's that?" I asked.

"Because that young Vance, the boy they put into the
hospital? The story was he kept a very special collection.
Apparently when one of his injured critters died, he would
keep the skull, like a picture of an old friend."

"That would explain the squirrel skull you found in
Beatrice's box," said Natalie.

"Before they shut down my investigation," said Delores,
"I found out that the young brother, who's our current
chief, told a friend they were looking for the collection for
some reason. Don't think they ever found it. So a missing head would explain the search. A missing head would
explain so much."

Yes it would, including the shiver that was snaking up
and down my spine.

RUNNING GIRL

I am running, this time not on four legs, but on two. I dash through a wood lit by a full moon, the soft light slipping past leaves and branches. I run between tree trunks, I leap over bushes, I slip on dead leaves. My shoes are covered with mud and my heart is breaking. I am angry and hurt. I feel doubly betrayed, doubly humiliated. I want to see no one and nothing, I want to leave all my crushed hopes behind me. And so I run. Through the woods. Away from my life.

This was the last of my nightmares. I had been wondering when it would come. That shiver in my spine was a clue that it was on its way. The dreams about the squirrel and the snake weren't just the most vivid of visions. They were messages from the other world, preparing me for one message more. Preparing me for this.

For now, here, in the middle of this nightmare, I am Beatrice Long.

My sister has betrayed me. My boyfriend has betrayed me. My life has been ripped to shreds, and now they are laughing at me. What else is there to do but run?

It almost feels good, this mad dash through the woods. To fill my lungs, to pump my arms, to feel the soles of my mother's old saddle shoes slam upon the earth is comforting. Maybe I am faster than I thought I was. Maybe I should give up cheerleading and run track. There are some cute guys on the track team. Everett Mason is on the track team and he has long blond hair that trails after him as he runs around the turns. Wouldn't Anil be jealous of that?

I look behind me to see if anyone is coming. To see if Anil is coming. Is Nilly chasing after me? Is he trying to apologize? I look behind me and I see nothing and I keep running, but I keep looking, too. As if looking will make it happen. As if he will come to me and hug me close and kiss my forehead and tell me it was all a mistake, a terrible mistake. And then Everett Mason with the long blond hair will appear and punch Nilly in the face, and I will shake with laughter.

In front of me I see a rock shaped like a boat, the ones that took Christopher Columbus to America and then later the Pilgrims. Until I saw the rock I was lost—I spied the two of them, my sister and my boyfriend, kissing, and took off blindly. I could have been in any old wood, but the rock tells me where I am, and it is as familiar as the hill on which sits my house. It is the rock where we found the dying squirrel, the rock where we caught the snake, it is our rock.

I slow down and stop, lean against the rock, and try to catch my breath. I look back once more to see if Anil is gaining—I hope he is gaining—but he's not there, he'll never be there. And I realize I am crying.

I am alone, and I am crying. I miss my sister, but I can't go to her. And right then I know where I can go, a place so hidden that nobody will be able to find me. Only Vance and I know about it. I can stay hidden there until Vance comes, and I'll tell him what happened, and he will understand.

I push myself off the rock and march slowly forward. I step between the two narrow trunks of a single tree that shoot away from each other like a great V and continue on through the gloomy woods and up a path that rises above the creek. Even with the full moon it is dark beneath the canopy of leaves, but the path is familiar. I can hear the water gurgle to my left. Beyond this step, to the right, is the anthill. I can just make out the little cage Vance places on top of the hill so the ants can swarm over and clean the skulls.

I keep climbing and then head straight along the high path. Down to the left, the moonlight tickles the water. To the right is pure darkness. And straight ahead, glowing dully now, are the ruins of an old stone house that had collapsed in on itself. Tucked inside the ruins and hidden from the path is a little hut that leans against one of the stone walls. The

*hut's walls are painted green, the roof consists of rusted bits
of mismatched tin. The windows are shuttered, the door is
clasped with a padlock.*

But I know where Vance hides the key.

*Inside it smells furry and wet and familiar and instantly
I feel better. I can hear the animals breathing, scurrying
within their cages, alarmed at my presence. "It's okay,
sweeties," I say out loud into the darkness. With the hint
of light bleeding in from the open door I find the candle
and the matches. Pull, snap. The sweet smell of sulfur as
the match bursts into flame and the hut comes into view. I
light the candle and look around. At the back of the hut, the
shelves are full of Vance's collection of skulls. To my right
are the cages holding the live animals Vance has found. A
baby chipmunk with a bad leg, an injured bird, the snake
we caught, four little field mice he has trapped for the snake.
The field mice climb over one another in the light, as if they
know what awaits them.*

*I step to the mice cage, open the door, and reach inside.
Gently I pinch the fur at the back of the neck of the smallest
and cradle its belly in my other hand. I take the gray little
thing out of the cage and close the door. In my palm I can
feel its heart race. I gently rub its side with my thumb and
nuzzle its back with my cheek, before I lift it toward the
snake's cage.*

*The snake is hungry. The snake is always hungry. It has
a copper-colored head with brown patches over its body.
Still injured, it is curled in its cage, quiet, watching things,
waiting for the moment when it can strike and then eat.
We must either feed it or let it go, but Vance doesn't want to*

let it go. And neither do I. It is my favorite of his animals, it is lovely and wary and dangerous. Just what I want to be. So we keep feeding it. I carefully open the cage door to put in its meal when I hear a sound outside. I turn my head reflexively and call out.

  "Anil?"

THE HELICOPTER PAD

"**I** know where to find Beatrice's head," I said in a low voice in the lunchroom the following Monday. My hair hung over one of my eyes, and I held a sandwich in front of my mouth as I spoke. I was trying to be inconspicuous—trying and failing, based on Natalie's puzzled expression.

"How do you know that all of a sudden?" said Henry.

"I told you I've been having these dreams, but they're more than dreams. They're like messages." I lowered my voice into a whisper. "From Beatrice."

"Wowza," said Natalie. "How cool is that?"

"Not very, if you want to know the truth. It's pretty gross, and way too much drama. But there must have been a connection created when I shoved the alder stake into her heart, because that's when they started."

"And what does she say?" said Henry. "Anything about me?"

"Really?" said Natalie.

"I'm just asking."

"You know she's dead, right?"

"She doesn't say anything about you," I said. "But the dreams have indicated that the thing we're looking for might be in a rickety old hut on a hill above some creek."

"What creek?" said Henry. "Where?"

"Whistler's Creek, I'd bet," said Natalie. "It was the one in the articles."

"That's what I figured, too."

"But which part of the creek?" said Natalie.

I took a sip from my juice and kept the cup raised. "I think I have a way to find out."

"Why are you hiding your mouth?" said Natalie.

"I don't want anyone to read my lips."

"Well, stop," said Natalie. "You look like you're making out with your juice glass."

Natalie and Henry both laughed as I took a sip of juice. And these were my friends.

"So what do we do now?" said Henry.

"We go get it, of course," said Natalie.

"But first we have to find out the starting location of her run into the woods. We could go back and ask Beatrice's sister, but she'd just call the chief on us again, and I really really don't want to end—"

"Shhhh," said Natalie. "It's the Fraydens."

The Frayden twins in their plaid shirts, trays held just below their chins so they wouldn't spill, approached our table like frogs approaching the Sun King, bowing and scraping.

"Mr. Harrison, sir," said Charlie. "Could we possibly join you for our afternoon repast in the empty seats to your right?"

"If it's not too much trouble," said Doug.

"Not right now, guys," said Henry. "We're talking about something a little personal."

"Well, then, of course, we are sorry to disturb you," said Charlie. "We'll just back away."

"Don't leave," I said. "Henry doesn't mean it, do you, Henry."

"I don't?"

"Charlie, Doug, grab a seat."

"Are you sure?" said Charlie.

"Sit down before she changes her mind," said Doug, and just that fast they were sitting at our table.

A moan rose from the rest of the lunchroom. It was one thing for Henry Harrison to lower himself to eat with nothing-special seventh graders like Natalie and me—the lunchroom had sort of gotten used to that by now. But with the Fraydens joining Henry, it was as if some final barrier had snapped, sending the whole social hierarchy of Willing Middle School West into chaos. Revolution!

"So, Charlie, Doug," I said. "How goes debate club?"

"Words, words, words," said Doug.

"He's quoting *Hamlet*," said Charlie. "That was one of Shakespeare's plays, Mr. Harrison, sir, in case you didn't know."

"Thanks for the heads-up," said Henry. "I would have thought it was a kind of sandwich."

"Hamlet and a side of chips," said Doug. The Fraydens showed their chipmunk teeth and laughed their hyena laughs.

"Hey, Charlie," I said. "When you guys had that internship thing at Singh Electronics, did you ever meet the boss?"

"Oh sure," said Doug. "We were tight with Anil. Best buds."

"Really?" said Natalie.

"Well, maybe not the bestest."

"He sort of waved at us once as he walked by the office where they stashed us," said Charlie.

"It wasn't so much a wave as a glance," said Doug.

"He glanced at us," said Charlie.

"And we glanced back," said Doug.

"So you have a glancing acquaintance," said Natalie.

"Yes," said Charlie. "That's it exactly."

"How late does he stay at the office, do you know?" I said.

"He works late, until seven thirty sharp. Like clockwork. And everyone has to stay and pretend to be working until he leaves. Then they all celebrate."

"What about his car?" I said. "Do you know which car is his?"

"You mean the gray Porsche 611 with the spoiler in the back that he parks right next to the helicopter pad behind his building?"

"Yes," I said. "That one."

39

BAD NEWS

The beams of our three flashlights squirmed within the dark mist, painting jittery white ovals on rough bark and the mossy ground as we made our way deeper into the woods.

Henry was to my left and Natalie to my right. We tried to stay close as we hiked around trees and over scrub brush, spraying our beams every which way. The plan was to trace Beatrice's footsteps on the last night she was seen alive. It would seem an impossible task after so long a time, but we had a couple of tour guides: Beatrice Long in my dream and her former boyfriend, Anil Singh.

Earlier in the night we had been sitting cross-legged on the helicopter pad in the deserted but lit parking lot outside his building, playing ghost to kill the time—appropriate, no? A few minutes after seven thirty, while Natalie was stumped on G-R-O-T-E, a man who matched the picture on the Singh Electronics website came walking toward a gray Porsche. He was short, gray-haired, thin, and—uh-oh—accompanied by one of his security guards. We three stood right away. A few days before, the sight of two security guards had sent us running like rabbits, but things had changed.

"Stop right there," said the guard after Natalie, Henry, and I hopped off the helipad and started walking toward Anil Singh. The guard stepped in front of Anil Singh with one hand raised and the other reaching into his jacket. Gun? Taser? Cookie? I wasn't counting on the cookie. "Don't come any closer," he said.

"It's okay, Lawrence," said Anil Singh in a sharp, clipped voice that was all business. "They're not why I asked you to walk me to the car. You can go."

"Are you sure, Mr. Singh?"

"Yes, I'm sure. Thank you, Lawrence."

Anil Singh waited as the security man glared at us for a bit before turning and heading back to the building. When the guard was out of earshot, Mr. Singh said, "You shouldn't be here."

"We just have a few questions," said Natalie.

"I know why you're here," he said. "The chief told me about your fake history paper. Which one of you is Stephen Scali's daughter?"

"That's me," I said.

"Your father represents us in patent litigations. He's a terrific lawyer. It's Elizabeth, right?"

"That's right."

"And what you want is for me to tell you all about Beatrice. Is that right, Elizabeth?"

"Yes," I said. "If you can."

"Well, to tell you the truth, Elizabeth, I don't think I can. The chief was very clear in instructing me not to talk to you three."

"We heard that the last time you saw Beatrice you were kissing her sister," said Natalie, "which is, I have to say, way cold, and a little hot at the same time. Is that true?"

"You're Natalie, I suppose. Well, Natalie, things are always more complicated than they seem."

"But is it true?" said Henry.

"And you're Henry, the swimmer, right?"

"Yeah, that's me," said Henry.

Anil Singh, who collected first names like he was selling lemon pops door-to-door, just shook his head. "Elizabeth, Natalie, Henry, I think it's time for you three to go home and forget all about Beatrice."

"Like you have?" I said.

"Go home," he said, "before I call the chief."

"She forgives you," said Henry. "She wants you to know that."

He tilted his head and stared, as if Henry had just stolen his lunch.

"She called you Nilly," I said.

He startled as if a squirrel had just run over his shoe.

"And she forgives you," said Henry.

"How do you guys know that?"

"We just do," Henry said. "We're only here, the three of us, because we're trying to help her. And she knows you want to help her, too."

Anil turned away from us and looked up to the sky, bright with the moon. He stayed there, looking up, for a long while, as if searching for something in the moon's face. When he turned around again, he was wiping at his eyes.

"So, here's all you need to know about me and Beatrice," he said, choking back what looked like a hiccup but which I realized was a sob. "She was my first love and I messed it up. I used to think I could fix anything. That's why I became an engineer. But I messed it up with Beatrice, and she was killed before I had a chance to fix things with her. I've never really recovered. She still haunts me."

"She's good at that," said Henry. "So, it's true about you and Beatrice's sister?"

"Yes," he said, simply, "it's true. I was young and stupid."

"You were in high school," said Natalie. "What else could you expect?"

"Well, maybe I could have expected more from myself," he said. "I often wonder how things would have gone if I hadn't been such a jerk that night. But Robbie's parents were gone, the music was loud, and then Roberta took my hand and bit my ear. What was I going to do?"

"Say 'yuck'?" said Henry.

Even with his wet eyes Mr. Singh smiled. "Well, maybe you'll be smarter than I was, Henry. I sure hope so."

"Where was the party?" I said.

"The party?" said Mr. Singh.

"The Halloween party where you last saw Beatrice."

"Robbie's house," he said. "Robbie Heegner? He lived down by the woods, the last house on the left on Dartmouth before it dead-ends. I think it burned down or something, but the foundation is still there."

"When Beatrice saw you and ran, did you chase her?"

"I tried. It wasn't so easy to get free of her sister. That Roberta had the grip of a weight lifter."

"I don't doubt it," said Henry.

"Which way did Beatrice go?" I said.

"Directly away from the back of the house, farther into the woods. I tried to follow, but I never found her."

"You didn't see her in the hut?"

"What hut? I don't know of any hut."

"Just something we read in the newspaper articles."

"I don't remember reading anything about a hut. All I know is that she ran away and I never saw her again. I still think about her every day." And then he smiled at Henry. "It's nice to imagine that she still thinks of me. But it's late, and you kids ought to get home now. It's not safe."

"What's not safe?" said Natalie.

"I didn't have the guard walk me to the car because I was afraid you three would show up."

"Then why?" I asked.

"Because of Vance, Vance Johansson," he said, suddenly looking around in a way that creeped me out, as if he was fearfully searching for a ghost of his own. "Didn't you hear the news?"

We hadn't then, but now we had, and that was why we were tracing Beatrice's path in the darkness, waving our flashlights across the landscape as we made our way ever deeper into the woods.

He had escaped. Vance Johansson had escaped from the maximum-security hospital four weeks before. That was why Anil Singh asked a security man to walk him to the car, and that was why the chief was trying to stop our investigation. Vance Johansson was on the loose. He had been the main suspect in Beatrice's murder. He was still considered extremely dangerous. There was no telling what he would do to anyone who crossed his path or what the police would do if they found him.

And so of course we were deep in the woods, waving our flashlights in the night, searching for Vance Johansson's hut of skulls.

It was my decision to do it right away. My father was somewhere on the other side waiting for me to do something, and my grandfather had told me the Court of Uncommon Pleas was due back in the city within a few days and then might be gone for months. We couldn't wait until the police found Vance. I figured going at night would be safer than during the day. If Vance Johansson was still around, he wouldn't be out there in the dark. And if he was out there in the dark, we would see his light in time to run.

So off we went in search of Beatrice's head.

It was actually a nice moment, the quiet of the search in the cool, misty night, with my best friend, Natalie, and our new friend, Henry Harrison. Our flashlight beams crossed like swords in the haze. I might have appreciated it more if I hadn't been scared out of my gourd by the image of the boy in my dream wandering these woods, and of what horrors we might discover in that hut. But still, being part of a team reminded me of when I was young and my mother—

"I think I found something," said Natalie.

My attention snapped back to our search. I aimed the beam of my flashlight to where Natalie's beam was pointing. And that was when I saw it, a landmark I had never laid eyes on but was still as familiar to me as the lines on my palm: a great piece of gray rock shaped like the *Mayflower*.

"That's it," I said.

When we reached it, I put my hand on its side. This was where the squirrel had hidden after being chased by the dog. This was where the snake had set up its burrow before being snared in the trap. This was where Beatrice had rested after running from the party. All three dreams had led me here, and were now telling me in which direction to go. I slipped my beam back and forth until I found the old tree with two thick and mottled trunks diverging like a V. I aimed my light right into the gap.

"She went thataway," I said.

Walking now in a row, we moved forward as straight as we could, passing through the diverging trunks and continuing on, until we came to the creek and then turned to the right.

A bit farther along, our waving beams caught the base of a hill.

We moved away from the creek and climbed, keeping our lights focused now on the ground ahead of us, trying not to light up any of the tree trunks like flares. At the point where I thought the anthill might have been I flashed my beam, but saw nothing except a mound of leaves. When we reached the crest of the hill we turned off our flashlights. The gaps between the treetops were filled with stars and moonlight, but all around us was a darkness without the barest glimmer of artificial light.

"There's no one here," I said, flicking my light back on. "The hut should be just ahead. We have to look for the ruins of a stone house."

And then, just ahead, there they were.

You know Pop Rocks, the candy that fizzes on your tongue? When I caught sight of those ruins, the way my blood started bubbling, it felt like someone had poured a pack of Pop Rocks right into a vein.

Blue Razz.

THE HUT

As the three of us stood inside the remains of a long-gone farmhouse, the bright circles of our lights intersected on a small hut leaning against one of the house's rough stone walls.

The hut, well hidden within the ruins, was a misshapen gray thing with nooks and crannies and a tilted roof. It looked like it hadn't been touched in years, in decades. Whatever paint had been applied to the wood had worn away, and the tin roofing was so thick with gunk that it was hard to distinguish from the night sky. A spindly tree grew out of one of the old farmhouse's stone walls, pointing to the sky like a finger of warning.

"Well, that's certainly creepy enough," said Natalie.

"You think it's there?" said Henry.

"If my dreams are indeed messages," I said, "then it's there."

"How are we getting in?"

"I brought a screwdriver," I said.

"That should do it," said Henry. "A screwdriver can open anything. I once opened a can of corned beef hash with a screwdriver. My mom fried it right up. Pretty good."

I looked at Henry. In the light reflected off the hut he appeared oh so eager to get inside. I felt connected to the squirrel and the snake and to Beatrice. All three might have died here. This hut was a place of sorrow and loss, and it deserved to be explored with respect.

"I'll go in," I said. "By myself. You guys should stay as lookouts in case someone comes. Natalie, go around to the other side. Henry, you stay here. Turn off your lights and keep your eyes open for anyone showing up. I don't want to be surprised while I'm inside."

"Are you sure?" said Henry.

"This is the safest way."

"How should we warn you?" said Natalie. "Birdcalls? I can do a duck."

"Please don't," I said.

"How about we just knock?" said Henry.

"Perfect," I said. "I'm so jittery, it won't take much. Toss a pebble and I'll be running like a rabbit."

"Are you sure you'll be okay?" said Natalie.

"No, but if something's wrong I'll let you know. Did you bring what I asked you to bring?"

She reached into her jacket, pulled out the whistle that

had been given to her by Beatrice's mother, and handed it over. I hung the chain around my neck.

"If I need you, I'll blow the whistle. Otherwise, I'll just grab the head and we'll go home."

"Let's hope that's the last time you ever say that sentence," said Natalie before walking to the other side of the ruined farmhouse. When she got there, she turned off her light. Henry did the same.

I looked around before stepping forward, around one pile of stone and then another, making my way, however hesitantly, to the hut.

The door had the remains of chipped green paint, and there was a rusted padlock on the clasp that was still locked. I would have used the screwdriver to wedge the clasp off the door, but time had done the work for me. Most of the screws were already free of the wood and the hardware dangled.

I grabbed the little iron handle and slowly opened the door. The hinges moaned.

Inside was so inky black that the beam of my light was swallowed whole. The smell through the open door hit me like a fist, a stale, moldy odor cut with a scent that reminded me of the lion house at the zoo.

I put a hand over my nose, ducked down to get through the low doorway, and stepped forward into the darkness.

When my light finally took hold, the space I saw was smaller than in my dream, and far messier. Everything was scattered, filthy, covered with mud and bits of dead leaves that had blown in through gaps in the boards. The wall of skulls had collapsed into a pile mixed with the filth on the floor. The cages on the right were silent. I flashed my beam into them one by one and saw a few tiny bones and bits of fur, but nothing else.

I walked to the pile of skulls, stooped down, and went through them slowly. Most of the skulls were tiny, coming from small animals and birds. There were a couple of long, narrow skulls, most likely of deer, and something canine that looked positively terrifying, like a dinosaur with a fierce underbite. But as I went through them, one by one, I found nothing even vaguely human.

I stood and waved my beam around the mess on the floor of the hut. The table was overturned to the left of the door, the chair on its side. There was a canvas bag, a slingshot, an old BB gun. Then something within a mess of clothes in the corner drew my attention.

I aimed my flashlight, walked over, stooped down. Between two old T-shirts rose twin leather handles. I shoved the shirts away and saw a leather bag attached to the handles, a filthy thing that had originally been blue with white highlights. It looked like a bag made for a bowling ball.

A bowling ball. Get it?

I grabbed the handles and lifted it free. There was something inside all right. I put the bag in front of me, pulled open the zipper on top, aimed my flashlight inside. When I saw the thing bound like a mummy, I swallowed a spurt of vomit.

I didn't have to look twice to recognize Beatrice Long's preserved head. She had rolled it at me, after all.

I was filled with sadness and terror, the two emotions

mixing inside me so that all I wanted to do was cry and run, run and weep. I closed the zipper, grabbed the bag, and spun around to the door. As I turned, and my light swirled, I caught just a glimpse of something peculiar in the far corner of the hut.

I wanted to ignore it but I couldn't. Something pulled me back. A lawyer's responsibility? Does that make sense? I don't know anymore. But slowly I turned, aiming the flashlight's beam into the corner.

It was hanging from the wall, as if from a hook. I took a step forward and realized the hanging thing was vaguely human, like a stuffed set of clothes, a scarecrow maybe, or a dummy. Then my light hit the face: pale, gray-whiskered, with hair wild and white, scarred cheeks, and a flat nose. The eyes were closed. The hanging figure was as dead as the skulls on the floor. As dead as the bones in the cages. As dead as wax. Instinctively I took another step forward.

The eyes opened.

41

THUNDERER

I didn't scream and I didn't throw the head—though if ever there was a head made for throwing, it was Beatrice Long's.

Instead, keeping my light focused on the face, I backed away, slowly, stepping over the piled mess on the floor. All the while the open eyes tracked my movements.

Then, with its lips moving barely at all, the face spoke. The voice was soft, a slurp of wet sounds.

"She said you would come."

I stared in horror for the briefest moment, then dashed for the door.

I almost made it.

He moved impossibly fast, catching my arm and yanking me back. The flashlight fell clattering to the ground. Its beam, now caught on the floor, cast shadows across the hut. I grunted as I swung the bowling ball bag, hitting him hard on his side. The thwack traveled painfully up my arm, but his grip stayed tight.

"I won't hurt you," he said in his soft, wet voice. He was thick and misshapen. His face was the face of the boy in my dreams, only older, paler. Vance Johansson. Of course he was. "I promise," he said.

I hit him again with Beatrice's head and he lost his balance, letting go of my arm for a moment as he fought to remain standing. We had spun around so he was now between me and the door. With my arm suddenly free I grabbed the whistle, bit down hard on the metal, and blew the thing with every ounce of breath I had left in me.

A bright, musical scream sounded out.

The whistle split the night quiet like an ax through ice. We were both frozen by the sound when a fierce thing leaped through the hut door and sent the man sprawling. It took me a moment to realize it was Henry, responding to my call, diving at my attacker.

As Vance fell to the floor, Henry flipped beyond him into the overturned table.

Vance struggled to his feet, blood now staining his gray whiskers. He took a step toward me. I was waiting for Henry to stand up and save me, but he stayed on the floor, shaking his head as he tried and failed to rise. I darted toward the door, but Vance cut off my exit. I put the whistle back in my teeth, took the screwdriver from my pocket and gripped the bowling ball bag tight. I was ready to defend myself and Henry as best I could.

Then I felt the breeze.

It flitted through the space like a bat, darting here and there. Through the foul stink of that hut a new scent arose. It was sweet and bright, flowery and full of hope.

A grayish light shimmered in the middle of the hut before the ghost of Beatrice Long began to appear. First her eyes, then her face, then the whole of her. She let out a moan. The attacker, illuminated by her ghostly light, fell to his knees and reached out to her, as if to a memory.

"I waited like you told me," he said. "And she came."

Henry, too, still on the ground, became lit by Beatrice's supernatural light. She raised a hand and, with his face filled with all kinds of wonder, Henry stood. Beatrice looked at Henry and me, and her smile was angelic.

Then she took off her head with one hand and, instead of rolling it, she held it right out in front of me. The glowing head said, *"Save me, save him. Save me, save him."*

With her free hand she pointed at the little birthmark below her eye. I thought it had been something pretty and distinctive, that dark dot, but I saw now it wasn't just one mark, but two, the other hidden in the shadowy edge of her nose.

Then the most magical, horrifying, and beautiful thing happened. She reached a hand through my chest and into my heart, just as I had thrust the alder stake into hers. It felt warm and shaky and full of light, that hand. I don't know how else to describe it. Maybe this: It felt like friendship. And as something passed between us, I finally understood.

"Save me, save him," she said for a final time, and this time I knew exactly who she meant.

She disappeared into an explosion of sparks just as I

heard the voices outside. Loud official voices, calling our names. "Elizabeth?" "Henry?" Even Natalie was calling out my name. And my mother, too. It was like a posse on horseback had come to save me.

But by then I knew it wasn't me who needed saving.

42

A MESSAGE
FROM THE DEAD

They reburied Beatrice Long, this time with her head, in a small ceremony at her gravesite at the Mount Lebanon Cemetery. It should have been raining, I thought. The burial scenes in my imagination happen in the rain, water dripping down black umbrellas like all the tears of the world—but it was bright and sunny as we formed a circle around the open grave.

Henry stood to one side of me with his hands clutched together, leaking some sort of misery. He had jumped without hesitation into the hut to save me, living up to the name of his war-hero great-grandfather. But he seemed empty, as if he had lost something inside the hut. Maybe it was an aftereffect of the knock he had taken to the head, but I think he was still overwhelmed by his feelings for a dead girl, and I feared he might be for a long time.

On the other side of me stood Natalie, with a guitar and a smile. It was Natalie who had heard the police tromping through the woods with my mother and Anil Singh and rushed to lead them to the hut. "I sure wasn't going to jump into the fight like Henry," she said afterward. "I just got my nails done." I always thought Natalie was too concerned with stuff, if you know what I mean: the right shoes, the right sweater. But what I found out in our Beatrice Long adventure was that I would trust her with my life any-where, anytime, because, in bringing her with me to that hut, I already had, and she hadn't let me down.

Also in the circle were Beatrice's sister, Roberta, and Beatrice's mother, who had been so grateful to us for mak-ing her daughter whole. "You don't know what it means to me," she said, and she was right. I couldn't imagine what it meant to bury a daughter—it was tough enough burying my dead hamster a few years back. It was Mrs. Long who asked Natalie to bring her guitar. "How nice would it be to play something that Beatrice might have known," said Mrs. Long.

"I have just the song," said Natalie.

Along with Beatrice's family there was Delores Baird, standing with an aide as she watched the final chapter of the story she reported, and Anil Singh, his eyes wet, still mourning the loss of his first love. I wanted to slap him on the back of his head and tell him to get over it. It was Anil Singh, actually, who ended up bringing the police and my mother to the scene.

After our meeting, Mr. Singh grew concerned over what we crazy kids might end up doing and placed a call to his patent lawyer, Stephen, who was working late. Stephen relayed the story to my mother, who, finding me not at home, immediately got on the phone with Chief Johansson. Together with a squad of police and Mr. Singh to lead them, they went to the burned-down house, where the infamous Halloween party had been, and followed our path until they heard the whistle. As they ran toward the sound they met up with Natalie, who took them to the hut.

That was where they were, the police with guns drawn, my mother with her hands over her heart, all of them calling out our names when the three of us walked out of the ruins of that old farmhouse. Henry was in the lead, waving his hands, telling everybody everything was okay and not to do anything crazy. I followed behind Henry, one hand holding the bag with Beatrice's head, the other gently holding on to Vance Johansson's arm. Together, Vance and I walked right up to the chief.

"Your brother didn't kill Beatrice," I said. "It was a snake. It bit Beatrice right below the eye. And the proof might just be in this bowling ball bag."

I handed Vance over to his brother, along with the bag, and then I rushed over to give my mother a hug.

Chief Johansson was also at the cemetery. He stood with my mother and Stephen and my little brother, Peter. Even Charlie and Doug Frayden showed up, since they were a part of what had happened, too. We were all there to pay our respects to a girl from our township who had died before her time. And along with all of us was Vance Johansson, wearing an ill-fitting suit, his rough cheeks clean-shaven for the occasion. The chief had intended for his brother to stand by his side, but Mrs. Long insisted that he stand with her. They held hands during the priest's eulogy, linked together in irretrievable loss.

Finally, after the priest was finished, Mrs. Long, still holding Vance Johansson's hand, spoke:

"I want to thank you all, especially the children, for showing up today. This isn't a sad occasion. In fact, I can't remember when I've been so happy. Roberta and I, and Anil too, and Vance, of course, all of us have been mourning my child ever since they found her body that terrible day so long ago. But since then I've also been strengthened by remembering her love and spirit, the way she cared for every living thing, especially the weakest and most in need. That's what today is about, the remembering. And that you, Elizabeth, and Natalie, and Henry, and your family and friends are remembering her, too, even if just for a day, gives me so much joy. I hope that her being whole, finally, will put her spirit at rest. Be at peace, my Beatrice."

And after Mrs. Long said that, one by one we said it ourselves.

"Be at peace, Beatrice."

"Be at peace, Beatrice."

I don't know if it was as effective as a chant in Latin that Barnabas could have recited, but it seemed to work, because I smelled something fragrant and just above the site a gray light shimmered. Henry looked at me, and Natalie did, too, with wide eyes, and Vance seemed to grow upset, stamping around like something was coming.

"Be at peace, Beatrice."

"Be at peace, Beatrice."

When it was her turn, Natalie handed me the guitar and stepped forward and dropped the silver whistle she had taken from Beatrice's box into the grave. "Be at peace, Beatrice," she said, and then came back into the circle. I handed her the guitar and as she hung the strap over her shoulder she said, "This song was being played on the radio the year Beatrice died." Natalie started strumming, mostly minor chords that seemed to match the mood, and then began to sing.

It was a song about summer love and saying good-bye. I had never heard it before, but the older people had, and you could see them nodding, even my mother. Mrs. Long smiled. Mr. Singh started blubbering. I looked at Henry, who seemed dazed as the glow over the grave became brighter.

I'll see you in the sunlight
I'll hear your voice everywhere.
I'll run to tenderly hold you,
But darling, you won't be there.

As Natalie sang the song's sad chorus, out of the shimmering light Beatrice appeared.

She smiled and spun around slowly, as if taking in the beauty of the day and the people in the circle. Natalie smiled when she saw her and kept strumming and singing. Henry waved. My mother seemed to notice nothing, as did Stephen, but a curious expression flitted across my brother's face. Petey looked at me and I could tell, right there, that he had seen Beatrice, too. I put a finger over my mouth and he nodded.

Beatrice swooped around the circle until she stopped before Mrs. Long. She bowed her head and touched her forehead to her mother's and there was a moment when Mrs. Long seemed to shudder. Then Beatrice hugged her sister and Roberta started bawling as if being touched with forgiveness. Then Beatrice put her hand on Anil Singh's cheek and he sobbed again. None of them saw the ghost, but they all grew brighter, as if they had started glowing themselves.

When Beatrice reached for Vance Johansson's free hand, he gave it to her and she brought it up to her lips. As she kissed his hand and pressed it to her cheek, Vance gave the first smile I had seen from him and he said out loud, "Good-bye, Beatrice."

The story that Chief Johansson eventually told was a painful tale of a father suspecting that his son might have killed the one child who had befriended him. While he never found enough evidence to convict the boy in a court of law, he had Vance placed in the state mental hospital to protect his community. Fifty years later, when Vance wandered away from the hospital, his older brother, now chief of police, and aware of his father's concerns, authorized his officers to find and capture his brother, with violence if necessary.

Word must have reached Beatrice on the other side. It wasn't a coincidence that Vance had escaped four weeks before the night at the hut, which was the same time Beatrice started haunting Henry.

The guts of this story lie somewhere in the relationship between a sweet girl and a troubled boy and a devotion that lasted way past death. Don't get me started, because I still cry when I think about it.

When Beatrice let go of Vance's hand she nodded at Natalie, who kept singing, and then swooped over to Henry. Just as Natalie sang the last line of the song, about sealing a pledge with a kiss, Beatrice did just that with Henry. He staggered back and fainted dead away. My mother and stepfather and Chief Johansson rushed over to him as the ghost of Beatrice Long came to me.

She spread her arms and hesitated a moment, staring into my face, before she swooped right through me. It felt as if everything inside me, my stomach, my kidneys, my spirit were rising. It felt as if I were swooping, too, as if I were flying through time and space. Something filled my heart, and I realized it was a gratitude that wasn't my own. Beatrice was thanking me, and her gratitude vibrated in my soul. I had freed her and saved Vance, and she was so grateful. It was the sweetest thing I have ever felt in my life. I spun around and saw the ghost of Beatrice Long floating away from us all. She turned her head, smiled, and then she disappeared, for good.

It was only later that night, in a moment just before I fell asleep, that I bolted upright in bed and realized Beatrice had given me more than just her gratitude.

43

THE GREAT WRIT

"Oyez, oyez, oyez," called out the great ram's head affixed atop the five-pointed star on the wall of the Court of Uncommon Pleas. As the ram bellowed, the scent of licorice wafted over the benches.

When the ram finished his call, he stared at me in the back of the courtroom and stuck out his tongue. But I wouldn't be chased away by a black-stained tongue, not today, not when I was in court to save my father. The empty cage hanging from the ceiling was a symbol of my father's imprisonment. On one side of me stood Barnabas and my grandfather. On the other side stood my mother.

Yeah, my mother.

"What are you doing here?" I had said to her when I saw her waiting for us inside the courtroom. "How did you even get through the door?"

"Oh, Ivanov's a sweetheart," she said, looking down as she fussed with a large bag. "I knitted him a sweater once. It didn't take much yarn."

"You shouldn't have come," I said.

Her head rose quickly. "Why not? I went to your soccer games, even though you were more interested in the clouds than the ball. I went to all your band concerts, thank heaven for earplugs. This is what I do, Elizabeth, I show up, which is more than you can say about your father. Besides, your grandfather called and told me you were trying to bring your father back from the other side. I felt I owed it to both of you to be here."

"But you hate my father."

"Oh, Elizabeth, how little you know about love. You should get some experience sometime, but maybe wait until high school. So, are you excited? Your first trial."

"My second. I lost my first."

"Oh yes, I forget. But you didn't invite me to that one, did you?"

"Or to this one, either," I said.

"Nevertheless."

I had purposely not asked Natalie or Henry to accompany me to this session of the Court of Uncommon Pleas. If I were to lose again, I preferred to do it without seeing the pity on my friends' faces. It felt like my mother had stepped over a boundary by barging in like this. I should have been angry at her for just showing up, but I wasn't. She was my mom. Kind of pathetic, I know, but there it is.

"I don't really know what I'm doing," I said.

"You know more than you think you know. Anyone who

can find a dead girl's head after fifty years can handle a little court thingumajig. After all, you are part Webster. Here, I brought this for you." Out of the bag she pulled a black robe and held it up to my neck to judge its length. Two wide purple stripes fell down from each shoulder, a purple that was the same shade as the walls in my room. "It was your father's."

"Mom?"

"I fixed the zipper, took it in, shortened the overall length, and sewed on the stripes. It needed some color, don't you think?"

"Mom," I said as I took hold of the robe and lifted it to my shoulders to judge the length. It was perfect, as I knew it would be.

"My sweet little barrister," she said. "There was something your father once told me about being a trial lawyer. He said that you don't start with the questions and move forward, instead you start with the answers and work backward."

"It sounds a little like cheating."

"Or like being a teacher," she said. "You have that in you, too, you know. Now, are you ready to give them heck?"

"Heck?"

"Shhh," said my mother as the ram blasted out his trumpetlike bellow. "It's beginning."

We stood when we were told to stand, and we waited quietly as the ram jabbered on about the court, and then we watched the whole cheap Vegas smoke-and-dance show bring the judge, red-eyed and red-faced, into the courtroom.

"Be seated," spat out the judge between coughs.

We sat. My mother patted my knee. At least she didn't pinch my cheek.

The right honorable Lord Judge George Jeffries, First Baron Jeffries of Wem, shook his long wig, twitched his long nose, and stared out at us with those red marble eyes. "Be brief in your pleadings or there will be consequences, don't you doubt it," croaked the judge. "We have much to accomplish and the fire pits are hungry, so let us not delay. Any emergency motions? First call, last call, come forward and be heard, or forever hold your tongues. As there are apparently no emergency motions, then the clerk—"

"Not so fast, you scurrilous British interloper," said my grandfather, in the aisle now, slapping his cane on the floor as he stepped forward at his fastest speed, which was slow as a snail, a bundle of scrolls held in a raised hand. "We have an emergency motion to be heard forthwith."

"If my eyes don't deceive me," said the judge, "I see a mangy gray rodent named Webster scurrying about my courtroom. Bailiff, order this rodent to be ejected with all due haste and appropriate violence."

The ram was about to speak, but my grandfather cut him off. "Eject me if you will, but not before you hear our motion."

"And what do you have for us today, Ebenezer," said the judge, "an emergency motion for clean undergarments? Now that would be a notable improvement." The judge laughed and the ram laughed and the flying babies overhead laughed with them and there was great hilarity until my grandfather hushed it all with two words of Latin.

"Habeas corpus," he shouted, and, bam, just as if he had unleashed a bolt of lightning, the courtroom silenced.

"Ahh," said the ram into the hush, its booming voice filled with awe. "The great writ."

"Why does everyone say that?" I whispered to Barnabas.

"Because it is the cornerstone of freedom," said Barnabas.

"I should have known."

The judge glared at the ram for a moment before turning back to my grandfather. "Habeas corpus, you say? And whom, may I ask, are you seeking be brought before this court?"

"My son," said my grandfather. "Eli Webster."

"And who do you claim is detaining him illegally?"

"The fallen angel Abezethibou," said my grandfather. "More popularly known as Redwing."

There was a murmur in the court at the name and a familiar lawyer in his white wig rose from the line of lawyers sitting on the front bench of the courtroom.

"As attorney for the fallen angel in question," said Josiah Goodheart, "I object, I say I must object, to this foul accusation." He turned around for a moment to take in the spectators with his arrogant smile. "Typical slander from a Webster. But as you know, my lord, no motion can be heard without appropriate counsel, and as you yourself have barred the very elder Mr. Webster from appearing before this court, the petition must be dismissed."

"Mr. Goodheart has a valid point," said the judge.

"We have counsel," said my grandfather, "admitted to this court just a short time ago. Elizabeth Webster."

"The sprite?" shouted the judge. "The girl who made a mash of things last time she appeared here? You are reaching low, Ebenezer."

"I am reaching higher than you know, you prideful rascal. Elizabeth Webster, duly admitted through her blood as a member of the bar before this great court, will represent my son, who happens to be her father."

"Elizabeth Webster," shouted the judge. "Are you here, in the courtroom?"

With shaking legs I stood.

The judge's red eyes scanned the courtroom until he saw me and then his lips twitched as if a piece of rotting meat were stuck between his teeth. "Are you ready to handle this matter?"

"I suppose," I said more softly than I intended.

"Speak up, girl," he barked. "I'll have no mealymouthed barristers here."

I stood up straight and shouted, "Yes, sir."

The judged winced and swiveled a finger in his ear.

"And this time have you a robe?" said the judge. "I'll not have an attorney stand before me without the proper cloak."

I held up the robe that my mother had given me.

"Well, put it on, girl. Put it on."

And so I did, slipping my arms into the sleeves and letting my mother zipper the front closed. The robe felt both light and heavy at the same time, like a suit of armor made of smoke.

"I hereby declare," said the judge, "that the matter of *Webster v. Abezethibou*, an emergency petition for a writ of habeas corpus, shall be dealt with forthwith. Miss Webster, come forward and be heard. We have much to do this evening, but I expect it won't take long for Mr. Goodheart to best you once again."

Before I stepped into the aisle, my mother squeezed my hand. "Be great," she said. I wanted to roll my eyes but I was too frightened to pull it off. Instead I smiled meekly.

In the aisle, I stood frozen for a moment. Barnabas, also standing, gently put his hand on my shoulder and pushed me forward. Together we walked to the front of the courtroom. My grandfather gave me the bundle of scrolls. Barnabas took one and handed it to the tall green clerk, who passed it to the judge, who in turn gave it a quick look.

"Fine, fine, the paperwork seems to be in order," said the judge. "Now counsel will announce themselves for the record."

"Josiah Goodheart for the defendant, the great fallen angel Abezethibou, protector of his granted domain and the unfortunate souls of those sinners within it."

"And you, young lady," said the judge.

Barnabas whispered in my ear and I said out loud what he told me to say. "Elizabeth Webster, representing Eli Webster."

"And for what relief are you asking, Miss Webster?" said the judge.

Barnabas whispered again. "We ask that Eli Webster," I said, "who is being illegally detained on the other side, be brought to this court and the validity of his detention under law be proven by the defendant or he be freed."

"There is no evidence, no evidence at all, that the younger

Mr. Webster is being detained on the other side," boomed Josiah Goodheart. "For all we know, he could be on a jaunt to the Caribbean. This court has ruled eons ago that due to the great breadth of the other world, in order to bring a habeas action the exact location of the petitioner must be declared. Otherwise the search for the moving party could tie up the court and its minions for years, nay for centuries."

"What Mr. Goodheart says is quite true, Miss Webster. If we are to bring your father into this court for your motion, we must know his exact location. What say you? Where be your father now? Tell us or be forever silent."

Josiah Goodheart stared at me with a gleam of victory in his smile. I turned to look at my grandfather, who urged me on with a little rise of his cane.

This time Barnabas didn't whisper in my ear, this time I was on my own. But in the moment when Beatrice Long, at her second funeral, had passed through me, along with her sense of gratitude she had also left a location imprinted in the recesses of my brain. *Save me, save him,* Beatrice had said three times, and true to her word she had given me the chance to save Vance, and then to save Henry from his haunting, and now to save my father.

"Petitioner is being held in the domain of Abezethibou, Your Honor," I said. "Level Eight, Island of Lost Souls, Village of Flatterers and Sorcerers, House of Faltenbrunner, Basement number four."

"A fabrication," shouted Josiah Goodheart. "A bluff to waste this court's time."

"We shall see, Mr. Goodheart, we shall see. The proof, as they say, will be in the Yorkshire pudding. Bailiff, search the location detailed by Miss Webster and bring back her father if he be there."

"Lower the prison coop," bellowed the ram.

As soon as these words were spoken, squeaks and creaks filled the courtroom and the cage, suspended by a single thick chain, was slowly lowered until it disappeared through the hole in the floor.

And then silence, nothing but silence. The judge peered at me with those hard red eyes.

"What if he's not there?" I said softly to Barnabas.

"We must trust in Beatrice," said Barnabas. "You protected her friend and gave her the gift of peace. She would never betray that."

"But she might have been mistaken," I said. "Or Redwing might have moved him."

"We can only wait with patient and hopeful hearts, Mistress Elizabeth. That is our fate in this world, to wait."

"Silence," said the judge with a bang of his gavel.

And having no choice, we waited in silence. But we didn't have to wait for long.

A great shaft of light flashed out of the hole and then slowly, squeak by creak, the chain was raised and the cage along with it.

At first the cage seemed as empty coming up as it did going down, but then as it was finally raised out of the floor we saw a figure slumped forlornly, its arms resting on its knees and its head resting on its arms. As the cage continued to rise, the slumped figure lifted its head, and there were gasps in the courtroom, from my grandfather and Barnabas, from my mother, and from me, too.

Inside the cage sat my father, looking through his round glasses with haunted eyes. The bottom half of his face was covered by an iron muzzle held in place by leather straps across his forehead and below his ears. When the cage came to a halt, my father weakly rose to his feet, stooped so as not to hit his head on the cage's low ceiling, and peered out from behind the iron bars.

When he saw me, his eyes behind the glasses crinkled with what might have been a smile, and he gave a hesitant, awkward little wave that broke my heart.

Have you ever thought that your life had been leading up to one single moment? Maybe when you performed a solo for your a cappella group, or you lofted a foul shot with the game on the line, or you finally leaned in to kiss the person you'd been crushing on for the last two years. That's what I felt just then, when my dad gave me that pathetic little wave—like my whole life had been leading me to this one moment, when my father stood in a cage with half his face bound by iron and it was up to me to save him.

And who was I kidding to think that I could get it done?

Barnabas leaned forward and whispered in my ear. I turned and looked at him, no doubt with horror on my face, but he simply nodded.

I looked at my father in his cage and then at the judge, who was staring at me with his red eyes, as if waiting for me to pull a rabbit out of a hat.

"Your Honor," I said, with the most confident voice I could manage, which was actually as squeaky as my clarinet, "petitioner calls to the stand the fallen angel Abezethibou, better known as Redwing."

44

THE LITTLE MAN

Josiah Goodheart spread his arms wide and bellowed his objection as shouts and murmurs rose from the crowd behind us.

"Why, this is raw insolence," shouted Goodheart in his shocked, shocked tone. "This is foul impertinence. This is high impudence. How dare opposing counsel burden such an eminence as Abezethibou with her mewing little pleadings? I say, I say nay, nay to this unqualified usurpation of—"

The judge banged his gavel and quieted the crowd and banged it twice more to quiet Josiah Goodheart and then looked at me out of those hard red eyes. "Elizabeth Webster," said the judge, "you have been charged with raw insolence, and foul impertinence, and high impudence. How do you plead?"

"I'd sort of like to deny it," I said, my voice breaking with the uncertainty of a question. "To be truthful, Judge, I'm not even sure what those words mean. But I'll admit to being accused of all three in the last few days, so, yeah, I guess that's me, all right."

Judge Jeffries stared at me for a long moment and then growled out, "Excellent."

"Sir?"

"There isn't a lawyer worth his salt without all three. Ebenezer, you might have found one here, though we will soon see for sure. Mr. Goodheart?"

"Yes, my lord."

"Your objection is denied. The prisoner was found in the domain of your client, which means the petitioner can call the demon to explain why the prisoner should still be held in a Level Eight dungeon within that domain."

"I take exception," said Goodheart.

"And I take exception to your ascot. But we have wasted enough time on this. Either the demon Abezethibou appears in this courtroom within a minute's time, or I will order the petitioner released, forthwith. Bailiff, call the witness."

The great ram lifted his chin and called out in his loud, neighing voice, "The fallen angel Abezethibou is hereby called to the witness stand."

The ram's words resonated with an echo, as if the order was being announced not just in the courtroom but simultaneously in all the corners of a far-off land. Even before the echo quieted, two spectators dashed out of the courtroom.

The seconds audibly ticked—one, two—as if some great clock was keeping time—seven, eight. Or was that just the beating of my heart—eleven, twelve. With each second tocked, my father was getting closer to freedom. The judge's fingers tapped impatiently on the desk, the ram chewed, Josiah Goodheart's smile grew tighter as the seconds continued to fly by—twenty, twenty-five.

"Call him again," said the judge.

The ram lifted his chin and repeated his order with that same echo. We waited with a growing sense of excitement as it looked as if our strategy was going to work—forty-five, fifty, fifty-five. The judge raised his gavel, ready to order my father's freedom at the count of sixty, when the rear door of the courtroom flew open.

A little man in a brown suit that hung loosely from his narrow shoulders rushed through the door. He had round glasses, a bushy gray mustache, and a brown briefcase. He hurried through the courtroom like a busy man with much to do, much to do, and not much time to do it. He passed right by us and hopped onto the witness chair as quick as all that.

"What are you doing there?" said the judge.

"I received a summons," said the little man in a high tweety voice, as if his appearance in that chair was as obvious as the ram on the wall. "And now here I am. What could be simpler?"

"We summoned the fallen angel Abezethibou."

"So you did," said the little man. His mustache twitched. "How can I help?"

"Mr. Goodheart?" said the judge. "What say ye?"

Josiah Goodheart simply shrugged. "What I say, my lord, what I say is that the witness has been called, the witness chair has been filled, and it is time for the petitioner's young counsel to proceed." He turned to me and gestured with exaggerated politeness. "Your witness."

"Bailiff," said the judge. "Administer the oath."

As the clerk brought out the golden skull and the ram gave his instructions, I looked at Barnabas, who nodded at me calmly, as if this was exactly as expected. The witness swore to tell the truth on the skull of the beheaded king. Barnabas then whispered in my ear and I repeated his words.

"Please state your name for the record," I said.

"My lord, I must object most strenuously," said Josiah Goodheart.

"To the question, Mr. Goodheart?" said the judge. "It seems innocent enough to me."

"To the travesty of a trained bird representing the petitioner," said my opponent. "Counsel is merely repeating the words of Mr. Barnabas Bothemly, who as we all know is not eligible to practice before this court. I wasn't aware that parrots were now being admitted to the bar."

The ram on the wall bleated out his laughter and the rest of the courtroom followed, before the judge banged everyone quiet.

"To allow this is to turn this court into a mockery of itself," said Josiah Goodheart, "and to turn this proceeding into a shammy sham. It can't be allowed."

"Yes, I believe you have a point, Mr. Goodheart," said the judge. "Mr. Bothemly, back to the benches with you. You'll sit down and stay quiet. Miss Webster, you will form your own questions, do you understand?"

"But I've never done it before," I said.

"Splendid. Then this shouldn't take long."

Barnabas patted my shoulder before he retreated to sit by my mother.

I looked up at my father in his cage, who stared at me with a frightening calm. Where did that come from? Why was my father so sure of me when I was full of doubt? The only thing I was sure of was that I wasn't ready for this, not at all. What wouldn't I give to be back in the benches, sitting next to my mother, nothing expected of me? What wouldn't I give to be back in the lunchroom of good old Willing Middle School West, with no question more pressing than where to sit?

"Proceed," barked the judge.

THE BIG SQUEEZE

"U h . . ." I said. "Um, well . . ." I said.

And then I remembered what Barnabas had last whispered to me.

"P-please state your name for the record?" I said, my voice rising nervously at the end of the sentence.

"I am," said the little man with a quick rhythm to his words, "whoever it was you called."

"We called the fallen angel Abezethibou."

"And here I am," he said. "As you must surely know, I have many names and many forms."

"Uh, okay," I said. I looked down at the scrolls on the table before me, shuffled them a bit, opened one. Amid a storm of Latin I saw my father's name. "And are you the one responsible for keeping my father, Eli Webster, on the other side?"

"I would say that he's the responsible one," said the witness. "He broke the law. The law was enforced. Consequently, as you can see, your father has been lawfully detained. Is that sufficient, Judge? May I be excused? I have oh so many souls to care for and so little time. A demon's work is never done."

"The testimony is as clear as rain, Your Honor," said Josiah Goodheart. "The witness testified that the detention is lawful. Can we now end this frivolous charade?"

"Miss Webster," said the judge, "anything else?"

"What did he do?" I asked the witness. "What did my father do?"

"He violated the law," said the witness. "I already said."

"What law?"

"The law. Didn't you hear? The law, miss. I could find out the specific violation if you wanted, but it might take a moment, and I wouldn't want to waste the court's precious time."

"I think maybe," I said, "if that's all right, sort of knowing the specific law that you say my father broke might help."

"My lord, must we?" said Goodheart.

"Miss Webster has asked the question, so I think we must," said the judge. "Go on."

The little man opened his briefcase, rifled through what was inside, peered closely at something without pulling it out, and then closed the briefcase with a bright snap.

"He interfered with an agreement," said the witness.

"Is that a crime?"

"Oh yes," said the man. "Under the common law, yes.

Men have been hanged for less. And he, as you can see, has not. Mercy has been exercised. May I now be excused?"

"What agreement did he interfere with?" I said.

"An affair of the heart that was none of his business. And if I may say so, Miss Webster, your father was detained not only pursuant to the law but for his own protection. As Mr. Bothemly could tell you, sometimes those who interfere in affairs of the heart come to the most unfortunate ends. You can think of me as Mr. Webster's benevolent guardian."

"And we thank you for your service," said Josiah Goodheart. "Are we done here, Judge?"

"It appears that we are," said the judge. "Anything else, Miss Webster?"

I didn't know what to do, where to go. Without Barnabas whispering in my ear I was lost. What kind of lawyer was I, anyway? My blood had gotten me admitted to argue before the Court of Uncommon Pleas, yes, but as my grandfather had pointed out, it wasn't enough to make me a lawyer. I was still just me.

As all my tactics and strategies rattled on the floor about me, I remembered what my father had told my mother about being a trial lawyer. *You don't start with the questions and move forward,* he had said. *Instead you start with the answers and work backward.* It had sounded like cheating to me, as if I had been given the solution to a math problem and was merely required to build the right equation to get that result. But the thought calmed me. Maybe this could be as easy as math. All I needed was to know what I wanted the fallen angel to say and work backward.

I looked up at the judge, peering at me now with red eyes

that were losing patience with every second. What answer could possibly win my father's freedom? I didn't yet know, but something the witness said echoed in my brain. And it reminded me of one of the stories my grandfather had told me. The beginnings of an equation began to form. Without any other choice, I would start there.

"Do you know a woman named Isabel Cutbush?" I asked the witness.

As soon as I mentioned the name something happened to the fussy little accountant on the stand. He began to stretch his neck, as if the loose suit he was wearing had tightened, and his wrists bulged out of the jacket cuffs.

"Isabel?" he said. "Cutbush?" His voice, at first just a high twitter, was now accompanied by another voice in a lower key.

"That's right," I said "Isabel Cutbush. She didn't pass over to the other side the usual way, did she? She didn't get hit by a car or die of some horrible disease. You tricked her and then brought her over."

"Something like that might have happened," said the witness. "But, as you may not know, being so young and inexperienced, it is allowed to bring someone over in the proper circumstances for short periods of time. In this case it was all done legally."

"You brought her over because you loved her and then you made a deal with her."

"Yes, we had a contract binding on all sides," he said. "An agreement was made and the laws were respected."

"Was my father on the other side representing Isabel?"

"Your father was interfering with a lawful agreement."

"But your agreement was deceitful."

"That is a lie," he shouted.

His voice went from double to triple tones, not unlike the voice of the great metal Pilgrim who had attacked me in the courtyard. His suit shrank even more until it burst into shreds. The little accountant was now a giant on the witness stand, with only scraps of fabric covering his broad chest and thick legs. His feet became so huge they split his leather shoes into scraps.

"You're changing," I said as his hands melted into huge claws and his feet formed into pointed hooves. His mustache burned away with a twist of flame and smoke.

"You've angered me with your rudeness," he said. Red scabs started rising from above his ears. "It's not as if I didn't warn you. It doesn't pay to anger me, girl."

"Like my father angered you?"

"Let him be a lesson."

A single red wing spread out behind him, stretched and fluttered. The rising scabs behind his ears grew and hardened into great spiraling horns. The demon now sat in front of us without his costume. I backed away and tried to stop my shaking.

"I have many forms," he said. "When I am angry my base form is called forth. You have questioned my integrity, but the agreement was fair. And the proof is in this very courtroom. Barnabas Bothemly still prowls this foul world."

At this Barnabas stood and shouted out, "You misled us, demon."

"You wanted to be misled," said Redwing. "You wanted to trade her life for yours, and so you did."

"You are lying still," shouted Barnabas.

"Quiet in the courtroom," barked the judge with a bang of his gavel. "I'll not have any more interruptions."

"The deal was made," said the demon. Its eyes were blazing and puffs of black smoke rose from the flames. "The price for Isabel staying with me was to bring Barnabas back to life. And there he is. The proof of my honesty is the presence of that coward sitting in the back row next to your mother. Your sweet, loving mother. Oh, I know her, too. Be careful what you say from here on in, child, for anything can happen to those we love."

"My lord," said Josiah Goodheart, a weariness injected into his rasp. "We're not here to discuss matters of contract law, of which Miss Webster is sadly ignorant. Can we get to the matter at hand before another millennium slips through our fingers?"

"Mr. Goodheart is right," said the judge. "Miss Webster, we're not here to argue about an agreement."

"But Your Honor, I believe—"

"Your belief is not important here. My ruling is. We will not argue about that agreement, do you understand?"

"Yes, Your Honor."

"Do you have anything else?"

Did I? No, I didn't, or at least I was sure just then that I didn't. But as I shrank from Judge Jeffries's awful stare, I began to realize that his red-eyed glare provided me a glimpse of the final answer I might want from Redwing. And was I wrong to think my friends and family, over this whole bizarre adventure, had given me the equation to get me there—this plus that, divided by that, added to that?

It was simple algebra, and if there was one thing I could always ace it was algebra.

"Well, Miss Webster?" said the judge. "Are we finished here?"

"Not yet, sir. I have just a few more questions."

"Be quick about it," he said.

"So, Mr. Redwing—can I call you Mr. Redwing?"

"Call me what you will," said the demon with the smile of a cat who had just eaten a boatful of mice.

"Mr. Redwing, you have accused my father of interfering with your agreement with Isabel."

"That is what I said, yes."

"How was he, like, interfering?"

"He was meddling," said the demon. "Talking to Isabel, my darling bride-to-be Isabel, searching my palace uninvited, asking questions of my other brides."

"Other brides? How many brides do you have?"

"Innumerable," said the demon.

"Yikes alive," I said. "I guess that puts the 'F' in 'Fallen.'"

There was a spurt of laughter in the courtroom, even the ram joining in, and as the laughter rose Redwing's horns glowed with an intense heat.

"Did my father ask your brides embarrassing questions?" I said.

"He was meddling, like I told you." It took me a moment to remember when I had heard that word just recently before. As it came to me, I couldn't help but smile. It was like another side of the family had joined the party.

"Was my father, like, meddling on his own, or was he told he could meddle by a court on the other side?"

"There might be some trivial thing."

"A legal case?"

"A farce," said the demon. "Something started to spread his lies."

"And so when he was searching your palaces, was he doing that because the court told him he could investigate things by, what is the term, Judge—taking discovery?"

"That it is," said Judge Jefferies.

"Well?" I said.

"The court had no right," said Redwing.

"And when my father was talking to Isabel and a few of your other brides," I said, "was he doing it because the court told him he could take depositions?"

"What part of 'meddling' don't you understand?"

"But it seems like the court was meddling as much as my father. So why was it my father who ended up in your dungeon and not the judge?"

"Your father's manners were poorer—as poor, frankly, as your own."

I looked up at my father, still peering out through the iron bars, muted by the iron muzzle, looking as innocent and helpless as a dove in its cage. I stared long enough so that the judge couldn't help but follow my gaze.

"You locked my father up because of poor manners?"

"He was being insolent," said the demon. "To me. In my domain."

I snapped my attention back to the demon. It was all right there in front of me.

"Oh my, he was being insolent," I said, using all my sarcastic middle school powers. "The big, strong, fallen angel got upset because the mean little lawyer was being insolent."

"That's what I said," growled the demon. As it spoke its horns glowed hotter and the flames blazing from its eyes rose to lick its brow. It focused its gaze on me as if there were only me and it in the courtroom, having a private argument, which it would not allow itself to lose.

"And impertinent, I suppose, the mean little lawyer."

"That he was," it said.

"Not to mention impudent."

"Now that you mention it, yes," it said in a voice so deep and angry my throat almost closed with fear.

It stood from the witness chair, stepped a great hoofed step forward, and leaned on the table in front of me. The pincers of its claws dug into the wood. Its long narrow tail writhed behind it like a burning electric wire. We were so close now I could smell the sulfur on its breath.

"And I can see," it said, "to your imminent peril, that the serpent's apple has not fallen far from the tree."

"Thank you," I said through gritted teeth. "I'll take that as a compliment."

"You should take it as a warning, little girl," said the demon.

"So, like, just to be clear, Mr. Redwing. You have locked my father in your dungeon because he was being impudent, impertinent, and insolent."

"That's what I said."

"So really, you only locked him up because he was acting like a lawyer."

"If you mean because he was acting like a meddling dog, then yes."

I turned again to look up at my father. "But I suppose one of the things my father has taught me—both my fathers, actually—is that lawyers are, at heart, meddling dogs. We see a wrong and we bound forward in an eager attempt to right it. We chase after fairness like a dog chases after a tennis ball. We see an injustice and we can't help but interfere, no matter the price to ourselves, or to our families, or even to our little girls. We are meddling dogs in service of the law, even if it takes us through the very gates of your domain."

"What does a whippet like you know of the law in my domain?"

I turned back to stare at the demon. It had just given me the final divisor of the equation to get exactly the answer I wanted. All I needed to pull it off was a touch of Charlie Frayden–type servility.

"You're right," I said. "I know nothing of the law in your domain. So teach me, Mr. Redwing, sir, please."

"You could use some teaching, that is evident."

"Explain it to a girl as dim and silly as me. I've been hearing about legal cornerstones until I'm about to puke. Patent law, or habeas corpus, or the common law, or whatever, it's like a blur. So tell us all, what constitutes the cornerstone of the law in your domain?"

"It is quite simple," growled the demon. "In my domain, I am the law."

"There are no other cornerstones?"

"None."

"No legal books? No statutes?"

"Trifling things in the face of my power."

"And so you have no need for lawyers?"

"They are a plague upon the land."

"Or courtrooms?"

"Think of all the dungeons we could build in those use-less spaces."

"Or judges, even?" I said, fighting not to look up at Judge Jeffries as I said it.

"Foolish, self-important windbags not fit to hold my cloak."

"What are they fit for? Your dungeons?"

"If they forget their places, yes."

"And Isabel will be another of your brides, no matter what they say is right or lawful."

"I say what is lawful. I say what is right. And I say she will be mine, forever and for always," said the demon Redwing, who then proceeded to give another of those mouse-eating smiles. "I suppose you could say I am a fool for love."

"Or maybe just a fool," I said.

And that was when the demon Redwing, horns bursting into flame, caught my throat in its claw and began to squeeze.

46

THE VERDICT

"I've heard enough," said the judge, banging his gavel twice so that two sounds like twin gunshots ricocheted around the courtroom. As the demon turned his head to look at the judge, the fire spouting from his horns subsided and the squeeze on my throat eased. "The witness will return to the stand without counsel's neck in its claw."

Redwing released its hold on me and bowed to the judge. "As you wish," it intoned darkly before retreating to the chair.

Judge Jefferies shook his head at me while I rubbed my neck, as if remarking on my utter foolishness at baiting a demon—a live, stinking demon with horns of fire—before saying, "Mr. Goodheart, make your argument."

"Thank you, Your Honor," said Josiah Goodheart as he put his right thumb into his armpit and dropped his left hand on a fat legal volume open upon the table before him. Just the sound of his raspy, jazzy voice filled me with despair. He knew the law better than I did, he knew the judge better than I did, he was ready to once again stick a skewer through me and roast me with onions and chunks of zucchini. "The standard of proof in a petition for a writ of habeas corpus, as this court has already noted, is extraordinarily high. And it is indisputable—indisputable, I say—that the junior counsel representing petitioner has failed to provide even the most rudimentary—"

The judge banged his gavel once, stopping the speech.

"I've heard enough," said the judge. "Sit down, Mr. Goodheart, and you too, Miss Webster. I've made my decision. This is not a difficult case. It is assumed, until proven otherwise, that a detention on the far side is in accordance with the law. The burden of proof of a violation, as Mr. Goodheart has noted, is extraordinarily high."

The judge cocked his head and stared down at me as if staring down at a cockroach. I slumped in my chair and looked at my father in his cage. His eyes behind his glasses seemed so tired and lost. My grandfather, sitting beside me now, put his hand over mine. I smiled weakly at him, all the time wanting to cry.

"Under questioning by petitioner's counsel, however," continued the judge, "the witness has made it clear that it pays no deference to any law other than its own. It has no respect for statutes or learned treatises which have been the cornerstone of the law for centuries. It has no respect for lawyers or courtrooms, and it has no respect for self-important windbags on the judicial bench. It is fitting, therefore, that this self-important windbag has no respect for its detention of petitioner."

The judge banged his gavel so loudly my heart leaped into my throat.

"The relief sought in Mr. Webster's petition for a writ of habeas corpus is hereby granted, and the petitioner shall be released forthwith."

There was a moment where I wasn't sure what had happened, where the commotion in the court and the creak of the chain lowering the courtroom cage seemed to meld with the assumption of disaster that follows me like a rain cloud. But then a loud whoosh erupted and Redwing burst into flame, an immense bonfire that licked the ceiling dome. The flying babies painted there flitted away from the blaze, twittering loudly in fear. When the fire abruptly died, the fallen angel Abezethibou had disappeared from the courtroom.

A great bout of cheering and hurrahs came from the spectators, the babies on the ceiling and the ram's head on the wall joining in. Along with the celebration came the sound of the cage's door swinging open, letting me know that my father was to be freed.

I jumped to my feet. My grandfather pounded me on the back. I turned around and saw my mother beaming at me with pride—imagine that—and Barnabas nodding with the slightest of smiles, the first time I ever saw such a thing on his long, mournful face. By the time I turned to look at the cage, my father, free now of his iron muzzle, was walking into his freedom.

"My sweet Lizzie Face," said my father, hugging me. "I'm sorry, so sorry."

"For what?" I said.

"For dragging you into this, but I knew you could do it."

"It was mostly Beatrice," I said.

"No, it was mostly you. When Beatrice came to me about saving Vance Johansson, I sent her your way because I knew you were the one to help her. And she seemed so miserable without her head."

"Can you blame her?" I said.

"I knew if you helped her, you could help me. You would have made our great ancestor so proud, but not as proud as you have made me. Now let's get out of here before the old windbag changes his mind."

I was rushing out of the old gray building and into the locked courtyard with the tails of my robe flowing behind me, still full of the elation of victory, when Redwing came for me one more time.

He was sheathed again in the great bronze figure of the black-hatted Pilgrim from the City Hall tower. The metal animate slithered again through the gap over the locked gate and came at us with its noisy wrench of metal—scritch clank, scritch clank—and it was pointing its metal scroll not just at me but at my mother and my father and my grandfather and Barnabas.

"You were warned, girl," it said in its three mismatched voices, the same voices we had heard on the witness stand after Redwing assumed its pure form. "All you Websters were warned not to get in my way. It's time to wipe out the entire repugnant clan. And how lucky for me I have you all right here."

Barnabas ran out in front of us, raising his hands. "Begone, monster," he shouted. "You've been beaten in a match of wit and law, accept it."

The Pilgrim swatted Barnabas aside as if he were nothing more than an annoying housefly. My father dashed forward to act as a shield for the rest of us, but the monster picked him up in his fist as if my father were a squirming mouse.

"I fear neither you nor your runtish father, Webster," snarled the demon at my father. "But know this, the one who will bear the brunt of the Webster treachery will be the vile trickster Elizabeth Webster. Who is laughing now, little girl?"

My grandfather placed his arm around me and pulled me close even as the most surprising figure stepped forward with utter confidence to stand before the metal monster.

"You'll take no one," said my mother. "Put Eli down and go."

"Mom?" I said.

"Ah, Melinda," said the demon. "Miss me?"

"Like the plague," said my mother.

"What could be merrier than the plague?"

"Mom?" I said again.

"If you touch my daughter you'll regret it."

"Why should I be afraid of a mewling little kitten like you, Melinda?"

"Because I know who you are afraid of, Redwing, and you know the things I could tell her."

"You can't. You wouldn't."

"Put my husband down and go."

The metal Pilgrim sneered before yelling "Hellsfire!" so loudly the very stones of the massive building vibrated in their places.

But even as the dust of shaken mortar fell to the stone courtyard, it backed away, and as it did it gently placed my father upon the ground. "One more false step from any one of you," it said, "and mark my words, the Websters will be no more."

And then with a harsh, metallic scritch clank, scritch clank, the Pilgrim strode defiantly away before climbing over the gate and through the round gap beneath the arch. It must have kept climbing like a great iron spider to his spot above the great clock on City Hall tower, because after we picked up Barnabas and dusted him off—sadly unharmed, he informed us—and we ducked through the gap he swung open in the south gate and onto the street, there it was, fixed in its spot high on the tower, staring benevolently upon the city as it had for over a century.

We all ended up back at my house. Talk about awkward.

The adults sat in a tight circle in the living room—my mother, my father, my grandfather, and Barnabas—savoring my success and figuring out what to do next, along with my stepfather. Stephen had been shocked to see them all: the bent old man, the odd-looking clerk, and, most surprising, my father. After saying hello he backed away, but then I spoke up.

"Just so you know, Grandpop," I said, "Stephen is a lawyer, too."

"Is that so?" said my grandfather. "Splendid. What kind? Criminal? Constitutional? Extranatural?"

"Patent law," said Stephen.

"Oh, I see," said my grandfather. "I suppose that counts, too."

"Stephen told me patent law is a cornerstone of the law."

"A small one, maybe," said my grandfather. "A brick, perhaps."

"It was Stephen," I continued, "who taught me the rules about serving a complaint on the defendant. And when we were taken away by the police, it was Stephen who marched into the chief's office and got us released. That's where I first heard about habeas corpus."

"Well done, Stephen," said my father, smiling at the current husband of his ex-wife. How does that even work? "Why don't you join us?"

"Thank you, Eli," said my stepfather to my father, "but I think Peter just woke up. All the excitement down here. I should help him get back to sleep."

"I'll go," I said, and quick as that I was out of there and up the steps, which, let me tell you, was a relief. I couldn't handle a grand family reunion just then. I couldn't bear sitting stiffly as my bizarre extended family tried to make sense of each other. Especially since I had too many mysteries still raging in my head.

How did my mother know Redwing, and what kind of blackmail did she have on him? She had rebuffed all my questions with a "Not now, Elizabeth." I let it go because I was so stirred by her bravery—but all my suspicions about her had been confirmed. I would have to get to the bottom of her story.

And also, what had my father meant with the cryptic comment he made as he pulled me aside after Redwing, in his Pilgrim guise, had left? "This isn't the end of it," my father had said softly to me. "Redwing has big plans that need to be stopped. It's up to the Websters, all of us, to do the stopping."

"What kind of plans?"

"We'll talk later. Now's not the time," he had said, being as purposefully mysterious as my mother.

It was all enough to have me feeling paranoid and alone. But I had a solution.

Peter's room was dark, and as I stood in the doorway I felt a wave of disappointment at the thought he might have gone to sleep, but then I heard his voice.

"Lizzie?"

"Can I come in?" I said. "I need a hug."

"My stuffed bear is in the corner. You can hug him."

I laughed, and jumped on the bed beside him as he giggled ferociously. I gave him so tight a squeeze he couldn't squirm free, though he didn't try very hard.

"What's going on downstairs?"

"A Webster-Scali reunion," I said. "Talk about strange. It's like Frankenstein's monster meets the mommy."

"Dad was so worried the whole time you were away."

"He's worried a lot."

"Not always," said Petey. "Usually he's just reading or

talking about what it was like when he was young. But tonight he was walking back and forth, back and forth. Where were you?"

"In the city," I said.

"With the girl?"

"What girl?"

"The girl that was floating around at the cemetery."

"So you did see her."

"I didn't tell anyone. But I really wanted to tell Tyler. He thinks he always has the best stories, even though his are made up."

"I knew I could trust you. That was Beatrice."

"How come I could see her, when no one else could except you and your friends? You're a Webster, so from what Mom says that lets you do all kinds of cool stuff. But I'm not a Webster, I'm a Scali, which is not cool at all."

"Wrong. Being a Scali is the coolest thing ever. But I figure if you could see Beatrice and I could see Beatrice, then maybe it was because of the one thing we have in common."

"Mom?"

"With Mom, there's always more going on than we know. Hey, Peter, can I ask you something?"

"Go ahead."

"Did she seem happy?"

"Who?"

"Beatrice."

"I think," he said. "Especially when she breezed right through you. Then it was like she was one big smile. What did that feel like?"

"You know how when Mom gives you a hug and all the things that bothered you all day disappear and all you can feel is Mom squeezing the air out of you?"

"Yeah?"

"It felt like that."

BACK TO THE JUNGLE

After the case of Beatrice Long, I no longer wandered the jungle of the Willing Middle School West lunchroom like a lost meerkat looking for a safe spot to park my tray. Now I carried my lunch to a table in the center of the lunchroom and sat with a motley crew of regulars.

There was Natalie, of course, and Henry Harrison, too, who had moved from being a client to being a friend.

Also sitting with us—surprise, surprise—was Debbie Benner. That final kiss at Beatrice Long's gravesite had burned away Henry's dazed love for a ghost and he was back with Debbie. You would have thought Natalie would have been upset, but she and Debbie had become fast friends. Natalie helped Debbie pick out shoes, and Debbie was training Natalie in, get this, tennis. Apparently, Natalie had a killer backhand. It wasn't uncommon to see the two of them walking together in the hallway in their tennis skirts, heads leaning one toward the other, chat-chatting away.

Joining the four of us were the Fraydens, who were no longer just friends but now teammates. Yes, I had gone and done it: I had joined debate club. It was actually a suggestion from my stepfather. "I did it myself in junior high and then through high school," said Stephen proudly. "Gosh, Lizzie, it's great practice for a lawyer." I rolled my eyes, of course I did, but then I gave it a try. For me it wasn't about the competition so much as forcing myself to speak up, to speak out, to develop a skill that might be needed in the future.

Redwing has big plans that need to be stopped, my father had said. *It's up to the Websters, all of us, to do the stopping.* I still didn't know what he was talking about, but when the time came I wanted to be ready.

"Big match tonight," said Charlie Frayden. "You ready, Elizabeth?"

"I suppose," I said, poking the mysterious filling inside my tacos.

"You better be," said Charlie. "We need you."

"She's a tiger," said Doug. "Elizabeth Webster is a tiger at debate."

"I could have told you that," said Henry. "She just needs to get her hair out of her eyes every now and then."

"Her hair's her secret weapon," said Natalie, who had slept over one recent night and convinced me to change my hair color. "Hot pink to hide an assassin's heart."

"What's today's topic?" said Henry.

"Supernatural spirits, fact or fiction," said Doug.

"I think Elizabeth will do okay on that one," said Natalie.

"We'll probably get the negative," I said.

"That's the easy side," said Charlie. "Ghosts are just figments of our overactive imaginations. We see ghosts because we make real what we want to be real. Who hasn't left a molar for the tooth fairy?"

"Ah, yes, the old tooth fairy argument," said Doug. "It works every time."

"She doesn't like that," I said.

"Who?"

"The tooth fairy. Pretending she doesn't exist makes her very angry."

"Did she tell you that?" Charlie asked, his voice soft with wonder.

"As a matter of fact, yes," I said. "And she mentioned your name when she said it."

We were laughing at Charlie's frightened gulp when I looked up through my dyed-pink hair to see a girl standing before me, black pants, black shirt, long black hair, and a steel ring in her nose, holding one hand in the other. We didn't know each other, but I knew she was an eighth grader, and I recognized the look in her eye.

"Uh, Miss Webster?" she said.

"Call her Lizzie," said Natalie.

"Do you have a minute?"

"Take my seat," said Charlie, who was sitting across from me. "Go ahead. I'll just move over here. Right over here."

"Thank you," she said, before sitting down, her gaze nervously resting on the tabletop.

"Hey, Young-Mee," said Henry.

"Hi, Henry," she said without looking up at him.

"You mind if they stay and listen," I said, "or would you prefer we talk privately?"

"No, they can all stay. Debbie was the one who told me I should come to you."

"Good." We leaned in, all of us, forming a huddle. "What's this about, Young-Mee?"

"Well," she said, "there's this thing that's happening in our house? It's like creepy and scary and I don't know what to do about it?"

"You've come to the right place," said Natalie. "Lizzie is the reigning queen of creep."

"Maybe it's not real," said Young-Mee. "Maybe I'm just going crazy."

"You're in the right place for that, too," said Debbie Benner with a smile.

"It's like one day a month I hear this shrieking in our basement? At first, I thought it was the shutters squeaking in the wind, but it happens even on the calmest day. And my parents don't hear it, or my brothers. Just me . . . and the dog. Yeah, the dog hears it, I can tell, the way she runs around in circles when it comes."

"What does it sound like?" I said.

"Like a cat has its tail stuck under a rocking chair and the chair keeps rocking. And now it's like I'm a wreck for a week before it comes, dreading it, and a week after because I get so worked up and scared."

"You said it comes once a month?"

"It's the same day, the fifteenth. Every fifteenth of the month I hear it."

"Ah, the ides," said Charlie Frayden, nodding. "It's like something out of *Julius Caesar*. That's Shakespeare, Mr. Harrison, sir."

"It sounds to me like a Class Two banshee," said Doug Frayden, who lately had been studying my grandfather's copy of *White's Legal Hornbook of Demons and Ghosts*, the definitive guide to the dead and undead.

"What's a banshee?" said Young-Mee.

"An unhappy spirit," I said. "A banshee is trying to tell us something but doesn't know how to express herself like a human being, because she's not a human being anymore. We just have to figure out what she is trying to say."

"So it's a she?"

"If it's a banshee," said Doug, "it's a she. And Irish, too."

"Why is an Irish ghost haunting me?"

"We'll have to ask it," I said.

"How do we do that?" said Young-Mee.

"I know," said Natalie. "Let's have a party!"

"That's your answer to everything," said Henry.

"Lighten up, Henry," said Debbie. "You've got to show some spirit if you want to battle in the spirit world."

"And I have just the right lipstick," said Natalie. "Estée Long-gone."

"So, Lizzie," said Young-Mee, "what should I do?"

Think about this for a moment. An eighth grader with a ring in her nose was asking me, a seventh-grade math geek, for advice. You never know what you'll find when you look closely at yourself. I would have liked to have found a brilliant singer, an actor who would leave them weeping in their seats, a painter, an acrobat, something artistic, something normal, but that wasn't to be. No, instead what I discovered was this bizarre lawyer thing. But when I looked around at my team, that didn't seem so bad.

"Go home tonight," I said, "and tell your parents you're having a Julius Caesar party for some kids in your English class. Then, on the fifteenth, we'll all show up in costume."

"Toga party," said Doug.

"Totally," said Natalie.

"We'll all get together wrapped in sheets, play games, drink punch, dance a little, and maybe, when the screaming starts, we'll try to have a discussion with your banshee. I have someone who can teach me the Latin that might get it done. If you have any questions before then, just get in touch with me."

I gave her my shiny new card.

```
WEBSTER & SPAWN
ATTORNEYS FOR THE DAMNED

ELIZABETH WEBSTER, ESQ.
```

"Webster and Spawn?" said Young-Mee.

"The family firm," I said. "I'm the spawn."

ACKNOWLEDGMENTS

I've had the bones of this story for years, for decades actually—ever since I went to work in my father's small and peculiar law office—and I spent thousands of words trying and failing to bring those bones to life. Truth is, they never started dancing until Elizabeth Webster carried her lunch tray into my office and asked if she could eat at my table. I'm so grateful that she was willing to sit with someone so low on the pecking order, but that's just the kind of kid she is.

Elizabeth might have shown me the route, but I also received much-needed help on the way to making this novel what I wanted it to be. I want to thank my agents, Wendy Sherman and Alex Glass, whose unwavering enthusiasm for the novel, and careful guidance toward the market, were instrumental in the creation of this book. I also want to thank Laurie Morrison, a terrific novelist herself, for encouragement and advice, and Tamson Weston for help with the tone and voice. My editor, the amazing Tracey Keevan, has not only made the book much stronger, but made me a better writer, too.

There are so many others to thank as I make my way toward a new audience. Alison Dasho, a friend and inspiration, was one of the first people to see the book and I am forever grateful for her faith in me and the story. *Multas gratias* to Anne Smith, of the Shipley School, who gently corrected my Latin. I also want to thank the students at Mighty Writers in Philadelphia for keeping me connected with the kind of kids I'm writing about, especially Mosadi Pearson, Lauryn Dorsett, Makayla Jordan, Moriah Lahr, Eric-Ross McLaren, Emanual Marquez, and Ayah Pearson. Your talent and commitment are a constant inspiration.

My sons, Jack, a physicist, and Michael, an engineer, told me I needed more math in the book. Their skills are proof that some things are not genetic. I also want to thank my daughter, Nora, for being strong and funny, sarcastic and steadfast, independent and caring. There's a lot of her in both Elizabeth and Natalie, which is why I love them so. My wife, Pam, has been my greatest supporter, from writing school through every twist and turn that has followed. Thank you for letting me share your life.

Finally, I want to acknowledge two historical works that lie at the foundation of Elizabeth's world. "The Devil and Daniel Webster" is a short story by Stephen Vincent Benét, first published in the *Saturday Evening Post* in 1936 and beloved by kids everywhere since then. Benét won the Pulitzer Prize in 1929 for his epic poem *John Brown's Body*. And then there is a treatise that remains a cornerstone of American legal practice, *The Common Law* by Oliver Wendell Holmes, Jr., published in 1881. Ebenezer Webster stands on a volume of *The Common Law* when he reaches for his hat.